Wayfarer Universe: Into the Void Realm of Behemoths

REALM OF BEHEMOTHS

TAYLOR GREGORY

Thank you Mom and Dad for giving me a love of stories, and the creativity to tell them. And thank you to my wonderful wife Maci for inspiring me every day.

Chapter 1

It was almost too much for Halis to believe. If it had been anyone but Calia telling him, he wouldn't have believed it. As he looked out of his bedroom window, admiring the sunrise coming up over the trees that surrounded his estate, he pondered the information that his sister had dropped at his feet.

The idea that there was a sixth realm hiding out there in the ways was not a new one. In fact, it had been pondered over by every great scientist and philosopher for the last few centuries. But if what Calia said was true, then it was no longer an idea. It was right under their noses, and always had been. His sister, whom he had always thought a little batty for wanting to devote her life to the study of the ways, had made the biggest scientific breakthrough of the millennium. And she didn't even seem to care.

"Keep this between us for now," Calia had told him.

Halis couldn't believe his own ears. This was a gold mine of opportunity, and she wanted him to stay silent and still? How could he?

Of course, she knew nothing of what he had been doing in the year that she had been gone. If he was honest, Halis didn't remember much of it either. He'd let the newfound wealth go to his head. Now it was all but gone. Blown on parties, drink, and women. They'd all wanted to be around when he was spending marks like they were going out of style, but they'd disappeared once his fortunes dried out.

But this was the perfect chance to turn the family fortunes around. Halis knew that he could leverage this into some kind of deal with the emperor. If only his family knew the secret of travelling into this new realm, they would have a monopoly on the realm. Explorers, settlers, and kings alike would have to come to them to reach this realm of behemoths. Even a fool could take that kind of an opportunity and set themselves up for life.

Halis was desperate for any kind of financial security. Most of the privateers his father had employed were well-known or well-liked enough to get their letter of marque from someone else. Many of them had taken offense at his attempts to strong-arm them into accepting better terms and had left rather than negotiate. Halis always believed that his father had been too soft when it came to negotiating business deals. But when he'd begun his campaign to rein in the privateer fleet his father had endorsed, he'd cut his family's main source of income in half instead.

And Calia wanted him to pause it all for a single man. Halis would have never suspected such an emotional response from the rational and unfeeling Calia. Looking back, he supposed it was possible that he only felt that way because he didn't know her well enough. It was likely that this emotional side had always been there, and that Calia had hidden it away from the world. Halis might never know.

And now he was stuck with a choice. He could either agree to his sister's wishes and postpone any attempt to profit off this discovery until they could rescue her lover. Or he could ignore her and try to press the issue. Fortunately for him, she had not been particularly secretive around the estate when she had been planning her expedition. Halis wouldn't be surprised if every servant in the manor had been told about the xheiat tea method of piercing the void. Any leverage she could have gained by withholding that information had been broken before she'd ever set out.

What was worse was that she was hoping that he would fund another expedition. Captain Akos had estimated that they would need at least one more ship and a sizable mercenary company to have a chance at rescuing his wayfarer. Halis half believed that he would pocket the money and run, but Calia seemed to trust his assessment. The man had sailed her into the void after all.

The thought of the privateer captain caused a sigh to escape Halis's lips. That was another problem that he had no way of dealing with at the moment. He'd never believed that the captain would take his sister into the void. Now that he had, and had successfully returned no less,

Halis owed him a substantial reward. A reward that he could not afford. From the way Akos and his sister had been talking, they were planning to use that reward as a way to at least help finance their return expedition.

His thoughts were interrupted as the door creaked open behind him. Halis turned to see that his aide and bodyguard had stepped in. The hook-nosed man was without his twin brother, whom Halis had asked to keep track of Akos's movements. Despite the early hour, the dour individual already looked as if he'd been awake for some time.

"Good morning sir," Lusalin Carralt said.

"Is it?" Halis replied. "I swear I thought the world was upside down when I looked out my window this morning."

The normally dour man smirked for a moment before his face returned to a neutral expression.

"Still thinking over Lady Calia and Captain Akos's proposition?" Lusalin inquired.

"Of course I am." Halis turned from his window, throwing up his hands in disgust. "I hardly slept a wink last night for their 'proposition.' I've no idea what to do about it, and no time to decide either."

"You could always say no. We know the recipe for reaching the void now."

"And be known as the man who cheated his own sister out of the discovery of a lifetime? That certainly won't appear in any history books."

"Then it seems you have no choice but to fund them."

"You know I can't do that." Halis glared at his manservant. There was something going on behind his spectacles. A light in his brown eyes that Halis rarely saw.

"There is always a third option, even if it takes some time to see."

Without another word, Lusalin stepped back into the hall to retrieve a pot of tea. He poured a glass for his master, and Halis considered his words as he sat down. Nothing sprang to his tired mind. The shock of the story he'd been told, combined with the sleepless night, seemed to have rendered him dumb. Halis allowed the tea to cool for a moment after Lusalin poured it and looked up at him.

"You've clearly got an idea," Halis said. "Spit it out."

"Outside of the family, Akos and his crew are the only ones who know the secret," Lusalin explained. "If they were to be removed from the equation, I'm sure that your sister would see reason. We would have time to gather investors. I'm sure that the privateer captain is the one pushing her to accelerate her schedule anyway."

"If we were to rescind Akos's letter of marque," Halis thought aloud, "he and his crew would be arrested as pirates. They've a prize tied up in court at this very instant. They could hang."

As much as he wanted to regain the family fortune, the thought of men hanging for crimes they didn't commit did not sit well with Halis. Especially when those men had put their lives on the line to help his sister out of a predicament she had put them all in. It didn't seem like something that would rest easy on the soul.

"I doubt they'll hang," Lusalin replied. "Considering Akos's service to Macallia and the situation, the judge will let him off with a warning. It could still take years to process though, what with the courts in Geralis all being terribly overbooked."

That eased Halis's mind. Still, something nagged at the back of his mind.

"Calia won't like this decision," Halis stated.

"No, but I'm sure she'll see the wisdom in it given time."

"I'm not worried about her. I'm worried about her handmaiden."

"Beralin and I can handle Valesa. And don't forget, her loyalty is technically to you."

"And technically I have a contract with Captain Akos that would prevent me from revoking his letter out of hand."

"A fair point. But if worst does come to pass, either Beralin or myself would be more than a match for her."

"You would be able to stomach that? I thought the three of you came from the same . . . school."

"The first thing they teach you at that school of ours is how to make difficult decisions. In our line of work, they are all too often necessary."

Halis took a sip of his tea to steady his nerves. This whole thing was starting to get out of hand. He knew that it was his fault that the family fortune was gone. His heart had been equally torn between fear that Calia might never come home and dread of what she would say when she did. Lusalin was right, though; the difficult decisions did need to be made. The family fortune needed to be rebuilt. Halis couldn't let such an opportunity slip out of his hands.

"Send Beralin down to the magister's office first thing and see to it that Captain Akos's letter of marque is officially rescinded today. He'll need to move quickly. The man is notoriously difficult to pin down."

"Right away, sir."

Lusalin left Halis alone with his thoughts. He picked up his teacup and wandered back over to the window. The gardens beneath him were bare, a sign that the season had finally changed. He absentmindedly wondered how cold it would get this year as he sipped his tea. Halis realized that he had better prepare for a long day. Calia was going to be livid when she found out what he had done. Her temper was much cooler than his, but she had a stubborn streak that rivaled any he had ever known.

Halis also needed to begin his plans to round up investors. Even if only the family and the servants knew the secret, it would spread soon enough. Things like this did not stay secret for very long. He would need to act fast to make sure that he was the first to move on this newfound information. Halis finished the rest of his tea and set the cup down. It was time to get started.

***

Calia was not known for patience. But if her recent time in captivity had taught her anything, it was how to endure long stretches of boredom. The luncheon she was suffering through had been thrown in her honor by her peers at the Geralin Royal University. It didn't need to be a boring event. She could have regaled them with the tale of her voyage to the other side of the one impenetrable void. Unfortunately, she had promised Halis that she would keep the word between them for the time being.

Instead, she got to listen to others prattle on about their own research while she had to bite her tongue and not speak a word about the scientific discovery of a lifetime. It was almost more than she could bear. Calia could have turned the invitation down, but after spending so much time and effort trying to get her peers to accept her, that seemed like a waste. As Valesa had reminded her, it wasn't as if they would be able to dash off and begin their rescue the exact moment they returned to Geralis. Akos needed time to get a line on the supplies, ships, and crew they would need to begin their return trip.

The captain could not work fast enough as far as Calia was concerned. He'd claimed that he had a personal errand to run this morning, but that he would begin his preparations before nightfall. Calia wanted to argue, but there was no point. She felt that Akos would only resent her for trying to tell him how to do what needed to be done. And the last thing they needed was any enmity amongst their own ranks.

So Calia fumed in her mind as she accepted another empty platitude from someone who had most likely helped to keep her out of the university's peerage in the first place. It was times like this that she wished she gave off the same dangerous and unapproachable air as her maidservant. People rarely bothered Valesa with idle chatter.

The maidservant sat at her elbow. She sipped at her tea as her gaze swept the crowd in a continuous scan for any threats. Even here, in the heart of one of the safest places in the Macallian Empire, Valesa was alert. Though she was a maidservant, there was little doubt left in the minds of anyone who saw them together that her main role was one of a bodyguard.

Her unflinching demeanor and cords of muscle only served to amplify that fact to any onlooker. If anyone were to mistake her catlike grace for mere courtly training, the scars that crisscrossed her arms would advise them otherwise. And if even that didn't do the trick, there were very few people who would not be intimidated by her piercing brown eyes.

Calia, on the other hand, knew that she was anything but intimidating. She stood a head shorter than the average man. Her face was soft, and she'd never mastered the same cold stare that Valesa could deliver. She'd never wanted to be intimidating before now, but she could see how it might be an advantage in her current situation. If only to stop every professor from coming over to offer empty words of praise for her bravery in even making an attempt at piercing the void.

I did *pierce the void and live to tell about it,* Calia wanted to scream in their faces. Not that she had anything that might serve as proof. Not yet, anyway. On their return trip she would have to find something that would serve as definitive proof that they'd actually accomplished what so many said couldn't be done.

Instead of screaming, Calia nodded and thanked them for their kind words. She might not be the model of a lady of the court, but her recent experience with putting on a smiling face and lying through her teeth helped to sell the politeness. If she had to guess, the majority of the people here were only around for the free food anyway. Hopefully once that was gone, the crowd would fade away.

"I must admit"— deep voice startled her from her reverie—"when you announced your intentions to the board, I didn't think we'd ever see you again."

Calia turned to see the wide, familiar smile of Duke Galith. The portly man was a patron of the sciences, particularly of the theoretical study of the realms, and was a frequent visitor at the university. He'd attended many of the same lectures that she had, and over the course of time had become the closest thing that Calia had to a friend at the university. He'd been one of the few who didn't scoff at her proposals when she'd brought them to the university's attention.

"I must say that I have never been so happy to be wrong."

"It's good to see you, Lord Galith," Calia replied, allowing him to kiss her hand.

"Are you enjoying the festivities?" Galith asked with a smile that told her he already knew the answer.

"Of course," Calia lied. "The tea is delicious."

"I've noticed that you haven't corrected any of the people who have wandered by, offering their condolences on your failed experiment."

"Why would I correct them?"

"Because your experiment wasn't a failure, of course."

Calia felt her jaw drop. How could Duke Galith know? She'd made sure to tell no one outside of the estate, and she'd sworn all the servants to secrecy. Of course, word would get out anyway, but she could usually count on the servants waiting at least a few days before they ran to spread their rumors. The man's raised eyebrow told Calia that he hadn't known a thing, but had merely been guessing. Her expression must have confirmed it for him.

Damn it Calia, she chided herself, *you need to find out how Akos maintains that 'mask' of his.*

"Why have you not shouted this news from the rooftops, milady?" Galith asked as he sat down in the empty chair next to her. Valesa raised an eyebrow, but Galith was as friendly a person as Calia had ever met. And he wasn't exactly a physical specimen either. With Valesa right here, Calia was under no threat of harm from him. Even so, Valesa kept an eye on him as she resumed her scanning of the crowds.

"Well . . ." Calia began.

"This could be earthshaking news. This could change everything we know about the realms, about the universe itself."

"Yes, but—"

"Even if it is naught but empty space, it would shorten trade times. Your methods would cure the sailors of their fear of sailing too close to the void. The economic implications alone—"

"Galith," Calia said sharply. If she didn't get him under control, he'd launch into a full lecture. As much as she liked the man, she didn't have time to listen to his ramblings today.

"You'll have to trust me when I say that there is a good reason that I haven't announced my findings yet," Calia continued.

"Please, for the sake of my curiosity, tell me one thing," Galith begged. He did a remarkable impression of a puppy begging for treats. "Did you find it? The sixth realm, that is?"

Calia considered lying to him. But news would get out. And perhaps if that news came from the right source, it would hustle Halis along on his decision-making process. She would need the family treasury open to her if she wanted to make a rescue a reality, and she didn't have much time to waste if she wanted to save Vibius before something happened to him.

"I'll say this," Calia responded instead. "There is a very good reason that I was gone for so much longer than I planned."

"I knew it," Galith said, leaning back in his chair. His eyes glazed over as if they were trying to fix on something a million miles away. A slight smile cracked his lips.

"Now I must ask a favor of you," Calia said. "Do not tell a soul of this for one week."

"One week?" Galith repeated, his mind still elsewhere.

"Just one. After that, come back to me and I'll tell you everything."

That snapped him out of his thoughts. The prospect of knowing everything that Calia had learned about the sixth realm was something that he would never pass up. If Halis continued to push for time to think, then the entire realm would soon know of her journey. Most would doubt everything she said, but enough would be willing to risk it all to throw a damper on his plans to monopolize the realm. This gave her some leverage.

"Lady Hailko, I must confess to something," Galith said, leaning in conspiratorially. "I am a member of an . . . organization that is highly interested in these kinds of things."

"Are you about to ask me to join a cult?" Calia asked.

The humor in her tone brought a smile to his face, but it quickly vanished. That was odd. Calia had never known Galith to be serious about much of anything.

"No, nothing like that," he replied, waving a hand through the air. "It is a fraternity of philosophers. You may have even heard of us—the Brotherhood of Sogost?"

Calia hadn't heard of any such brotherhood. She glanced at Valesa, who gave a brief shrug of her shoulders. Calia turned her attention back to Galith.

"I'm afraid not."

"Well," Galith continued, "the brotherhood is founded on the teachings of the ancient philosopher Sogost, who postulated on the best way to govern a society. He hated kings and emperors. In fact, he believed that a modified form of democracy was the best."

"I'm afraid I don't see how this is relevant, Lord Galith."

"Bear with me. The brotherhood has long craved a place where we might carry out what we call 'the grand experiment.' To this point, it has been nothing but a thought exercise. But if a new land, unclaimed by any of the kingdoms of the realm of man, were to present itself..."

"You want to set up a new nation in the void?" Calia asked, not bothering to hide the surprise in her voice.

"Well, yes. That would be our ultimate goal. And I'm sure some form of . . . recognition could be arranged for. My brotherhood is populated with generous—and wealthy—men and women."

Calia took a moment to organize her thoughts before replying. The offer was clear. If she were to help them establish a foothold in the void, they would make her a rich—or richer, anyway—woman. Not that she particularly needed the money, but the offer was intriguing.

It did conflict with Halis's interests. Galith probably wouldn't want to share his offer with her brother, given his own machinations, and Calia knew that would be true of her brother as well. Calia had always been raised to put family first, but she had the feeling that Halis was going to drag his feet on this one. Something about the way he had reacted to her news didn't instill her with confidence that he would do everything in his power to help her get Vibius back.

"Let me consider your offer for a day or two?" Calia said.

"Of course, milady." Galith smiled again and took her hand, bowing over it as he rose. "You know where to find me once you decide. Of course, the choice if up to you, but I'd prefer you let me know either way?"

"I will," Calia promised.

With that, the duke was gone. For a rotund man, he was surprisingly graceful as he picked his way through the thinning crowd. Thankfully, it seemed that the caterers had run out of food, and the people were growing bored of each other's company. Before long, Calia would be able to go about her day.

She continued to accepted platitudes as her mind raced with the implications of the deal she'd been offered. Of course, Galith had not offered specifics, but Calia was sure that he would help her to get Vibius back if that was the price of her aid. If it were true that the brotherhood as a whole would be willing to chip in to help her, then the prospects of a successful rescue went up astronomically.

Of course, if Halis offered to help her, then the point would be moot. She wouldn't turn her back on family for the offer of money. But if, for whatever reason, Halis decided that he couldn't help her with her task, then at least she had options.

CHAPTER 2

Akos was getting tired of trying to dress with one hand. Especially the frilly shirts and tight pants that were in style amongst the elite of Macallia. Krallek assured him that the sling on his arm would be coming off within the next month and he would soon have free use of his left hand. Until then, Krallek swore that he would rebreak the arm himself if Akos took off the sling. The surgeon might only stand as tall as Akos's chest, but he had forearms like ham hocks and Akos had no doubt he would see the threat through.

As he finished dressing, Akos looked toward the door as if expecting someone to walk through. No one appeared, and he silently berated himself. What he was really looking for was an excuse not to have to do what he was about to do. But there was no putting this off any longer.

Akos strode toward the end of the docks and waved down a carriage, giving them an address before settling in for the ride. There was nothing to be afraid of. He was making a social call, nothing more. Still, his heart pounded ever faster despite his self-assurances. There was a good chance that Lord Varrie would turn him away at the door, and he didn't have a backup plan if that happened. He would just have to make the old man see reason.

The carriage rumbled down the streets of Geralis, eventually coming to a stop before the Varrie estate. The building was in the heart of the city, smashed between dozens of other mansions. Though it was nowhere near the grandeur of the sprawling Hailko country estate, it was a match in elegance. The Varries had spared no expense when they'd designed their opulent home, and it showed in every facet of the building, from the massive front door carved with scenes from Macallian history to the guardhouse that was shaped to resemble an old turret.

Akos wasn't used to seeing the building from the front. He'd never taken the opportunity to admire the loving work that the carpenters and masons had dedicated to making the mansion such a masterpiece. His entrance was farther around the back, where there was a crack in the wall wide enough for him to shimmy through without soiling his clothes. It was difficult to see from the interior, and Akos could wait until the light of a lantern had passed to know that the guard's patrol route had taken him away from that area. Then it was up the grate providing the framework for the vines that covered the eastern wall and into Anastasia's room.

But not today. The guard at the gatehouse eyed the carriage with a look straddling apathy and curiosity. Akos swallowed hard to keep his his heart from beating its way up into his throat. He'd faced blades, guns, and behemoths without flinching. *One old man shouldn't terrify me so much*, Akos thought to himself.

So Akos steeled himself and stepped out of the carriage. The guard's look changed from mild curiosity to one of intense scrutiny. Akos searched his memory to see if he could place the man's face, but he didn't think he'd ever been thrown out of the mansion by this particular man before.

"Name and business please?" the guard demanded.

"Captain Akos Freedman," Akos replied. "I've come to speak with Lord Varrie."

"Lord Varrie is a very busy man. Do you have an appointment?"

"No, but he'll want to speak to me. It's about his daughter."

"I'll let him know that you are calling. Please wait here."

The guard turned on his heel and marched off, leaving Akos to stand on the street. Akos allowed his annoyance at having to give his full name to help him calm himself. He hated having to use it, but he knew that Lord Varrie would not even consider seeing him unless he gave it. Varrie was a lord of the old breed, and a family name was everything to a man like that. At least the annoyance was drowning out his anxiety.

It only took a few moments for the guard to return. Akos braced himself for a refusal, but instead the guard opened the gate and ushered him inside. He led him down the path to the front door, where another man was waiting to receive him. The pencil-thin mustache and the look of general disdain were all too familiar to Akos.

"Good afternoon, Jalston." Akos tried to be as polite as he could. "How are you?"

"Captain Akos," Jalston sneered. "Lord Varrie is between meetings and has graciously decided to hear what you have to say. I would advise you to not waste his time."

"I'm doing well, thank you for asking."

Rather than reply, Jalston turned and opened the door. Akos thought that he could have picked at random from his crew of veteran killers and found a more delightful person to receive his guests than Jalston. But perhaps that was part of Varrie's plan to keep unwanted visitors away. If the reception was rude, it might deter the less determined from attempting to bother him.

The entrance to the house was as grand as the exterior. The sight gave Akos pause as he stepped in. The polished marble floors and soaring columns gave him flashes of memory of his first time seeing the atrium of Ferundun Keep. Akos did his best to hide his shiver as he waited for Jalston to make sure that the lord was ready to see him. At least this room didn't have a massive painting dominating an entire wall glorifying Lord Varrie.

The guards standing at either side of the door eyed him with interest. At least one of them had thrown him out of the mansion before when he'd tried to call on Anastasia. Akos flashed him his best smile and hoped that he didn't seem too threatening. It took him a moment to realize that the real reason the guards were giving him such ugly looks was because he was still wearing his sword.

It was there as nothing more than a reassurance. Akos had worn a blade at his hip since he was seventeen years old. It was his left arm bandaged up after all, and Akos was right-handed. However afterwards, he'd have to face Krallek, who had a strict no swordsmanship policy while he was recovering. That was a terrifying prospect, and one he'd sooner avoid altogether.

Instead of clinging to his blade, which was his right, Akos decided to extend a gesture of goodwill to the guards. He unbuckled his sword belt and handed the weapon over to one of the men. The man took it with a grateful nod. Hopefully they would remember that if this meeting went south. Akos would prefer that they were gentle with him if they were ordered to throw him out again. His arm and ribs were almost fully healed, but still tender.

Thankfully, Varrie did not keep him waiting long. Jalston returned and ushered him forward into the next room. Akos took a deep breath before striding into the sitting room. He'd been there a time or two, but never for long. It was well furnished, with plush couches and chairs dotting the magnificent Illyrian carpet.

Lord Varrie sat in one of the chairs, and he rose as Akos stepped into the room. He was not a tall man, and age had stripped him of any weight he may have once carried. Still, the wrinkles and lines age had carved into his face had done nothing to dull the wit behind his deep brown eyes. And he still held himself with a regal posture, despite the fading wisp of white hair that clung to his head, looking as though a stiff breeze may blow it away.

"Captain Akos Freedman," Jalston announced, derision dripping from his voice.

"Lord Varrie," Akos said, stepping forward to shake the older man's hand. "You honor me with this meeting."

"I thought I'd reward your courage in asking for it," Varrie replied. "And my sons tell me that you are single-handedly responsible for more damage to Vanocian shipping than any other privateer alive. That is worth something."

Varrie motioned for Akos to take a seat. Akos did, almost sinking into the luxurious softness of the chair. He was forced to wiggle to the edge to sit up straight and look Varrie in the eye while he spoke.

"Well, I won't mince words," Akos said after a long and uncomfortable silence. "I've come to speak to you about your daughter."

"I thought as much," Varrie said.

"Soon I'll have enough to fulfill the price you've set."

"Oh?"

The only indication that the man had any feelings about that was the eyebrow he raised. Otherwise, his face could have been carved from marble. Akos didn't think that the man believed him. It was true, although there was a chance he would have to spend a good chunk of it

14

to fund his rescue of Vibius. However, Varrie didn't need to know that right at this moment.

"Yes," Akos continued. "I've just completed a contract for Lord Hailko, and the payment will put me well over your number."

"You've just returned?" Varrie asked. This time there was a note of something else in his voice, slmost as if it had softened somewhat. Akos wasn't sure what to make of it.

"I have."

"Then you won't have heard. I hate to have to tell you this. Lord Hailko really should have been the one to deliver the news."

The bottom dropped out of Akos's stomach as he braced himself for whatever Varrie might have to say. He felt like he could take a good guess based on the man's demeanor.

"Lord Hailko has spent the last few months since your departure with his sister, steadily drinking and partying away his fortune. I'd be very surprised to hear that he has enough money left to hold up his end of the bargain."

The news hit Akos's chest like a hammer. He knew that Halis had been acting odd. The signs were all there if he'd bothered to pay attention. There had been far fewer guards and servants at the estate when they'd arrived. Thinking back on it, many of the pieces of art in the collection had disappeared from their pedestals as well.

"That certainly is a setback," Akos admitted. "But I think you'll find that even without that, my finances are more than enough to take care of your daughter."

"If the number hasn't been reached—"

"With all due respect, Lord Varrie, a lump sum of money was never what this was about."

"You don't think so?" The softness that had previously appeared on Varrie's face was gone now.

"No, I don't. You've all the riches in the world. Another fortune in dowry will do nothing to soften your life. This demand has always been about ensuring that your daughter goes to a man who can keep her in the lifestyle that she is accustomed to."

Akos wished that he could claim credit for that analysis, but it had all been Vibia. She'd always had an insight into things that escaped him. Akos had always appreciated having a point of view that he couldn't see himself. It had served him well in the past, and he had a feeling that it was about to serve him well now.

"That is an interesting opinion," Varrie said, neither his face nor his voice indicating assent or disagreement.

It was easy to see why Lord Varrie had a reputation for being a tough man to do business with. He was unreadable. This was difficult enough, made even more difficult by the news of Halis's destitution, and Varrie seemed determined not to make it any easier on him. *Lucky for me*, Akos mused, *I've no idea when to quit.*

"I think we both know that it's no mere opinion. It's the truth of the matter."

"The truth, you think?" Varrie steepled his fingers and leaned back as if considering this. "Do you want to know another truth?"

"Yes," Akos lied.

"You are a privateer. That in and of itself is no mark against you. In fact, in another situation I might be singing your praises and clapping you on the back. But the truth is that you are here inquiring after my daughter, my world, whilst pursuing one of the most dangerous careers in the realms. Do you think that is what I want for my daughter? A life of worry and wonder? Loneliness for months at a time, filled with the fear that this time her husband might not come home at all? And the final truth, the truth that I don't think you'll be able to deny in your heart, is that you have no intention of giving up such a life for her."

"You could not be further from the truth, my lord."

Akos had always intended to put his wild ways behind him when he finally won Anastasia's hand. He knew it would be difficult. He loved the sea and the adventure that it held. But he loved her more.

"Perhaps you really think that you mean that," Varrie said. "But I've known too many men like you to believe it. Void son, I've raised two of them. My daughter will never know a peaceful or happy life in your hands."

"What does she think?" Akos asked.

"Excuse me?"

"What does Anastasia think of your analysis of me? I'm sure that she's made it clear by now that none of the suitors that you've brought before her are what she wants. Your daughter and I love each other. I may not be able to give her peace of mind, but I can give her happiness."

"We'll see. I'll have to think on what you've said here before I make my decision. Rest assured, Captain Akos, that my opinion of you is much higher now than it was before."

"Wait," Akos said as Varrie rose from his chair. This was his last chance, and he knew it. He would not be around long enough for Varrie to make a final decision. And Akos was sure that would influence any decisions that the lord made. "May I speak with her?"

"I knew you were bold when you showed up on my doorstep asking to see me." Varrie shook his head in bewilderment. "But now I know you are a madman."

"I beg you, Lord Varrie."

"A humble privateer. I never thought I'd see the day. Very well. You may speak to her for a moment. Jalston, please fetch my daughter."

Jalston looked as if he would burst a vein in his shiny forehead, but he bowed and turned to obey without comment. Lord Varrie stepped out of the room to give them privacy to speak. Akos was thankful for that. If the lord had heard what he was about to say, he would have him shot on the spot.

"Lady Anastasia Varrie," Jalston announced after an agonizing wait.

Akos stood and turned to see her. His heart skipped a beat at her familiar face. She was beautiful. Artists and sculptors the world over would have killed to have her as their model and muse. Her dress showed far too much of her perfect, pale skin to be considered proper, but Akos doubted anyone would ever complain. Her raven black hair fell in ringlets halfway down her back. Her dazzling blue eyes lit up when they fell upon him, and he registered the flash of concern that crossed them when they slid across the sling binding his arm.

"Captain Akos, how lovely of you to pay me a visit," Anastasia said as the door closed behind her. "Through the front door no less," she continued once they were closer. "In the *daytime.*"

"I'm always full of surprises," Akos replied.

He bent to kiss her hand. Anastasia pulled his face up so that his lips could meet her own. She kissed him with such passion that for a moment he forgot all about the world—about his duties, about his worries, and about the void. But guilt began to flood his heart the moment they broke their embrace. In that moment he'd forgotten Vibius, and that was something he swore that he would never do.

Anastasia was looking at him with growing curiosity as he stood there, holding her hand. Akos was frozen with uncertainty. *This is new.* Akos was not one to be hesitant. Something about Anastasia turned his mind to clay, though, and he had trouble remembering what he was here for in the first place. He forced himself to sober, and looked down into her inquisitive gaze.

"Marry me," Akos said, wondering if he should drop to one knee. It wasn't as if he'd brought a ring. He didn't think he'd need one tonight. Akos decided that he should stay standing.

"My father approved?" Anastasia gasped.

"Well . . ."

Anastasia broke from his grip and moved to sit in one of the chairs. Akos followed her and took the seat across from her. She looked deep in thought.

"You know that I cannot marry without my father's approval," Anastasia said.

"You could . . ."

"I thought you said that after you returned you would have the dowry that my father required."

"I will. But I'm going to have to . . . reinvest much of it for one last voyage."

"Reinvest? What does that mean?"

"We found a new realm, but there were some complications. Vibius was taken, and I have to go save him."

"And it will cost that much?"

That simple sentence wrongfooted Akos almost as much as the kiss.

"Damn the costs," Akos declared.

"How do you even know that Vibius is still able to be saved?"

Akos couldn't believe what he was hearing. He had expected some pushback, but this was more than he'd ever imagined. He and Anastasia had often lain in each other's arms speaking of their dreams to run away together. To drop everything and disappear.

"I just know," Akos said. "How could you even suggest that?"

"I know that you love Vibius, but if you've been all the way to the void and back, then it's been months since you've seen him alive. If you left him in another realm, there is no telling what's happened to him. Why spend the dowry we've waited so long on to go after someone who may not be able to be saved?"

"I have to try, regardless of the chances."

Akos rose to his feet despite his spinning head. He didn't know where this was coming from. Anastasia certainly was not as close to Vibius as he was, but that didn't excuse her writing him off as another casualty of their journeys.

"But if you do this, who knows when you will be able to make the dowry again. It's taken almost a decade to gather it this time. I can't wait forever, Akos."

"Then don't," Akos said. "Come with me now."

"What?"

"Elope with me. We've talked about it often enough. Run away with me and live aboard the *Mist Stalker* until this last voyage is over. Then we can figure out the rest."

"That was all just pillow talk."

"Ana . . ."

Anastasia rose from her chair, refusing to look him in the eye. Akos tried to glean what she was thinking, but her face had hardened much like her father's. She held her head high as she began to walk away from him toward the door.

"Wait," Akos begged.

"No," Anastasia replied simply. "If you have the funds now, then there is no reason to put it off any longer. I need a man who can take care of me, Akos, and if it isn't you, then it is high time that I began to explore other options."

"What are you saying?"

"That if you feel you must choose Vibius over me, then you can have him. But you will no longer have me. So which will it be?"

"Ana, this is madness."

"Do not call me that anymore. I am Lady Varrie, and you will address me as such. And do not call on me again."

Akos was too dumbfounded to manage any more words as the woman who was his world took her leave and strode out the door. Her beautiful visage was replaced with the sneering face of Jalston as he stepped back in. The contempt written across his face only deepened as he took in Akos's state.

"Not the answer you were hoping for, Captain?" Jalston asked.

Akos didn't deign to reply. His usual wit had fled, chasing after Anastasia he was sure. Jalston motioned for him to follow. Before he knew what was happening, Akos was standing on the street in the afternoon sun, wondering what to do now. *Nothing for it but to go back to the Hailko estate*, Akos thought, *and pray that Calia has more luck than I do.*

The shock of Anastasia spurning him was so deep that Akos didn't realize he hadn't called for a carriage to take him back until he was almost to the Hailko driveway. The sun had set almost an hour ago, but he hadn't noticed that either. Akos blinked, trying to snap himself out of the shock, but it was no use. His mind was still reeling as he made his way down the driveway to the manor.

Another surprise in the form of Lusalin Carralt was waiting for him at the door. The dour-faced man was not the first person that Akos was hoping to see. Though to be fair to the butler, Akos wasn't in much of a mood to see anyone at the moment. Still, there was a little too much of Jalston's superior attitude in Lusalin's terse smile for his liking.

"Lord Hailko has requested your presence in the library," Lusalin said.

Akos didn't even bother to respond. Hopefully Halis had finally decided to help them. He trudged up the stairs and through the open door to see what the man would say. It couldn't make his evening any worse. *That's the spirit*, Akos thought to himself.

The now-familiar twists and turns of the Hailko mansion passed in a blur as Akos made his way to the library. If Halis was waiting to talk to him, that meant that he had probably already spoken to Calia. He wondered how she would take the news if her brother decided not to help them. Unless Akos missed his guess, she would take the news as poorly as he would.

Lusalin hurried ahead of him as he stomped his way through the corridors and opened the door to the library for him. Akos thought that the man was worried that he might throw open the door and damage it. In his mood, he might. But as the butler ushered him through the door, Akos realized that there had been another reason: Lusalin was trying to distract him from what was waiting for him in the other room.

Halis did indeed sit in his favorite chair in the center of the room. But Akos didn't notice the guards on either side of the door until he'd passed by them. Uniformed members of the Geralis City Guard were stationed all around the room. Akos's heart skipped a beat as he realized that there was only one reason Halis might have summoned them.

"Captain Akos Freedman?"

One of the guards stepped forward. Akos immediately pegged him for an officer. His uniform was covered in far more medals and ribbons than anyone else's in the room. Akos wasn't sure if it was just his current mood or his innate stubbornness, but he refused to answer the man.

"This is him, lieutenant," Halis said when it became clear that Akos wouldn't answer.

"Right," the lieutenant said. "Captain Freedman, your letter of marque has been revoked. With a prize in court, that means that you are a pirate. I'm afraid you'll have to come with us. Sword please."

It was at that moment that Akos realized he had in fact left his sword at the Varrie's. It was almost enough to draw a wry chuckle out of him. The idea that the dozen or so armed guards, each of whom had their hands already on their weapons, might need to relieve an effectively one-armed man of his sword did force him to laugh. The lieutenant hopped back a step nervously, and several blades came an inch or two out of their sheaths.

I wonder what stories they've been told about me? Akos mused.

"I'm afraid I've misplaced my blade," Akos replied.

"Very well then," the lieutenant said, his face reddening. "If you'll come with us."

Akos allowed the men to lead him out of the room, but not before casting a glance back at the man who had put him in this situation. Halis looked as though he'd just gotten away with the most cunning plan of the century. A grin split his soft face. Their eyes locked for a moment, and the grin wavered. Akos allowed his gaze to linger until the man broke eye contact and looked away. Then one of the guards shoved him forward, and he lost sight of the traitor.

As the group made their way out to a waiting prison wagon, Akos could only wonder how Calia would take *this* news.

CHAPTER 3

"You what?" Calia shouted in surprise.

"Understand, sister, this is a necessary step to ensure—" Halis began.

"Necessary to ensure what, Halis? To ensure that he didn't tell anyone? To ensure that you have the monopoly on this new land?"

"Yes! He is a *pirate,* Calia. He would have betrayed your trust eventually. He was doing nothing but using you for his advantage, to accomplish his own goals. I'm sure that once this Vibius was rescued, he would immediately return and spread your discovery to the world, or at least to whoever would pay him the most."

"You don't know the half of what you're talking about. I demanded that we return for Vibius before he even suggested it."

"I'm sure he's led you to believe that. But this is his goal, not yours."

"I love Vibius!"

That finally seemed to take Halis off guard. Calia hated when he got like this. So sure of his position that he was unwilling to allow any opposing viewpoint to creep into his mind.

Calia stood without allowing him to say another word. Halis started to stand as well, but Calia held up a hand to stall him.

"Surely you know that some pirate wayfarer is no suitable match for a woman of your station," Halis managed to say after a moment.

"He was a noble before he was a wayfarer," Calia shot back. "And even that would be enough if you hadn't already written him off for dead."

"I'm sure if you take some time, you will see that this is the proper course."

"Then I'll take that time. Away from you."

Calia stormed out of the library without another word, Valesa falling into step behind her. She didn't even know where she was going, she just knew that she needed to be somewhere away from her brother. She couldn't believe what she'd heard from his little explanation.

"Milady, I need to speak with you," Valesa said.

Calia snapped her head around. She hadn't realized it, but she'd marched all the way to her room. Valesa stepped in behind her and closed the door. Something must have been serious if Valesa was calling her milady without anyone around to hear them.

"What's wrong?" Calia asked.

"I've been speaking with the other servants during the day when you didn't require my services," Valesa said. "There's something about Halis that you should know."

"You mean other than the fact that he had Akos arrested and killed our plans without so much as a second thought?"

"Yes. The servants tell me that he's been blowing through the family fortune. None of them were sure of the exact amount, but if they're correct, there can't be much left."

Calia turned around and put her hands on her writing desk. She stared down at the wood without seeing it, her mind churning as she tried to process everything that was happening. There was a lot to think through.

It shouldn't have surprised her to hear, but for some reason it did. Calia knew that Father had always tried his best to teach them the value of money. The lesson had stuck with her better than it had with Halis. He'd always been a spender, but she thought that he would change his ways once he was forced to deal with the entire inheritance rather than just the allowance that their father gave to each of them.

But the idea that he would break a contract to prevent someone from threatening a possible source of wealth had never occurred to her. Much less someone who had saved her life and done everything that was asked of him. Regardless of their initial intentions, Akos and his crew had proven to be true and honorable men who deserved more than what Halis seemed willing to give them.

It did explain why he'd balked at their request to fund another expedition, and when Akos had asked after the bonus that he'd been promised. If Halis had the money, he probably wouldn't have even hesitated.

"All this for money, Halis?" Calia muttered to herself.

"People will do odd things for money," Valesa said.

Calia shook her head, wondering whether he would betray her if it would protect his precious fortune. She'd like to think that her own brother would never do that to her, but now she wasn't so sure. Calia knew that she couldn't let this stop her.

"We have to get to the *Mist Stalker* and warn the others," Calia said. "If they've arrested Akos, they'll be moving on the crew as well."

"I'll have a carriage prepared," Valesa said.

"No, that will draw too much attention. Halis will know. Have two of the horses prepared, and make sure to ask little Calstat to do it."

"Why Calstat?"

"He's always had a little crush on you. If you ask him to keep it secret, I'm sure he will."

"How do you know that?"

"I talk to the servants too. Now go; we need to move."

Valesa nodded and left, leaving Calia to her own thoughts for a moment. She could only hope that they managed to reach the rest of the crew in time. A storied privateer captain like Akos and a wayfarer like Vibia would be fine, but the rest of the crew would likely be hung as pirates. The idea of seeing Leodysus or Old Haroln swinging from the gallows turned her stomach. If there was anything she could do to prevent that, she had to at least try.

That was if there was still anything to be done. There was always a chance that when Halis summoned the city guard, they'd sent some along to the ship in case Akos returned there instead. If that were the case, the crew would already be in chains awaiting trial.

Calia shook the thought from her mind. There was nothing she could do about that. She needed to focus on what she *could* do to help. If she reached the docks before the guard, she would at least give the crew a chance.

Of course, she had no idea what they would do after that. Without the family fortune, she had no idea how they would get the money they needed to raise a force large enough to free Vibius from Anson's grasp. Akos had filled her in on his own personal finances, and though they were impressive, they would only get them part of the way there.

Calia's eyes lit up as she remembered the words of Duke Galith. Several wealthy backers were just what she needed. If she told Galith that they were going to prepare a way for them to settle a colony in the void, she was sure that he would be more than happy to provide her with funding. It seemed that the duke would not have to wait a week for her story after all.

Calia grabbed a pen and inkwell from her desk and jotted down a brief letter on some spare paper. She didn't even bother sealing it when she was done. It was an invitation for Galith to meet with her at nightfall in his mansion. Hopefully he would believe her story and provide them with the aid they needed. If they could manage to get Akos out of prison and keep the crew away from the gallows, that is.

There was simply so much to do. Calia turned away from her writing desk with the letter clasped in her hand. There was nothing for it now but to get started.

***

Calia slowed her horse as they reached the dense crowds that constantly surrounded the docks of Geralis. A trade hub for both international and interrealm trade, Geralis was one of the richest and busiest cities in the entirety of the Empire of Macallia. Calia had never had much reason to travel down to the docks before her errant adventure with the crew of the *Mist Stalker*.

Now she was glad to be on the back of a horse. From her vantage point, Calia could see clear across the bustle of the docks and into the forest of masts that swayed against their moorings. She stood up in her stirrups to try to peer through that mess toward where the *Mist Stalker* was docked.

They'd ridden as fast as they could without drawing any suspicion, but it seemed they were too late. Calia felt her heart sink as she realized that the men swarming the deck of the dark ship were wearing the bright blue uniforms of the city guard. There had to be at least two dozen of them securing the vessel. Calia sank back into the saddle, fear settling into her heart as she did so. All the friends she'd made in the voyage to and from the void would be tried and sentenced as pirates, all due to her brother's greed.

That fear began to turn to rage, blinding and hot. Calia's cheeks flushed as the anger found its way to her face. She turned to snap at Valesa, though she wasn't sure what she would say. The thought died in her throat as something across the street caught her attention.

Leaning against the outside wall of one of the string of taverns and inns that lined the docks was a short and stocky figure smoking on a pipe. Krallek the dwarven surgeon had a short but thick beard greyed by age and a hard face that time had only just managed to carve in to. He didn't say a word, but he raised his pipe and tipped his head in a salute.

Calia felt the anger begin to drain out of her even as she turned her horse to head back to the taverns. Krallek pointed to one with a hanging sign marking it as the Black Fish Inn with the stem of his pipe before returning it to his mouth and looking back out over the crowd. Calia motioned for Valesa to follow her as she rode toward the hitching post outside.

"Are you sure this is wise, milady?" Valesa asked after they dismounted.

Calia glanced over the façade of the dirty old inn. It was a wooden structure that looked as though it would fall apart at a stiff breeze. There was no door, but a curtain had been hung over the entrance to keep out the brisk wind. She could hear drunken laughter floating out from within, despite the fact that it was midday.

This was no place that a woman of her birth would be caught dead. None of her peers would so much as consider entering such a dilapidated establishment. But Calia was not her peers, and she'd long ago decided that she would never let propriety stop her from doing what needed to be done. She replied to her maidservant with a simple nod before pushing her way through the curtain and into the Black Fish.

The smell of the place struck her as soon as she whisked back the curtain. It was an odd combination of tobacco smoke and what could only be xheiat root. She had never smelled the smoke, but from her research she was familiar with the scent of the root, and it was distinctive to say the least. A pall hung over the main room of the inn.

It looked to be more of a bar than a place to sleep, though she could see bedrooms at the top of the stairs that led to a second level. Women wearing little more than corsets waved elvish fans in their faces to clear some of the smoke, though many of them were smoking as well. A band played a jovial tune in the corner for anyone who cared enough to listen, and a few dozen patrons drank away their troubles at tables in the main room.

It didn't seem that anyone had noticed their entrance. Certainly no one looked up from their drinks. A few of the courtesans at the top of the stairs began to whisper behind their fans, but Calia paid them no attention. Her eyes scanned the room for any familiar faces. Valesa stepped in behind her and did the same.

"I was wondering when you might show up," Leo's voice boomed from a side table.

Calia spun to see Leo sitting in the corner of the room. He rose to greet them, and Calia wrapped her arms around his waist in a hug. He patted her back gently before offering the two of them a seat.

"I figured it was only a matter of time until you came looking at the docks," Leo said. "What's going on?"

"My brother has lost his mind," Calia explained. "He's had Akos arrested, and I thought he would move on you too."

Leo waved his hand dismissively. "Wouldn't be the first time the guards came for us. We knew they were coming a half hour before they moved. It was easy enough to leave them an empty ship to look after."

Calia noticed that even while he spoke, Leo kept an eye on the door. Even if he was trying to play it off as if it were no big deal, the man was clearly rattled. She watched him glance up at one of the courtesans and gesture for her. She dipped into a different room and returned with Vibia, who smiled in relief when she saw them.

"I'm glad to see the both of you," Vibia said. "I didn't know how far this would go."

"Halis wouldn't have me arrested," Calia said with much more confidence than she felt. "But the rest of you aren't safe."

"I assume they've taken Akos?"

Calia nodded. Vibia's brow furrowed in thought. Calia hadn't spent near as much time around Vibia as she had Vibius on their voyage, but she knew that the woman was at least as intelligent as her twin. Her golden eyes danced in the muted lantern light of the inn as she thought her way through the situation. Calia trusted that between them, they would be able to think of something they could do to help their captain.

"Well, they won't hang him," Vibia said, "so that gives us some time. But we don't know how much time Vibius has, so we need to move now. And we need to get out of the city. The watch will eventually wise up and start looking for Leo and me in the taverns."

"I think I have an idea," Calia said. "I thought of it as we rode over here to check on you. I could go to the prison at dawn and attempt to have them release Akos to me."

"Do you think they would do that?" Leo asked.

"I don't know. But since it was my family that held his letter of marque, I could try. They might be confused enough to go along with it."

"And if they ask for bail money?" Valesa asked.

"I'll tell them to send the bill to Halis."

Valesa smirked at the thought. Calia had to admit there was more than a little pettiness to it. But the entire plan relied on her being able to bluff her way through the prison chain of command. Unfortunately, she didn't see any other options that would get Akos out of prison in a timely manner.

"Then what?" Vibia asked. "We'll need a new ship. The *Mist Stalker* is firmly within the hands of the guard."

"I don't know about that, but I do know what Akos was planning to do next," Calia said.

"Really? He never discussed anything with me."

That surprised Calia. Vibia was practically Akos's sister, and they'd had frequent discussions on the return from the void. She couldn't imagine why he might plan something and leave her out of the loop.

"He said he wanted to go to Tersun to meet with a man . . . a Maximillian I think . . . to discuss a ship he owns," Calia explained.

"Do you mean d'Maxilae?" Vibia asked.

"Yes, that was the name."

Vibia rolled her eyes and then sunk her head into her hands. Leo barked out a laugh at her reaction. Calia glanced over at Valesa, who shrugged.

"I detest that man," Vibia muttered.

"He doesn't detest you," Leo said.

Vibia turned to glare daggers at Leo, who was suddenly very interested by something on the ceiling.

"Either way," Vibia said, turning back to Calia. "If that is what our plan is, I suppose I'll have to suffer through it. But if your brother is having us arrested, I doubt he'll be funding our expedition."

"I have a plan for that as well," Calia said.

It only took her a few moments to explain her conversation with Duke Galith and the implications, as well as the letter she'd sent off to him before they'd made their way to the docks.

"Well, that might work," Vibia said. "It sounds like you've got things well in hand."

"I wouldn't say that," Calia replied.

"I would. Would you like us to accompany you to the prison or to your meeting with Galith?"

"I think I can handle them on my own. I don't want to draw any undue attention to you."

"Very well then. We'll begin to round up the crew and find a way to get to Tersun. I think it's best if we go by multiple ships."

"Agreed. We'll see you in Tersun."

CHAPTER 4

The term "gilded cage" came to Vibius's mind as he looked out over the island of Logathia from his princely chambers in Anson's keep. Despite his previous escape attempts, he had been treated with much higher regard than he'd worried he might. After all, it had been his ruse with the unloaded pistol that had cost Anson his chance to kill a traitor.

And as Vibius had come to learn, Anson loved nothing more in the world than killing those he deemed to be traitors. As of late, anything was a traitorous act. Vibius had watched as a man was executed via behemoth for forgetting to bring the right kind of wine with dinner. It had been a surreal experience. The idea that a single man held such complete power over the lives of so many sickened Vibius.

Mentally, Vibius could understand why Anson was treating him with such care. The secrets of travelling to and from the void were locked within his mind, and if Anson ever wanted to make his dreams of a multirealm empire a reality, he would need Vibius's help. Not that he would ever get it. Vibius had no desire to lift so much as a finger in aid of the monster that lorded over Logathia as a god.

But after witnessing the man call out his servants for the smallest actions and have them put to death, Vibius had a hard time reconciling the two views. Many of the men he'd seen put to death recently had been lifelong servants and had earned as much trust as a man could in this society. Perhaps the betrayal of Akos had shaken him more than he was willing to show. Or perhaps it had something to do with the more physical wound he'd given him.

From what little information he was able to ferret out, Vibius could piece together that there hadn't been a serious attempt on Anson's life in over a century. The gods of the various islands had been in somewhat of a stasis for centuries, each trying to goad the other into fighting on their home territory. The people of his island were so thoroughly convinced of his godhood that they dared not make the attempt. If the man had received more than a papercut in the last fifty years, Vibius would be amazed.

And it seemed that this aura of invulnerability had begun to seep into Anson's mind, blurring the line between his own carefully crafted lies and the truth of the world. When Akos had stood over him, ready to deliver the coup de grace, something in Anson's mind must have broken. The mental veil he'd wrapped over his eyes had been violently torn away, and for the first time in what must have been centuries, Anson was forcefully reminded of his own mortality. It was the only way to explain the paranoia that the man was exhibiting. As Vibius watched the soldiers in the courtyard go through some drill, he wondered which of them would be on the receiving end of the next tirade and accompanying execution.

Vibius leaned out of the window and, not for the first time, considered throwing himself out of it. The courtyard was far enough below that it was sure to kill him. It was, after all, the only surefire way to ensure that Anson never got the information that he so desperately needed. Torture didn't seem to be an option yet, but if that ever changed, Vibius would have to do something. He knew himself well enough to know that he would break under the pain.

Akos had told him once that no man could withstand torture forever. That eventually all men broke. Vibius had pointed out that in the first fifteen years of Akos's own life, the worst mental and physical tortures the slavers could inflict had not broken him. But something in the man's eyes told him otherwise. Akos said that he had been broken, and he'd only pieced himself back together when the Antonius twins had happened into his life.

Now, Vibius had to find a way to stay strong without his companions. Regardless of the appearance of the situation, Vibius knew that Anson was trying to torture him into revealing his secrets. Anson was taking a far different tactic than Vibius had anticipated, but he knew it nonetheless. This torture was insidious because it took the form of kindness. It took the form of promises of reward. It took the form of feigned comradery.

Vibius had seen through it so far. But he feared that he might not see through it forever. That one day, Anson might blind him with the promise of something that he couldn't resist. Or that the desire to see home might overwhelm him and overrule his sense. Or, far more likely, that he would wear out his welcome and Anson would switch to more aggressive tactics.

If Vibius was any judge of character though, that might take a while. Until recently, Anson had been very patient and meticulous in all things. His seeming immortality allowed him to take a far longer view of things than a normal man would. Even if it took a lifetime for Vibius to spill his secrets, what was that to a man who'd already seen twenty?

Vibius turned his view from the courtyard toward the sky. The sight caused a pang to run through his heart. The sky in the realm of behemoths was the same beautiful shade of blue as Calia's eyes. All it took was the thought of her crossing his mind to push him away from the ledge. Vibius couldn't conceive of a world where she still lived, and he didn't try to find his way back to her.

The thought of her turned Vibius's mind inward. Was his refusal to end his life a product of his hope that he'd see her again or a fear of losing that chance? Eternal optimism or simple cowardice? He liked to think it was the former, but he didn't know for sure. Neither option changed the fact that his heart was set on seeing her again. His mind would simply have to find a way to make that happen.

Unfortunately, Anson seemed to have learned his lesson. The deep scar on his wrist must be a continuous reminder. Vibius was at all times watched by at least two men, even in his own room. That in and of itself would have made planning anything significantly more difficult. But it was the ever-present shadow of a behemoth dogging his every footstep that gave him true pause.

After spending so much time around them, Vibius had come to understand their limitations better. Anson couldn't see through their eyes, at least not at all times, but he could gather a great deal of information from one. Vibius had noted that when Anson wasn't focusing on one in particular, it tended to act more like a tamed animal than an extension of the self-styled god's will.

None of that gave him any edge in an escape attempt. If anything, he now understood that Anson's lieutenants could use the creatures as monstrous bloodhounds even if Anson weren't directly involved. Still, knowing the limitations and capabilities of an enemy was the first step on the road to defeating them. So as he learned, he would continue to try to plan out an escape.

As if on cue, a knock on the door interrupted his thoughts. One of his guards opened it without so much as waiting for a nod from Vibius.

"Lord Anson requests the wayfarer's presence," the servant announced.

"This is unscheduled," the guard replied.

Vibius smirked. He hadn't been in captivity for too long before he'd tried to bribe the slaves that worked in the keep with promises of freedom and riches. Unluckily, it also hadn't been too long before the servants reported him. Now all his activities were scheduled, and any deviations had to come with the written approval of Anson himself.

The servant offered up a piece of rolled paper instead of a reply. The guard scanned through the note despite the fact that Vibius knew he couldn't read. All he was looking for was a seal—the official seal that Anson marked all his personal correspondence and orders with. The man nodded after he spotted it.

"Where are we to take him?" the guard asked as if he hadn't pretended to read the order.

"The docks," the servant replied. "Anson wishes for him to help inspect the new navy."

The guard gave little more than a grunt of affirmation. Vibius readied himself. This plan had been a long time in the making, feeling out which servants he could trust and which guards he could fool. His nerves were frayed from his long captivity, but he did his best to calm them for one more try.

The servant led Vibius through the now-familiar halls, flanked by his personal guards. As they walked, Vibius wondered what was actually written on the note that the servant had brought. It was probably something mundane, like a request regarding what he wanted for dinner. Very few of the common-born guards could read; that luxury was retained for the nobility, so it didn't actually matter what it said. So long as the paper had Anson's seal, they would have done whatever the servant told them to.

Vibius would have considered it a dismal state of affairs in Macallia, but he was glad for it here. He'd almost laughed aloud to himself when he'd realized illiteracy could be the key to his salvation. It seemed to be too simple a solution. Now, as they made their way to the gates and to his freedom, he felt like laughing again. Still, Vibius was careful to keep the mirth from his face, as difficult as that was.

It wouldn't be too much further before they came to the room that contained the slaves that would overpower his guards and don their uniforms. Then they would make their way to the docks, where the false guards would commandeer a boat for them to sail back to the realm of man and to freedom. It was a simple plan, but still Vibius felt sweat beading on his back as the tension of the situation tightened his muscles.

One more turn. If the guards suspected anything, they gave no indication of it. It helped that the room Vibius and the slaves had chosen for their ambush was on the way to the gates. They shouldn't know what was happening until the slaves' knives were sinking into their throats.

They rounded the corner and walked into the room. Vibius braced for the commotion, but nothing was forthcoming. The servant that was leading faltered a step and looked over his shoulder. Vibius didn't dare turn around. The group slowed to a halt as the servant's knees began to shake. The guards looked confused, but they fell to their knees as well when they looked around the room.

Vibius felt the bottom drop out of his stomach as he heard footsteps behind him. Slowly he forced himself to turn and face his fate. A behemoth stood in the corner of the room, clawed hands resting on the shoulders of the would-be assassins. It would have been almost paternal if it weren't for the lolling mouthful of shark-like teeth and crown of doll's eyes that surrounded the behemoth's head. How the creature had managed to squeeze itself into the small storeroom was beyond him. But the massive creatures had shown a dexterity that belied their size before.

As Vibius turned, a new figure strode around the corner. Anson had looked better. When they'd met, he cut a regal figure. His normally clean-shaven face was covered in stubble, and his smug smile had been replaced by a permanent scowl. His hair was pulled back in a ponytail like it usually was, but it was ragged, with loose strands falling about his face. His hands were clasped behind his back, and he looked over the group in the room as if inspecting soldiers on a parade ground.

"You should've known better than to trust a slave," Anson said coldly. "They told a dozen people to be ready to move minutes after you made your plan. They just can't help themselves."

Vibius ignored the man. This was an all too familiar dance. Anson would lecture him on the hopelessness of his situation, Vibius's guard would be doubled, and then they would go on about their lives. Vibius knew that Anson couldn't risk anything happening to the wayfarer, so he would face no repercussions other than being forced to watch the people who'd helped him be executed.

That would be punishment enough. It was why Vibius had tried so hard to keep other people out of his plans for so long. He'd taken the risk on this plot because he'd been convinced it would work out. Now he would have to live with all their deaths on his conscience.

Anson stared into Vibius's eyes. He tried to meet them. There was something wild in those brown eyes that troubled Vibius. He found himself looking down at his feet instead. He cursed himself for a coward. Akos would have stared into the man's eyes without so much as flinching.

"It seems that you have not learned your lesson," Anson said, anger creeping into his voice. "Always looking for a way out. Can you not see what I offer? What only I can offer?"

Vibius gave no response. He set his jaw and his shoulders and forced his eyes back up. Golden eyes locked with brown, and what Vibius saw terrified him. All reason was gone from those eyes. Anson began to pace the floor, eyes still locked onto the wayfarer.

"Kill them," Anson said.

The behemoth's claws curled inward, punching through the chests of the slaves like paper. It then forced them outward, ripping chunks of flesh, organs, and bone and flinging them about the room. Anson and Vibius were both sprayed with viscera, and Vibius took an involuntary step backward. The guards turned their blades on the servant that had led them there, cutting his throat and tossing him aside. Vibius stood amongst the carnage and barely kept the contents of his stomach down.

"He cannot see what he needs to see," Anson muttered to himself. "He is looking for things he should not. What to do?"

Anson's gaze snapped to the guards with such intensity that even they jumped.

"Take him to the dungeon," Anson ordered. "And once you're there, take his eyes. But keep him alive. I'll need him at some point. Even if it's just as an example."

Vibius did his best to fight back as the guards grabbed his arms, but it was no use. They dragged him kicking into the bowels of the keep.

CHAPTER 5

Calia stood before the Geralis Jail with growing trepidation. Her entire plan revolved around the guards not asking questions and allowing her to take Akos into her custody without any fuss. If they didn't acquiesce, she didn't know what she was going to do. She also didn't know what she would do if they asked for bail. Halis couldn't front her the money even if he wanted to, and she didn't have any of her own.

"Everything alright?" Valesa asked her.

"Just a little nervous," Calia admitted.

"You'd be mad not to be. You don't have to do this."

"I do."

"We don't owe him anything."

Calia disagreed with her maidservant on that point, but she didn't respond. She could see where Valesa was coming from. Akos had lied to them about his intentions for taking them into the void. But Calia knew that he'd done that in order to protect his crew, and she wasn't sure that if their positions were reversed, she wouldn't have done the same thing. And ever since then he had been honest and true to his word.

She knew that Valesa would view him as an untrustworthy pirate no matter what he did to redeem himself. So instead of trying to convince her of his worth as a friend, she changed tactics.

"Even if we don't owe him anything," Calia said, "we need him. He has the connections that we need to get back to Vibius."

Valesa pursed her lips as if she wanted to argue, but instead nodded her head to concede the point. Calia also knew that Valesa still wasn't convinced of the need to go back to save Vibius. But that point was not up for discussion.

Calia steeled herself for the inevitable confrontation with the guards and did her best impression of Akos. Vibius had told her how he adopted a "captain's mask" when he needed to avoid showing his true emotions. Calia tried her best to project an aura of confidence bordering on indifference. Her back straightened and her chin rose slightly.

As sure of herself as she was ever going to get, Calia strode through the front gate of the jail. Valesa stalked her heels, casting about for threats. For this trip, the bodyguard had decided to wear her sword in plain sight. Calia wasn't sure whether that was a show of force for the prisoners or the guards. It was always possible that she intended to intimidate both.

The front yard of the jail was pleasant enough, with manicured grass and benches. It might have fooled a casual observer into thinking that it was a park or the yard of a manor house. The high walls of the second level dispelled that notion. If an inmate somehow managed to climb the sheer face of smooth stone, they would be met with a row of spikes that resembled the tips of pikes in close formation. After that they would have a fifty-yard run through the front yard, which was crawling with armed guards, before finding any freedom.

It was unlikely that the people incarcerated here would risk making such an attempt. The Geralis City Jail was where they kept the nobles and high-ranking criminals. Lower-born criminals were kept outside of the city bounds. The nobles awaiting their court dates and bailouts in this prison wouldn't dare to soil their clothes attempting to escape. If Calia had to guess, the guards were as much to keep unwanted visitors and assassins out as they were to keep the prisoners in.

"Here to visit a prisoner ma'am?" a guard asked as they approached the inner gate.

"That's Lady Hailko to you," Valesa growled.

The guard immediately fumbled his morning paper and straightened up. Calia did her best to give him what she hoped was a disdainful look. The man bowed at the waist before speaking again.

"My apologies, Lady Hailko. Are you here to visit a prisoner?"

"I'm here to have a prisoner released into my custody," Calia replied.

"Ah . . . that is most unconventional, milady."

"A friend of mine has been imprisoned here wrongfully. I understand that his name must be cleared by the court, but I intend to allow him to stay at my estate until his court date."

"I understand, but that sort of thing has not been done in a while."

Calia could feel her mask slipping. The guard glanced between her and Valesa as if looking for a cue that this was all a joke. Calia wondered if her entire plan had been doomed to fail from the beginning.

"This is just ridiculous," Calia sighed.

"Excuse me?" the guard asked.

Calia resisted the urge to snap her hand to her mouth. She hadn't realized she'd spoken aloud. The guard was tensing up, bracing for what must be the all too usual tirade of an angry noble berating him for doing nothing more than his job. If there was any goodwill there before, it was fluttering away.

"I didn't mean anything you're doing," Calia scrambled to say. "I just mean this whole situation."

"I'm afraid I don't take your meaning, milady." Now the guard looked perplexed.

"I employed a prisoner here on the promise of payment by my brother. The prisoner completed the contract, but now my brother doesn't want to pay him and had his letter of marque revoked to avoid it."

The guard seemed to loosen up a bit as she talked. There was clear sympathy on his face. Perhaps this was the tack she should have taken from the beginning. She decided to press forward and hope that she could sway him.

"I just don't want him to suffer for my brother's greed," Calia said, clasping her hands in front of her. "I would *greatly* appreciate anything you could do to help me."

"I'd love to help you, milady, but it's over my head," the guard said.

Calia didn't have to fake the disappointment in her eyes. She should have known better from the start and come up with a better plan. She should have known that the only time her plot would have worked was in one of her sappy novels. She was about to thank the guard for his time and leave to come up with something else when the guard sighed.

"I'll speak with my commanding officer," the guard offered. "I can't promise anything, but I'll see what I can do."

"Oh, thank you, sir," Calia said. "You've no idea what this means to me."

"What is the name of your prisoner?"

"Captain Akos Freedman."

"Yes?" a voice said from behind the guard.

***

The light stabbed at Akos's eyes as the guards led him through the prison and into the processing room. A man went to fetch his personal belongings from a lockbox while he tried to blink the sleep out of his eyes. Of all the prisons he'd been thrown into, this was by far the nicest. It seemed that despite his new status as a criminal, there were still enough people in the justice system that recognized his contributions to the Macallian efforts to control the seas to earn him a comfortable cell.

Despite the comfort of his cot and the polite guards, Akos hadn't slept. He scratched at the stubble forming on his chin as they laid out his personal belongings on a table for inspection. It wasn't really bothering him yet. He'd learned to go long hours with little sleep a long time ago. Perhaps it was the unusual weight on his mind and heart that were making him feel so exhausted.

Without a word, Akos retrieved the few things that he'd had on him when he'd been arrested. There wasn't much to show for himself. A purse with a few marks in it. Not even his sword belt. He wondered whether Lord Varrie would keep it or if he would give it to the next guard that earned a commendation. It was a pity. Despite the antiquated make of the blade, it had a sharp edge and had been a trophy from his time in Logathia.

"Captain Freedman, you are free to go," the guard at the inner gate stated. "You will receive your official court summons soon. Failure to appear will—"

"I know the penalties," Akos stated.

The sharp words cut the guard's proclamation short. Akos was in no mood to deal with blithering formality right now. He needed to be moving. The crew would have gone to ground when they'd heard word of his arrest, but Halis might have moved on them before ever moving on him.

Akos knew that he was a prominent figure in the Macallian privateer fleet, enough so that he wouldn't be in danger of a piracy charge carrying the threat of immediate execution. His crew would not be so lucky. It was nothing more than blind hypocrisy, but it was the truth of the world. Though they'd served with as much distinction as Akos, they would be held to a different standard due to their birth and their place on the chain of command.

Only as he was stomping through the short tunnel that led to the outside world did he hear a familiar voice: Valesa, barking at a guard. Despite himself, Akos stopped in his tracks. That was not a sound he'd expected to hear. He crept forward to see what else he could hear.

As he listened, he realized that at least one of his worries was now over. He'd worried that Calia might have been complicit in her brother's plot. His rational mind kept telling him that there was no chance of that, but his heart cast doubts as he languished in his cell. It was good to see that he hadn't entirely lost his ability to judge someone's character.

Maybe I just lose it when I'm in love with the person, Akos thought. He tore his mind away from Anastasia. Akos had already seen what happened when he allowed himself to lose himself in his sorrow. He needed to stay in the moment until he could ensure his crew's safety. There would be plenty of time to nurse his broken heart later.

Akos decided that he'd heard enough and stepped around the corner as Calia announced his name. Valesa saw him first, and her eyes opened in uncharacteristic surprise. Calia's mind seemed to have some trouble processing what she was seeing. The guard seemed to be the least confused among them. He'd probably heard of Akos posting bail through the rumor mill.

"Ah, how?" was all Calia could manage.

"I posted bail," Akos said.

That thought seemed to take Calia a long time to process. That was almost enough to make his imprisonment worth it. Akos was used to the woman's quick wit. Seeing her floundering for words had enough comedic value to threaten to crack his melancholy.

"If it's quite alright with you," Akos said, "I'd like to leave. Lovely as the jail is, I think I've had quite enough of it for a lifetime."

"Of course," Calia said.

She turned without another word. Akos cast a questioning look at Valesa. The bodyguard gave a slight shrug before falling in step with her charge. Akos followed behind them, content to be well away from this place before they spoke of anything else.

Calia took them to a waiting carriage. The group embarked and were on their way with no words between them. Akos wasn't quite sure what to say. It was clear that he'd surprised them almost as much as they'd surprised him.

"Thank you," Akos said once the carriage was underway.

"No thanks are necessary," Calia demurred. "You got yourself out anyway."

"Well, the thought counts for something. I appreciate that you risked your brother's ire for me, anyway."

Calia shifted in her seat and looked out the window at the passing city. Akos could tell that she was uncomfortable receiving the praise, so he dropped the point. For a moment, they rode in silence.

"I have to get to the docks," Akos finally said. "I need to make sure that the crew is alright."

"They're fine," Calia said. "We spoke to them before we came to get you."

Akos listened while Calia filled him in on the things that had transpired while he'd been in prison. It didn't surprise him that the law had failed to catch Leo with his pants down. What did surprise him was that the first thing Calia had thought of was his crew. It raised his opinion of her significantly. Most nobles couldn't look beyond their own self-interest, but Calia was proving to be an exception to that rule.

"This Duke Galith is sure to help us?" Akos asked after she was finished.

Calia nodded. "He's already offered once, in a roundabout way. I doubt that he'll rescind that offer now."

Akos nodded and leaned back against his seat, deep in thought. If all went according to Calia's plan, this duke could certainly help. His friends in Tersun would be more than willing to assist him, provided he had the coin to get there. And he'd just blown almost all his money getting himself out of prison.

Of course, things rarely went according to plan. Their own recent experiences should have hammered that point home. Still, at least this plan had a better chance of succeeding than anything else he could think of. And if things fell apart, all they needed to do was get to Tersun and Akos could figure something out.

CHAPTER 6

The Galith estate was a sprawling manor skirting the limits of the town. It took up an entire block, walled off from the adjacent houses. Most of that space was dominated by a courtyard which was surrounded on all sides by the main house. Calia and the others were quickly ushered through by the steward and into Duke Galith's office.

The office was incredible. Maps and charts of all sorts papered the walls, so many that they overlapped each other. Calia wondered how Galith managed to read any of them. Or perhaps he had them all memorized. Whatever the case, he seemed to have dedicated a decent amount of his fortune solely to the collection of maps.

Galith was cradling a glass of brandy as they entered. When he saw them, he swept up and gave them a wide grin. Calia could see that he was very interested in what she had to tell him. His excitement was clear with every gesture and every word as he welcomed them in and bade them a seat.

"I knew that you would not be able to resist spilling the story before a week was over." Galith grinned. "Not that I'm complaining. It's only been a day and already the curiosity is killing me."

"Well, things have happened that have necessitated an . . . accelerated schedule," Calia said.

That garnered a raised eyebrow from Galith, but he seemed content to wait until she was ready to speak. Now that it was finally time to tell someone of their harrowing journey though, she found herself lost for words. It had been easy to tell Halis; she'd known that he would believe her. But Calia knew that even the thought of piercing the void beggared belief, and Galith had no proof other than her word that she had managed it.

Calia glanced to the others for support while she gathered her thoughts. They would be of no help, she decided. Akos was drinking the brandy he'd been offered much quicker than was prudent and staring absently at the various charts scattered across the walls. Valesa had taken up a guard's post by the door, and her expression made it clear that this particular task was up to Calia.

With no help forthcoming, Calia decided that there was nothing for it but to explain it all and hope that he believed them. She covered everything, from the conception of her theory to their eventual escape from Anson's clutches. Galith sat and listened with rapt attention, never stopping her to ask a question. When Calia wrapped up her story and took a fortifying sip from the glass of brandy, she realized that several hours had passed.

Galith seemed lost in thought, so Calia glanced around again. Akos had finally settled into one of the chairs offered and gave her an encouraging nod. She could never read the captain's expression, but it seemed to be one of approval and agreement. Still, his eyes seemed focused somewhere else. Calia wondered what might be on the man's mind that had him so distracted. That would be a conversation for another time though. For now, they had to convince Galith of their need for his aid.

"I have to admit," Galith said after gathering his thoughts, "that is a rather extraordinary tale."

Calia gripped her drink tighter as she braced herself for his denial of her story.

"You really faced down one of these behemoths?" Galith asked Akos.

"'Faced down' is putting a glorifying spin on it." Akos gestured to his sling. "Survived is more accurate."

"Amazing. This culture sounds as if it is entirely backwards. I can only imagine the implications of introducing widescale reform to their current systems."

Shock almost made Calia lose her breath. Galith was acting as though there were no doubt in the world that every last word she'd told him was pure truth. His mind already seemed to be picturing the inner workings of Logathia, as though trying to picture the culture of some distant land.

"You believe me then?" Calia asked.

"In all the time I've known you, Lady Hailko, you've never lied to me. To lie about this would be tantamount to throwing away every shred of academic dignity you have. And I just don't believe that you would do such a thing."

Now surprise did rob Calia of any words.

"I also think that this Logathia sounds like the perfect place for my brotherhood to begin its experiment," Galith continued. "I will call them together so that we can vote upon it at once."

"A vote?" Akos asked. "How long do you think that will take?"

"Well, they must be informed of the situation first, and then they must have time to ponder the—"

"How long?"

Akos jaw was clenched, and Calia could see fire in his eyes. That wasn't good. She'd never seen him so outwardly emotional. If he lost his temper, they might well lose any support that Galith would have otherwise given them. Calia needed to cool the situation down.

"What Captain Akos means to say," Calia said, "is that we have something of a ticking clock to work against."

"Do you truly believe that this Anson will harm Vitus?" Galith asked.

"Vibius," Akos growled.

"No," Calia interjected. She cast a pointed glance at Akos, but he didn't seem to notice. "We think that as long as Vibius is his only link to the outside world, he will remain physically unharmed."

"Then it seems to me that we have time."

Calia reached over and placed a restraining hand on Akos's arm before Galith even finished his sentence. A quick glance told her that it was the right decision. At least now Akos was glaring at her rather than their host. If there was any help that they could wring from Galith, they would do it with words rather than violence.

What is going on? Calia pondered the question for a brief moment. Akos was normally collected and calm. What had happened in such a brief time that had caused his captain's mask to crack, she wondered. Calia cast the question aside. They wouldn't be discussing it here and now. Right now she needed to focus on getting the help that Vibius needed from one of the few men who had both the capability and the inclination to help.

"Lord Galith, he might not be in immediate danger, but you must agree that every moment he spends in Anson's clutches constitutes a threat to all civilized society," Calia said.

"How so?" Galith leaned in.

"Lord Anson might not have the secrets of travelling into and out of the void unraveled yet, but Mr. Antonius does. And if there is even a small chance that he could crack him, it would unleash a danger on the realm the likes of which we have never seen."

"I don't see it as a threat to the realm. Your expedition faced down these behemoths and survived."

"We were very lucky. And Anson isn't the only one. There are at least a dozen other rulers there with the same-sized army as his, and the same control over the beasts. And none of them are stupid. They would recognize the opportunity that our realm represented to add to their own power base. They might face initial setbacks as they adapted to our advanced technology. But they would adapt, and they would bring their full might to bear. While in Logathia, I saw the skull of a behemoth that was the size of your main gate. I shudder to think of what it would take to kill one of those monsters, and what it could do to a regiment of men before it died."

Galith leaned back in consideration of this point. Calia removed her hand from Akos's arm, at which point he rose and removed himself from the conversation. He went over to the charts, inspecting a family crest which hung there, a pair of swords behind an old knight's helm in front of a shield. It was probably wise of him to go elsewhere. For whatever reason, he seemed to be feeling rather than reasoning, and that was liable to get them into more trouble than it saved. Fortunately, it seemed he had realized that as well.

"I understand your point," Galith said slowly. "And I do wish to help. I really do. But there is only so much that I can do without the full support of the brotherhood."

"Any help that you can provide would be appreciated," Calia said.

"Well, funding an expedition on my own would be considered a violation of our standards. But I am free to do whatever I want with whatever funds I keep in my own safe. I can give you at least enough to get to your friends in Tersun, and to help you once you get there if you must depart at once. But I would implore you once again to wait until the brotherhood has had time to mull their decision over. If they were to agree, we could send you back with an army of mercenaries and a flotilla of ships. There would be no doubt of your success."

Calia considered the offer. Her father had always taught her that it was best to stack the odds as much in her favor as she could when things were important. Halis III had always made sure that the odds were squarely in his favor before he tackled anything important. There was certainly something to be said for that line of thinking.

But there was also something to be said for action. Calia had always been a patient woman. Almost too patient. She'd waited far too long to challenge her superiors at the university. She'd waited far too long in her life to start taking agency and making her own way forward.

And no matter what she did, she could not shake the feeling of dread that had grown in her since she'd watched the silhouette of her love fade into the horizon. Something was not right. Calia couldn't prove it or put into words what was making her feel the way she did. But she knew that waiting was not an option. She offered Galith a tight smile as she shook her head.

"I'm afraid we must leave right away."

Galith sighed, but his eyes held at least some understanding. He stood, offering a hand to help Calia out of her own seat. Once they'd risen, he clapped his hands together, and his usual smile returned to his face.

"My safe is on the other side of the estate," Galith announced. "If you will all follow me, I'll fetch the funds at once."

***

Akos couldn't believe what had just happened. Calia had handled the situation well. That didn't surprise him; he'd already seen that she was more than capable of competence.

What shocked him was his own lack of decorum. He'd done everything short of threatening their host with violence. Not just their host, but the only person that possessed both the disposition and the ability to help them. His control had slipped and his temper had gotten the best of him.

No matter how hard he tried, Akos couldn't remember the last time he'd allowed that to happen outside of a swordfight. He silently cursed himself for a fool as Galith led them across the estate to fetch the funds he'd offered them. Calia had done well to even secure that after his outburst.

Akos couldn't imagine what they'd have done without Calia's rational mind and Galith's generosity. He might still have enough in his accounts to get them to Tersun, but they would be on their own from there. They would have had to beg, or steal, any help they could get. If what he'd heard via the rumor mill was true, there was no way that his old friends would give him what they needed on promises and nostalgia alone. They would need money, and plenty of it, to convince anyone to help.

Unless he completely missed his guess, whatever Galith considered spending money was likely to be enough. Akos had met his type before, and they thought nothing of throwing away money that would have been a fortune to any other man. They might not be able to do everything that they needed to, but they would have enough to convince the right people that they could. From there, Akos was sure that they could figure out the rest.

Akos and Valesa waited outside as Calia and Galith went to fetch the funds. Lanterns were being lit around the courtyard, where various statues and plants cast dark silhouettes. Akos stared into the square, watching the shadows dance and wondering how he could regain control of his own emotions.

When he was younger, bound by chains to a master that he hated, he'd struggled with self-control. He'd raged against his captors. Now he was raging against people who were, in their own way, trying to be his allies. He needed to stop. His mastery of his emotions had allowed him to command situations in the past that he'd had no business surviving. It had allowed him to thrive in a profession where men tended to die young.

Now it seemed he couldn't even control his own eyes. One of the shadows appeared to be dancing ever closer in the dim light of the lanterns. It was only once the shadow had closed to within a few paces that Akos realized it was no figment of his imagination.

Instinct threw him backwards and just out of range of a flicker of a blade as it flew through the space he'd occupied a heartbeat before. Akos hit the wall behind him with a gasp and a flare of pain through his ribs. It seemed they were not as healed as he'd hoped. Akos's mind struggled to make sense of what he was seeing. Where once there had only been shadow stood a man poised to strike again. Dark steel caught the light of a lantern as it plunged forward toward Akos's heart.

An instant before it buried itself in his chest, the blade angled away. It sparked off the wall as Akos tried to find somewhere to move. It wasn't until he'd sidestepped farther down the wall that Akos realized that Valesa had swatted the blade away. Valesa was now standing between him and the threat, allowing Akos to get a better look at who was assailing them.

Akos's jaw dropped as he recognized the figure. It was Lusalin Carralt. The tall, slender aid to Lord Hailko held three feet of dark steel with one hand while removing his spectacles with the other. He was looking down his hawkish nose at Valesa, annoyance plain on his face. His lip curled into a sneer even as he began to try to circle her to get to Akos.

Valesa held her ground, keeping herself in front of him. Akos wondered if it were genuine care for him, or simple training that made her put herself between them. Akos tried to get to the door of the office that Calia and Galith had disappeared into, but Lusalin and Valesa cut him off.

Akos reached up and slipped the sling off his shoulder. He threw the cloth away and flexed his hand, wondering if he had enough strength in it to be of any use. Fortunately he was right-handed, but if he had to fight with no weapon, he would still need the use of both his hands.

"Step aside, Valesa," Lusalin said. "You're standing in the way of Lord Hailko's orders."

"What are you doing here?" Valesa asked.

"I'll not waste my time bantering. Either step aside or I will add you to the list of problems that I am taking care of tonight."

Akos went for the door as they talked. If Galith could summon his guards, or even if there was a weapon in there, they could turn the tables on Lusalin. But the aid was too fast. He lunged forward with such speed that Akos was amazed Valesa had time to get in front of him and parry his strike. The two exchanged a flurry of strokes, with steel ringing off steel.

If the two kept it up, it would only be a matter of time before the guards were alerted. Akos glanced about while dancing backwards to keep from being under Valesa's feet as Lusalin drove her back. There were no guards forthcoming. Akos began to worry as he realized that he hadn't seen any of the guards that were wandering the estate since they'd left Galith's chart room. Then he spotted the still figure of a man splayed out on the ground. He ran over to check on him as Valesa and Lusalin dueled in the lantern light.

Akos slowed as he realized that the man was lying in a pool of his own blood. Light flickered on eyes glassed over with death. Akos cursed as he realized that his scabbard was empty as well, the blade tossed away or hidden by Lusalin. The hairs on the back of Akos's neck rose as he realized that there was a possibility that Lusalin had brought his twin brother or part of the Hailko guard with him, but a paranoid glance about did not reveal a second figure waiting to run him through.

Akos stood and looked back toward the duel. The combatants were inching their way toward him. The man was going blow for blow with Valesa, a feat that Akos knew from personal experience was not easy to manage. It stood to reason that wherever the late Lord Hailko had found a bodyguard for his daughter, he'd also found one for his son. The pair shuffled and hopped between the statues and columns that covered the courtyard in near silence, the only sound to mark their duel the ringing of steel against steel. The fight seemed to be evenly matched.

A fair fight was one of Akos's least favorite things. He needed a weapon to put the odds in his favor. It dawned on him where he could get one. Without a second thought, Akos sprinted back to the chart room.

***

Valesa had sparred with the Carralts before. It came to no surprise to her that neither of them had ever shown the full extent of their skill during their sessions. She certainly hadn't gone all out during their sparring sessions. They had all come from the same school, and that school taught that no one should ever see the full extent of their training. Unless, of course, that was the last thing they ever saw.

Lusalin was pushing her to her absolute limits now. Feints, parries, and counterstrokes were flashing at a rate that Valesa's eyes could scarcely follow. Each movement was as much instinct as it was thought. Lusalin had the element of surprise and preparation. Neither had managed to impart so much as a glancing blow against the other, but Lusalin was very clearly dictating the fight. Valesa had been on the back foot ever since he'd emerged from the darkness.

A lunge drove her to skip backwards, knocking the tip of the blade aside before whipping her own sword around to slash at Lusalin's face. The man expertly recovered and her sword sparked off his. Valesa used the opportunity to put more space between them by stepping behind a statue of one of Galith's ancestors.

As the fight dragged on, Valesa began to calculate the odds of success in her mind. Lusalin had the edge in physicality. Valesa was in excellent shape, but Lusalin was over half a foot taller and his slender form was covered in wiry muscle. He was like a spring, every movement exploding with barely controlled speed. Valesa could match him for speed, but her hand was beginning to go numb under the hammer blow that accompanied every block and parry.

Valesa believed that she had the edge in pure skill. His technique was far from sloppy, but it was nowhere near perfect. He had weaknesses. The only question was whether she would be quick enough to exploit them.

It was a good thing that Akos had gotten out from underfoot. He was skilled, but he hadn't practiced in months due to his injuries. If he'd tried to join in the fray to help her, he'd have done more harm than good. Especially unarmed. From the corner of her eye, she saw him duck back into the chart room. If he was smart, he'd barricade the door and only come out once the city watch came to see what all the commotion was.

The fight demanded her attention once more, and all thought of the world around her faded. Valesa's world narrowed down to the things that could help her win this fight. Nothing else mattered. Footwork, blade placement, and body control were the only important things in the world.

A flurry of blows probed her for a weakness. Lusalin was getting desperate. It was one thing to murder a handful of common guards, but to eliminate a duke would be another thing altogether. And if Galith emerged to see them dueling, he would have to dispose of Lusalin to prevent him from spreading knowledge of their school. The only one that was safe from harm here was Calia.

At least, Valesa hoped that was true.

The desperation of that thought fueled her, and she managed to seize some momentum for the first time in the duel. She drove Lusalin back, and for the first time he had to use the environment to escape her. Valesa didn't let up.

Her pursuit took them around several of the statues they'd already passed. Lusalin sprang against one as he leapt behind it, breaking the form off at the ankles and sending it hurtling toward her. Valesa had to spring backwards to avoid being pinned beneath the marble form. Lusalin used the distraction to gain precious distance and reevaluate his approach.

Valesa didn't realize that she was panting until she took stock of herself. She was free of any cuts, but there were several bruises where she'd been hit with the flat of Lusalin's rapier. Sweat poured down her face despite the cool night breeze.

"What are you doing, Ms. Laris?" Lusalin asked.

"I could ask you the same, Mr. Carralt," Valesa replied.

"Your contract is to Lord Hailko. When Halis III passed, that mantle was bestowed onto Halis IV. Your orders come from him."

"I'd rather eat pig shit than take orders from that entitled brat."

Valesa couldn't tell whether the sour look on Lusalin's face was his resting expression or the result of her words touching a nerve. Clearly Lusalin had thrown in fully with his master. *Knowing Halis, this was probably all Lusalin's idea*, Valesa thought. The boy hadn't stumbled over an original thought in years. It was far more likely that the bodyguard had placed the idea in his ear and let him think that he'd come up with the order.

"Regardless of your personal feelings on the matter," Lusalin continued, "he is our master. And his orders are to prevent Captain Akos from spreading word of Lady Hailko's ventures."

"I have a hard time believing that even Halis ordered the cold-blooded murder of one of his sister's friends," Valesa retorted.

"He ordered that we use any means necessary."

"Well, Lady Hailko has issued the order that her associates are to be protected by any means necessary."

Calia had done no such thing, but Valesa imagined that she would have if she'd thought about it.

"You do not work for her." Lusalin was speaking between gritted teeth now. How much of the red on his face was from exertion and how much was rage Valesa could only guess. "You work for Lord Hailko. Need I remind you of the terms of—"

Valesa cut him off. "You don't."

She was getting tired of this banter. Lusalin was stalling for time to decide how to work the situation to his advantage. There was nothing that he could say that would convince her to turn her back on her mistress. Valesa had made her decision long ago. Repercussions be damned.

"Then you know the punishment for turning coat," Lusalin said.

Valesa ignored him and began to circle once more. Lusalin was forced to resume the duel as well, lest he give up too much position. Whenever he opened his mouth to speak, Valesa struck, forcing him to remain quiet and focus on their duel.

Desperation and frustration grew obvious on Lusalin's face as the duel drug on. The dull burn of aching muscles told Valesa that she was getting near her own breaking point. The longer this dragged on, the less effective she would be. She could already feel her legs going leaden beneath her, and her steps were a beat slower than when they'd started. But so were his. Their battle of attrition was nearing its end.

As they exchanged a series of blows and counters, Valesa saw her opening. Lusalin wavered. He'd wrongfooted himself trying to extend for a strike. Valesa slipped inside his reach. She had the perfect chance to bury her own blade up to the hilt through his chest. The tip of her blade dug into his flesh below the sternum.

And then there was no more. Valesa had pulled the blow as though this were a training match. Valesa felt her mouth go wide with confusion as there was no follow up. Lusalin staggered backward, a spot of red staining his shirt. There was no physical reason that could explain his stay of execution. She was still trying to understand she would pull her swing when Lusalin came back at her.

Confusion led to sloppiness. Valesa felt herself being pushed back, and by the time she even thought to rally, Lusalin had her cornered. He'd maneuvered her against a column. With nowhere to go, Valesa felt her legs go out from under her. She sank to a seat. Lusalin towered over her, staring down the tip of his blade.

"I knew you didn't have it in you," Lusalin chided.

His sneer had returned, and his voice dripped with disdain. Valesa loathed the man. But she hadn't been able to kill him when she'd had the chance. She'd never hesitated before. It seemed that her school ties were not so easy to break as she'd thought.

Lusalin slipped the tip of his rapier under her chin and tilted her head back to look at him. Valesa met his eyes with as much defiance as she could, but her fighting spirit seemed to have left her. She felt a trickle of blood run down her neck as Lusalin pondered her fate.

"You've betrayed your master," Lusalin decreed. "You were trained better than that. Traitors cannot be allowed to live. To do so would be an affront to—"

A blur of movement drew Lusalin's eye. His blade came up a half second later—just in time to intercept Akos's own sword. Valesa could feel where the razor tip of the rapier had drawn a neat line through her flesh, though not deep enough to be dangerous.

A flurry of blows followed the first, and Akos managed to drive Lusalin back far enough that he could plant himself in front of Valesa. The man made no noise other than the occasional grunt of effort. Lusalin backed away far enough to get the measure of this new threat. What he saw clearly did not impress him.

"You think you can face me?" Lusalin asked. "How long has it been since you even held a blade, Captain?"

"The last time I held a blade, I maimed a god," Akos replied.

Lusalin let out a snort of derision.

"And he broke you in return. When was even the last time that you exercised? I may be tired, but I'm in far better condition than you and we've barely just begun."

Akos didn't bother to respond. Valesa could see that he was in fact sweating already, and his breath was coming in heaves. Akos was a fit man, but he had barely been allowed out of bed under Krallek's orders. His conditioning had surely suffered.

"Move out of the way," Lusalin commanded. "I'm feeling generous tonight. I'll end the traitor and then escort you back to prison."

"I'm feeling generous too," Akos replied. "Leave now and I won't kill you."

Lusalin barked out a laugh, and Akos wasted no time in trying to make good on his threat. Valesa watched the captain fight in awe for a moment. His blade wasn't even real. It was a decoration he'd ripped off the wall. Still, he matched Lusalin blow for blow. His condition might be down, but his skill was still there.

Valesa watched for a moment more before rage started to fill her chest. What was she doing? She was a bodyguard, a graduate of the elite Presby Academy. She'd trained her entire life for the sole purpose of protecting someone against any threat. And here she was on her ass with someone else doing the fighting for her.

That rage brought her to her feet with her blade in hand. Valesa was no fainting damsel that needed protection. The fire in her core surged into her limbs and renewed her strength. She strode forward, fatigue forgotten as she closed in on her target.

"On your left!" Valesa yelled as she came up behind Akos.

To his credit, the captain didn't so much as hesitate. The man sidestepped to the right while launching an attack to distract Lusalin. Valesa came in on his left side with an assault of her own. Soon enough, Lusalin was too hard pressed to do anything more than avoid their blades.

If the pair had ever fought together before, Lusalin wouldn't have survived a minute. His only saving grace was that they had to be almost as aware of each other's blades as they did their opponent's. Still, it only took a moment before the effects of their dual assault were felt.

Akos landed a blow against Lusalin's thigh. His blade was dulled though, and it didn't do much more than draw a grunt of pain from their opponent. Valesa used the momentary advantage to draw a long cut down Lusalin's sword arm. Lusalin started to panic, his arrogant expression fading away.

Lusalin made a desperate lunge for Akos's chest, which Akos swatted away with ease. Valesa took the opportunity while he was overextended to strike. The tip of her blade bit into Lusalin's underarm. This time Valesa didn't pull her strike. She put her whole weight behind the blow, shoving the blade deep into his chest. Valesa could feel the blade slip between his ribs and grate against the bones on the other side.

Valesa withdrew the blade and Lusalin stumbled. He had enough time to glance down at the bloom of blood against his shirt before his eyes glazed and he fell in a heap. His corpse twitched as his lifeblood pumped out onto the tile of the courtyard.

Akos dropped his own blade and put his hands on his knees, gasping for air. Valesa stumbled a few steps before catching herself against a statue. Her own breath was coming in ragged gasps, and it was a few moments before she regained any control.

A sudden thought interrupted Valesa's calm. If Lusalin hadn't come alone, his brother or someone else might be threatening Calia and Duke Galith right now. Valesa sprinted toward the office door, banging into it as it refused to budge. She hammered against it with a fist.

"Who is it?" a shaky Duke Galith called.

"It's Valesa. Is Calia alright?"

After a brief moment, she heard a lock turn and the door unlatched. Galith peeked through a crack in the door, pistol shaking in his hand. When he saw her, visible relief crossed his face, and he almost dropped the pistol as he sagged. Calia pushed her way around him as he opened the door fully.

"We heard sounds of fighting," Calia said. "And we found a guard dead in the hall. What's going on?"

Rather than answer, Valesa swept her charge up in a bear hug. Despite a grunt of discomfort, Calia returned the hug, patting Valesa on the back. The rush of the fight was over now, and all her emotions were amplified tenfold. Valesa couldn't imagine what she would have done if her charge had been harmed. Joy and relief flooded her heart.

"I'll explain later," Valesa promised. "For now, we should move."

"Alright," Calia said.

Her curiosity only increased as she saw the body that Akos was standing over, but she said nothing. Akos was inspecting the blade that Lusalin had used. When he heard them enter the courtyard, he turned to them and bowed slightly at the waist.

"Duke Galith, thank you for your hospitality," Akos said. "But I think it's time that we should be going."

"Now wait just a moment," Galith sputtered. "What in the hell is going on here? I deserve an explanation."

"I'll send you a letter and explain everything," Calia assured him. "But I think it would be better for you if we weren't here when the watch arrives."

Galith looked between them for any hint of an answer. Unhappy with what he saw, he sighed. His hands were still shaking as he mopped at his forehead with a handkerchief.

"Just what have I gotten myself involved in?" Galith asked no one in particular.

"I'll send you a letter once we've reached Tersun to explain all"— Calia waved a hand at the courtyard—"this. And another once Logathia is ready for your brotherhood to begin its colonization."

Galith considered that for a moment before composing himself. He managed a weak nod.

"Good luck."

Chapter 7

Calia didn't think a word had passed between her, Valesa, or Akos since they'd boarded the ship bound to Tersun. While still in Geralis, it made sense. They were too busy watching for Beralin to speak. But here aboard the cargo vessel *Macallia's Pride*, a hundred miles to sea, Calia was beginning to feel anxious for her friends.

The fight had drained Akos. Calia knew that despite the facade he tried his best to put on, he was in the worst shape he'd ever been. Krallek's strict orders had helped to heal his wounds, but they'd done nothing for his conditioning. The man she'd once watched scale ratlines and practice with his blade for hours on end had been completely exhausted by a few minutes of swordplay.

Valesa, on the other hand, had completely retreated into herself. Calia didn't know why. She'd never seen her handmaid act this way. Valesa wasn't a talkative person, but she'd never hesitated to confide in Calia. Her silence told Calia she was struggling with something, but for the life of her she couldn't place her finger on what it was.

If only she'd been able to witness what had transpired between the pair of them and Lusalin, she might understand better. But there was no way to change that now. Calia had to trust that when they were ready, they would open up.

Until then, she was alone with her own thoughts. Calia looked out at the wake of the ship trailing slowly behind them. The crew gave her an odd glance every so often, but she paid them no mind. It was unusual for a lady of her stature to walk about a ship unaccompanied, but Calia needed the fresh air. They were still several days from Tersun, and the cramped cabin she and Valesa had been berthed in had already begun to close in on her.

The thoughts in her head could not seem to settle on one subject, and that frustrated Calia to no end. Even at her most flustered at university, she'd been able to focus on one thought until she needed to shift her attention to something else. Of course, none of the problems or stresses she'd faced at university had been anywhere near the same magnitude as the ones she felt now.

Though if someone had tried to tell me that at the time, Calia mused, *I wouldn't have believed them for a second.* It still amazed her how quickly her entire world had changed. She'd changed the face of the scientific community forever, and it hardly seemed worthy of an afterthought to her. It was an achievement that would see her placed amongst the best-known names in scientific history, and in her secret moments late at night she almost wished that she'd never made it. That Akos's plan to fool her had succeeded and she'd returned home with Vibius to pursue her career at the university.

Calia had avoided those thoughts as best she could. The very idea of taking pride in something that had done direct harm to those she loved seemed abhorrent. Now, in the fading light of day, with no one to speak to and no tasks to busy her mind with, there was nothing to do but confront her thoughts and feelings for what they were.

Regret was definitely there. She'd already developed feelings for Vibius before they'd ever reached the void, and some part of her believed that they'd have fallen in love even without the added urgency of their imprisonment. If they'd failed the experiment and returned home, the two of them might be busy planning their wedding now. Or even married already and further pursuing their new life together.

But that hadn't come to pass. Her theory had held true, and a new realm had been discovered. Calia decided that she could not deny, even to herself, the fact that she took great pride in that. She'd done what everyone had said she couldn't. When grizzled sailors had balked, she'd stayed the course and held true to her beliefs. Her discovery would change not only the scientific, but the economic and even the theological landscape of the realms until the end of time. Fame had never been the goal of her expedition, but Calia had to admit that the idea of being remembered in the history books until the end of humanity had a certain appeal to it.

Calia could do nothing to change what happened. Nothing would change the fact that she'd placed them in this predicament. But she could do her best to help them out of it. Calia imagined that if Vibius could talk to her right now, he would tell her that she had every right to feel pride in her achievement. She just needed to make sure that she did everything in her power to give him the opportunity to express that opinion in person.

Her spirit sufficiently lifted, Calia raised herself from the railing and turned to head back to the cabin. As she turned, she caught sight of a looming form from the corner of her eye. The suddenness made her jump and yelp in surprise. Akos, for his part, merely raised an eyebrow in her direction. Calia placed a hand over her now pounding heart as she realized that she'd been so lost in thought that she hadn't even noticed the captain join her at the railing.

"You startled me," Calia said.

"My apologies," Akos said.

It was Calia's turn to raise an eyebrow. Akos sounded as if his thoughts were a million miles away. Even after everything they'd been through, she didn't think she'd ever heard the captain sound so deep in thought. Akos had always struck her as a decisive man who didn't dwell on things. But his attitude in the last few days indicated that he had something weighing on his mind.

"Looking for a place to think?" Calia asked.

"I suppose," Akos replied. "Tell me, do you know Anastasia Varrie?"

The non-sequitur caught Calia off guard. She couldn't imagine a single reason why Akos would want to know something like that. Despite her obvious surprise, Akos waited patiently for an answer.

"I don't know her well," Calia replied after some thought. "But I've met her in passing. And I know her reputation quite well."

"Her reputation?" Akos asked.

"Well, yes. The ladies at the academic functions I attended loved nothing more than to gossip about the nobility of Geralis, and it was hard not to pick it up."

Akos shifted his weight from foot to foot and looked back out over the bow. Calia had never considered herself an excellent judge of character, but she could tell that Akos wanted her to continue. Despite the fact that none of this made sense, she felt that this had to do with whatever was weighing on his mind. And Calia knew that they would need Akos focused on the task at hand in order to plan a successful rescue of Vibius, especially now with many of their advantages stripped away.

But even more than that, she felt that if she could help Akos, she should. Perhaps it was a false bond created by the urgency of captivity, but Calia felt a connection to the crew of the *Mist Stalker* that she'd never felt in the halls of the university. Regardless of where the feeling stemmed from, they were no longer mere acquaintances, nor were they simple business partners. Calia considered Akos to be a friend, and she thought the feeling was mutual. So she continued.

"Anastasia was the stuff of legends among the university staff," Calia said. "More than one professor's wife complained that she'd heard her husband calling her name in his sleep."

"She does leave quite the impression," Akos said with a tone that implied it was meant as anything but a compliment.

"It may be improper to ask—" Calia began.

Akos cut her off. "I asked her to marry me."

Understanding was slow to come. Calia knew what the words meant individually, but put together she struggled to form them into a coherent thought. Fortunately, Akos didn't seem to be looking for any kind of response, so she had time to process. Once her mind finally caught up to her ears, Calia couldn't help her eyes widening and her mouth hanging open.

"She said no," Akos said. "In case you were wondering."

"Ah, I wasn't aware that you two were . . . courting," Calia stammered.

"We weren't. Not publicly anyway. I've been visiting her for years though, whenever I docked in Geralis."

"And did she ever give you any indication that she would marry you?"

"We talked about it for years. I assume you're familiar with her father's dowry requirements."

Calia was. They were the stuff of legends. Many men who might have otherwise pursued Lord Varrei's daughter had been warded off by his strict requirements.

"That was the only reason for my wealth," Akos continued. "Before I met her, I didn't care how much was in my bank accounts. All I cared about was the open sea."

"Well, the sea is still there," Calia pointed out.

Akos tilted his head to acknowledge the point, but then shook it.

"I've spent so much of my life in pursuit of her that I don't know what to do now that she's no longer an option."

Silence settled in as Calia thought on that point. She didn't know what to say to comfort him, or if there was anything to be said at all. Perhaps he needed some time to himself. But Calia was hesitant to leave him to his sorrows. That seemed to be a cruel thing to do.

"Over the years, I think I replaced the ideals of a life of absolute freedom on the seas with her," Akos said. "She became the ideal that I strove for, and freedom lost its shine. I wonder what I will do without something to dedicate my life to."

"I understand how you feel," Calia replied.

Akos turned his gaze back to her. Calia could see that it wasn't a challenging gaze, looking to prove that his sorrow was deeper or different than hers. It was simply a questioning one, wondering what she'd been through to cause her to say that.

"I dedicated my life to the university," Calia explained. "Everything I've ever done has been in service to my academic career. Now that I've seen the world that lies beyond the mists, no matter how awful our experience with it was, I can't find it in my heart to care for academia anymore."

"Who would have ever thought that we'd end up two listless ships on strange waters?" Akos asked.

"If I might ask, what caused you to propose so suddenly?"

"I knew that I would have to spend at least the lion's share of my fortune to retrieve Vibius. It took years to amass that fortune, and after our trip through the void, I didn't feel like waiting any longer."

Calia felt a pang through her chest as she realized that this too was something she was responsible for. If not for her need to be recognized in academia, Akos would never have been in this predicament.

"I'm sorry for causing this," Calia said.

"Don't be silly," Akos replied. He straightened up, and Calia could see that the cloud had left his eyes. "If she truly loved me, she would have run away with me regardless of my wealth. And if you and I had never met and I'd married her, she would have broken the illusion eventually. The only thing you did was accelerate that process."

They stood in silence once more as Calia didn't know what to say. The wake churning beneath them trailed away and out of sight as the sun set on the horizon.

"I know this is an unfair burden to place on you," Akos said. "I just felt that you deserved to know where my head has been."

"Think nothing of it," Calia replied. "I can sympathize."

"I do want to assure you; this will not affect our current task. There will be time to grieve my lost love once we've retrieved yours."

Akos smiled as Calia blushed. Despite the truth of the statement, it still felt odd to hear it from someone else. Still, she hadn't hesitated to declare her love for him, so there was no reason to be embarrassed. That thought did nothing to ease the heat in her cheeks though.

"I think it's about time to eat," Akos said. "And I think Valesa would kill me if I allowed you to go about a strange ship unaccompanied. Would you care to join me in the galley?"

"It would be my pleasure," Calia replied with a smile.

***

The whetstone scraped along Valesa's blade with a satisfying rasp. The rhythmic sound helped to soothe her raw nerves. She hadn't been able to untense until they were several miles offshore. Even then it had been all but impossible until she'd managed to check out the crew and make sure that none of them were agents of Halis.

Lusalin's attack had caught her off guard, but it shouldn't have. Valesa should have realized that Halis would order Lusalin to do whatever was necessary to keep Akos from spreading Calia's secret if he thought there was even the slightest chance that he could monetize it.

Valesa had never liked Halis. He was nothing more than a spoiled child who thought the world owed him whatever he wanted. Unlike Calia, who'd forced her way into the profession that she loved, Halis couldn't be bothered to do much of anything if it meant having to put in any actual effort. Valesa counted her blessings daily that Lord Hailko had assigned her to his daughter rather than his son.

The headmaster of the Presby Academy would be livid if he could hear that thought. *He might be more upset by the fact that one of his graduates had killed another,* Valesa thought. Especially when both graduates were under the employ of the same master. Such a thing was unheard of. Vengefulness was not high on the academy's list of traits, but Valesa would have to step carefully if she ever found herself around another graduate, or they might take it upon themselves to defend the academy's honor.

Thoughts swirled in Valesa's mind as she went through the motions of sharpening her already razor-sharp blade. The academy had been her life from the time she was born to the time that she was an adult. She never would have considered going against her contract when she'd first left the academy. And yet, she'd done just that. Lusalin had died by her hand, all to defend a man she didn't even like.

Though, to be fair to herself, Valesa admitted she hadn't done it out of some loyalty to Akos. It was her dedication to Calia that caused her to act. That same dedication had seen her willingly follow her charge into the void itself. Alumni of the Presby Academy were expected to do whatever their masters asked of them, but Valesa knew that most of her peers would have balked at that. But she'd never even flinched at the idea. Once Calia decided on her course of action, Valesa knew without thinking that she would follow it without question.

Valesa glanced down the length of her blade as she wondered when her devotion to Calia had overtaken her duty to the academy. Graduates were expected to serve as bodyguards and aides for one person until they were no longer capable, but it was always understood with whom your loyalty was supposed to truly lie. The academy spent large amounts of money and time to ensure that each of their graduates was as close to a one-person army as they could be. That kind of service did not come cheap. In return, they expected complete obedience. And they almost always got it.

In the annals of the academy there were only a handful of cases of graduates breaking their contracts. *One more now,* Valesa mused. Though she wondered if they would ever find out it was her. The only other witnesses weren't going to volunteer any information. Perhaps she would get lucky and the academy would never learn of her betrayal. The idea almost seemed too much to hope for, but Valesa found herself hoping all the same.

Not that she wouldn't make the same decision again in a heartbeat. That thought paused Valesa's hand as she moved the whetstone along the blade. She sighed as she realized that Calia was the closest thing to a family that she had.

Valesa had no parents. It was one of the requirements of the academy—no family to return to. Valesa was sure that served some pragmatic purpose, such as ensuring that the graduates' primary loyalty was always to the academy.

The Presby Academy had forced her to give up a lot of things. Valesa had spent her life learning how to be the deadliest person in any given room at the expense of everything else. She'd never be a great academic like her charge. She'd never be a leader like Akos. Valesa had given up any ideas of romance for fear that it might blind her to a potential threat or divide her loyalties.

Yet when Valesa looked upon Calia, she knew that it was all worth it. The young woman was something special. Someone Valesa considered to be worth guarding with her life. As long as she had her, nothing else mattered.

Satisfied that her blade was as sharp as human hands could manage, Valesa rubbed some oil on the blade and slid it back into its sheath. She needed to rest. None of them had gotten much sleep since Beralin's assault, but Valesa had been particularly high-strung. This was the last chance they might get to sleep easy for a while.

Tersun was a pirate's town. Valesa had never been there herself, but everyone knew it by reputation. It was a dangerous place full of dangerous people who knew no authority other than that which flowed from the barrel of a gun. Valesa would have to stay on her toes to keep her charge safe there. But she would do whatever it took to do so.

After all, it was the only thing that mattered.

CHAPTER 8

Days dragged into nights, and it wasn't long before the two were indiscernible from one another to Vibius's mind. Not that he had any way of tracking time in the dungeon. He had the feeling that even if he could see, there was nothing but blackness awaiting him.

He supposed the occasional torch would have illuminated the world around him when the guards came down to give him meals. Vibius wondered if that would have been a good thing. If he got a look at the cell he'd been confined to, it might have driven him further toward the edge of madness. Not that he was very far from it as it was.

For the first several days he'd been too shocked and in pain to think much at all. They'd taken his eyes. Even as the guards prepped their torture devices and approached him, some small part of Vibius's mind had screamed that the whole thing must be a joke. That this must be Anson's sick way of getting back at him for his escape attempts. That before the poker dug its way into his eyes, the madman would pop through the door and tell them to stop, laughing at the look on Vibius's face.

Vibius should have known better. He'd never been a pessimist, but it was getting hard to see the light of hope at the end of this ordeal. *Not that I'll ever see the light of* anything *anymore*, Vibius thought wryly. He forced himself to chuckle at his own joke. The sound was weak in his ears. It dawned upon him that gallows humor was more fun when your neck wasn't the one in the noose.

Once the pain and shock of his situation had worn off, the cold reality of began to sink in. Vibius did everything he could to stave off madness. It was a futile effort, but he planned to give it his all regardless. It wasn't as if he had anything better to do.

That thought managed to wring a genuine smile out of him. Vibius knew that the only way his sanity would survive his imprisonment was if he stayed positive. After all, it was still unlikely that Anson would throw him down here and forget about him. Despite his antics, he was the only sane wayfarer in the entire realm of behemoths, and he was the only one who knew the secret of how to exit the realm safely. Anson needed that information if he was ever going to fulfill his grand plan.

That is, if the man had not gone so mad that he'd forgotten his own ambitions. Vibius tried to push the idea away, but it kept nagging at him. From the tidbits of conversation he'd managed to pick up from the guards as they came and went to deliver his food, Vibius had discerned that Anson was slipping ever closer to total madness.

When that happened, he would be easy pickings for the other gods. From his brief look into behmothian politics, Vibius knew that they were each constantly looking for some advantage over the others. Each god wanted to rule the entire realm. Adding the manpower and production capabilities of Logathia to their own would be a good first step for any of the other gods looking to advance their place in the realm.

When that inevitability came to pass, it might be better to be forgotten down in a cell. The other gods couldn't torture him for his secrets if Anson himself had forgotten he had him down here. Vibius could pretend to be a regular prisoner, claim that he was an escaped slave brought to justice or any of a thousand reasons he might be down there. Anything that would keep them from learning of his true capabilities.

Vibius wondered if he would even know when that came to pass. Would the feedings simply cease as he was forgotten, guards either abandoning their post or dying during the fighting? Or would they continue to come, making conversation about trivial things as usual, with nothing to mark the passage of time but a bowl of tasteless gruel every so often? The question wracked his brain.

Desperate to take his mind off such depressing thoughts, Vibius lowered himself to a seat in the center of his cell. Or, as near to the center as he could tell anyway. He'd spent what must have been an entire day pacing the cell, determining its length and width with the only unit of measurement he had left: his own stride. Three strides wide by four steps long. When he reached up, he could feel the ceiling about a foot about his head.

He supposed it could be worse. There was at least enough room to lie down without having to lean against the damp walls, and to stand without stooping over. Vibius had been on several ships that hadn't afforded him that kind of space.

Thinking of ships made him wonder where the *Mist Stalker* was now. It had been more than enough time for them to reach a safe haven. He wondered if Calia was alright. Vibius found that, now more than ever, his thoughts turned to her. She was the only beacon of hope left in his life. So long as she had made it home, he could rest. Of course, he had no way to know if she had, but his gut feeling told him that his friends had made it back.

That thought brought Vibius back to the present. He rolled his neck and tried his best to relax. It was difficult in a dungeon. The absolute silence transcended peacefulness to become disturbing. Vibius had spent some time yelling into the darkness to try to alleviate the feeling, but to no avail. He'd shouted himself hoarse, and it had done nothing to curb the dread that surrounded him.

The smell wasn't great either. There was a small chamber pot in his cell that the guards took away once in a while. But the infrequency of their visits made the whole cell smell putrid. Vibius had become accustomed to the scent, but it still was not pleasant when he was trying to clear his mind.

But he did manage to clear it. Thoughts of his friends, of his predicament, and of the world in general faded away into the background. They were still there, but not in focus. Vibius knew they would be there to greet him whenever he ended his meditation, but for now they were quiet.

Vibius didn't know how long he sat there. He didn't know if time passed at all when he was meditating. He didn't even know if he'd found some waking peace, or if he had actually started to fall asleep as he sat and tried to pass the time with meditation. It was possible that he was achieving nothing more than a nap. Something felt different though. Vibius's sleep was restless, and this was serene.

On a whim, Vibius tried to open his wayfaring senses. From the middle of a realm, nothing would happen except a headache. He'd be able to sense the nearest mist, no matter how far away, but that would be it.

If Vibius could get close enough to the edge of the realm, then he could theoretically shift himself into the ways. Pragmatically, that would be suicide. It was possible, of course, and Vibius had done it for several small trips when he was younger just to see if he could. But without a vessel of some sort to carry months of supplies and keep him afloat when he needed to sleep, it would be a very short trip indeed.

Not that it would stop him at this point. Given half the chance, he would dash toward the nearest way and throw himself headlong into it, with or without a ship. Anything would be better than spending the rest of his days rotting away in this dank, smelly cell.

Vibius shook his head to clear his thoughts, forcefully reminding himself that none of that mattered when he was meditating. He needed his mind clear to use his gift, and that wouldn't happen if he was thinking about the stench. Opening his wayfaring senses had always come easy to him, and his inability to do so now was frustrating him.

Rather than let his frustration win out and force him to abandon his idea, Vibius tried to press ahead. He pictured the last time he had used his ability. It had been to propel them into the realm of behemoths. He'd been standing at the shoulder of the *Mist Stalker*'s helmsman. With a grunt of effort, Vibius stood. Perhaps assuming the proper position would help him achieve the proper state of mind.

For a brief moment, Vibius wondered how foolish he must look, standing there in the darkness as if he were beside the helmsman of a ship. All in a vain attempt to *see* something. That was all it was. Ever since he'd lost his eyes, he'd wondered if he would even be able to see the ways anymore. He'd held onto the hope that even if he could no longer see the world around him, he'd still be able to see the ways like he used to.

If that was gone, he didn't know what he'd do with himself. Vibius had never wanted anything more than to explore the realms. His gift would have allowed him to live a life of relative leisure with minimum effort, but he'd used it to plow through the mists in hunt of prey that no one else could even see. He'd never bothered to worry about what he would do if he lost his gift, because he *was* his gift. Without his gift, what would he be?

The thought nagged at him. A wayfarer without the ability to read the ways was nothing more than dead weight. No better than any other sailor, except in Vibius's case, he was far worse than any other sailor. Without his gift or his eyes, he would be a burden on a ship. Someone to be taken care of and carted around like an invalid. As a child, Vibius had hated being taken care of by his father's staff.

He wouldn't go back to that kind of a life, devoid of any responsibility or adversity. Over the years, he'd found he loved the challenge of locating a ship in the ways. It had given him a unique purpose that made him irreplaceable even without the friendships he'd built over the years. Without it, without his gift, he was nothing but a drain on any ship that took him on.

Vibius couldn't bear the thought of being rescued only to be a burden to his friends for the remainder of his life. He hadn't dreamed of being rescued in some time now, but if there was even a half a chance that his friends would come for him, he owed it to them to at least know whether or not he could still perform his duties as wayfarer. He owed it to himself.

So Vibius stood just off-center of his cell, pretending that a helmsman was prepared to receive his instructions. He stood there until he could hear the guards coming, slumping back against the wall to avoid any suspicion on their part. Despite thinking that nothing they could do to him would be worse than what they'd already done, some part of him feared that wasn't true. They could come up with some new torture to finally break his mind. A few things with behemoths sprang to mind as he did his best to look miserable against the wall of his cell.

It wasn't hard. If the guards were even paying attention to what he was doing, they gave no indication. He heard the bowl of gruel hit the ground and grate as it slid under the bars and into his cell. Vibius feigned as if he didn't even notice what was happening. The guards whispered to each other, too low for Vibius to make out what they were saying, and didn't wait for him to take the bowl. Before the gruel had even stopped sloshing about inside, the guards were already making their way back upstairs.

Once he was sure that they'd left, Vibius slid over to the bowl of gruel. He spooned the slop down as quickly as he could. Standing for hours would have been routine on the *Mist Stalker*, but since his imprisonment here it had become an arduous task. Vibius would need his energy if he was to continue. And if he ate it quickly enough, he wouldn't have to think too much about the taste or the texture.

The gruel ran out far before his hunger was slated. Vibius wondered what the guards would do if he asked for more next time. *Probably laugh in my face and spill half of it on the way down*, Vibius thought. Better not to tempt fate. Despite the growling in his stomach, Vibius slid the bowl away and rose to his feet. He would find out if he still had the gift if it killed him.

Chapter 9

The morning sun was beginning to paint the sky when the *Derot's Pride* crawled into harbor. Akos watched the familiar docks spring into view. A forest of colorfully tipped masts waved in the gentle morning air. Dozens of ships from all corners of the realms were moored there, each bringing with them a different color and style of flag. Only a few cargo vessels were tipped with the official flag of any of the nations of the realms the rest were all pirate flags.

The sight filled him with a sense of nostalgic longing for the past, when life was simple. It hadn't been that long ago that Akos's life had revolved around bringing in bounties from plundered ships rather than planning rescue expeditions into the void itself. It wasn't hard to look favorably on the past when the present was so strange.

Akos allowed his thoughts to wander for a while as they made their way toward port. This was the town where he'd first met Leodysus. Akos wondered what the man had thought of them when they'd arrived. A freshly freed slave and a pair of gangly wayfarers must have stuck out as easy marks in a town full of conniving thieves. Leodysus had been the only person not to laugh in his face when he'd declared that he was a privateer captain looking for a crew. Without him, Akos doubted he would have been able to assemble his first crew, much less actually take their first prizes.

Thoughts of the big man led him to wondering where his first mate was. With any luck, Leo had already tracked down Felix and convinced the man to help them. *With my luck*, Akos mused, *Felix is dead in a ditch somewhere and Leo was arrested on arrival.*

That seemed unlikely on both counts. Leo was much too clever to allow himself to be arrested by the pathetic constables that Tersun offered. And there had never been a situation that Felix couldn't talk his way out of. Akos chided himself for being a pessimist. Then he checked to make sure that his new sword would draw easily from its scabbard.

After the fight, Akos had done his best to give the sword to Valesa. From what Akos had been able to gather both she and the aid had graduated from whatever school had taught her to be a bodyguard. It only seemed right that the blade belong to her. If nothing else, she'd been the one to actually kill the man. By rights, it was hers.

Valesa had refused it every time he'd offered it up. Despite her best attempts to make it look like pure pragmatism, Akos had seen the conflict in her eyes when he tried to give it to her. There was something else going on there, something deeper that had to do with her schooling. Akos hadn't pressed the issue, not in the least because he *did* need a weapon. Tersun was the most dangerous city in the entirety of the realm of man, full of predators looking for easy prey. Akos could prove that he was not prey, but he'd prefer to avoid the question being raised in the first place.

It also didn't hurt that this was one of the finest blades that he'd ever held. Akos had wielded dozens of swords of all types but none had felt half as well balanced as this one. The blade was almost three feet of dark dwarven steel, with the signature star pattern that marked a dwarf-made weapon. And it seemed to be the genuine article rather than some human-crafted knockoff.

Despite their fight, it still held a razor edge. Try as he might, Akos couldn't find a single chip or nick in the blade. The bright-silver, half-basket hilt stood out in stark contrast to the blade itself. The grip was simple, well-worn leather. It was a blade that any nobleman would be proud to wear at his side, but even from his limited window of experience with the sword, Akos knew that it was no mere showpiece. It was a weapon first and foremost, and any appreciation of its form was of secondary concern to its function.

Old experience reminded Akos that a sharp wit was almost as important in this town as a sharp weapon. Tersun was a place where there was no real law. The city council was made up of pirates that had somehow survived long enough to feel the need to retire, and they didn't give a damn about enforcing any law. The true government of Jerlasic, the island that Tersun was nestled on, didn't want to deal with the expense, in money or lives, it would require to clean the town up.

That created a place where men with more cunning than scruples could flourish. Akos knew he was once one of those men, when he had just broken his bonds and was still high on the freedom that he'd won. But it hadn't taken him long to realize he didn't belong here. Still, it was always a good place to lay low when you needed to hide, and he'd been back plenty of times over the years.

As the ship dragged its way into port, Akos and the group made their plans. Their first stop would be to check in along the port itself to see if any of the crew were staying there. That was always the plan, but if Leodysus had run into any trouble, he would have moved the crew farther inland. Akos didn't expect trouble, but this was neither the time nor the place to take chances.

Once they'd docked and settled up with the captain of the ship, they departed. The familiar sights, sounds, and smells of a dock welcomed them. The wharfs at Tersun were, perhaps, slightly more chaotic than their counterparts in Geralis, though it wouldn't be readily apparent to the untrained eye. Men still moved in ragged groups, loading and unloading ships with all the industrious frenzy of a beehive. Akos kept one hand on his sword as they made their way through the tight press of humanity, making certain that no one broke up the wedge their small group formed. Neither of the women following him had been to Tersun before, and it was a hell of a place to get lost. The streets twisted and wound together at random. Unwary visitors could easily lose their way in the warren of houses, shops, and bars that made up the town.

Akos made his way to the nearest portside inn and started their search there. As they progressed through the various inns, Akos noted an air of tension. Even the pickpockets, who usually swarmed newcomers the same way that flies buzzed around a fishmonger's stall, were unusually fearful. Akos would like to believe that was due to his and Valesa's withering glares, but he knew that even the roughest men were not above the predations of Tersun's street urchins. Something more was going on here.

It didn't help that all the portside bars seemed to be abandoned. The few that weren't boarded up had barkeepers who seemed scared to answer even the most basic questions. Akos could feel his frustration building each time he was stonewalled by an innkeeper who didn't want to say if they'd even seen Leodysus.

Akos debated whether he should even bother going into the last inn on the row. If it were another dead end, they would have wasted the morning with nothing to show for it. In the end, Akos bit back his frustration and stepped through the swinging doors and into the common room.

There were only three other people in the common room, despite the fact that it was lunchtime. Normally these inns would be swamped with people looking to grab something to wash down with a stiff drink before returning to their labor on the docks. The two patrons eyed the newcomers warily, while the innkeeper hardly glanced up from the glass that he was scrubbing with a rag that was definitely too grimy for the job. Akos sat down at the bar with the other two in tow.

"What can I get you?" the barkeep asked.

"I'm looking for my first mate," Akos said. "Big man, black as coal and covered in tattoos. Refuses to wear a shirt. Have you seen him around?"

The barkeep studied him for a moment. Akos did his best to look congenial, though it was difficult after such a frustrating morning. The barkeep looked like every other they'd met so far—a grizzled old man who had the look of a pirate that injury had forced into settling for a tamer profession. Though to be fair, being a barman in Tersun was at least as rough as life on the high seas. He had a short but thick grey beard with a long and jagged scar running through it on the left cheek.

"Can't say that I have," the man said after a long moment. "But if he's any kind of a fighter, he'll have been scooped up."

"By whom?"

"You just washed in, haven't you?"

Akos nodded, trying not to show too much curiosity on his face. He didn't want the man to think him overeager or he could dry up. Akos didn't want the only person who'd been able to give them any information so far to clam up.

"Well you'd best get back on the ship you came in on and head right back out. You and the angry one look like you could handle yourselves in a fight, and that's a look you don't want to have around here right now."

Akos glanced back at Valesa, who was scowling at the barkeeper. If it fazed him, he didn't show it. Akos fished a few coins out of his purse and set them down on the bar.

"Why is that?"

"There's a war going," the barkeeper said without even glancing at the coins. "And I don't mind telling anyone who'll listen to get out while they still have the chance."

"Then this is for an ale for me and the ladies."

The barkeeper looked as if he'd refuse anyway, but after a hesitant moment he grumbled and swiped up the coins. He turned away and poured them each a glass. Akos glanced about, noticing that the two patrons had left. They'd looked like dockworkers taking a break anyway, but Akos couldn't help but wonder whether his presence had anything to do with their hurried exit. A creeping feeling running up his spine told him that it did.

Once the barman set their mugs down, Akos took a swig. It was not what he would call high quality. In fact, the ale tasted like it was stale.

"Oh . . . my." Calia sputtered as she took a sip.

That finally managed to wring a slight smirk out of the bartender.

"You ought to leave," the barman said. "This town ain't no place for a gentlewoman in the best of times."

"Unfortunately, we have to find my crew and an old friend first," Akos said. "Last I heard he was holed up here."

The bartender sighed. "Look, I ain't seen your first mate, but maybe I know your friend. What's his name?"

"Felix d'Maxilae."

The bartender's eyes shot wide and he took an involuntary step back. Akos felt the creeping feeling make its way further up his spine. One hand fell to the sword at his hip. The room chilled as the man caught his involuntary backpedal and tried to steady his nerves. Akos didn't even need to glance at Valesa to know that she'd picked up on the strange behavior too.

"What's wrong?" Akos said.

"You need to go now," the bartender said.

Despite the words, Akos didn't feel like it was a threat. The tone sounded more like a plea. Akos raised an eyebrow as he rose from his stool. He stood, hands braced on the bar, and leaned over it as far as he could without losing his balance. He finally got the bartender to look him in the eye and fixed him with his gaze.

"Why?"

"Those two men will have run off to get the recruiters," the bartender explained. "If you're friends with d'Maxilae and they bring Garot's boys, they'll gut you like a fish. And the gods only know what they'll do to the women."

Akos examined the panicking man for a moment longer before turning away from the bar. Something was going on here, and it sounded like Felix was in the middle of it. *As usual*, Akos thought. The man could never seem to keep his nose out of trouble. They needed to be gone when the recruiters arrived. The bartender hadn't made it sound as if these recruiters were very friendly people, and Akos didn't want to find out for himself.

"A word of advice," the bartender shouted as Akos started for the door. "Don't use that name unless you know it's one of his boys."

"Akos," Valesa said.

The single word was said low, but with enough urgency that Akos snapped his head around to look at the woman. She nodded toward the door, a hand already on the hilt of her weapon. Akos looked at the door. He didn't see anything, but he could already hear the pounding of boots on the walkway outside. He sighed as he realized that it was already too late for them to flee.

"You wouldn't happen to have a back door?" Akos asked.

There was no answer, and Akos turned to see that he was talking to no one. The old man had slipped off as they watched the door. Akos weighed his options in the brief seconds he still had.

He had regained a lot of strength, and the desperate fight against Lusalin had proved that he could still hold his own if he needed to. Valesa was a good secret weapon to have in any brawl against unsuspecting men. The men who inhabited Tersun would underestimate her until she gave them reason not to. If it came to a fight, they might be able to cut their way out of here.

That option came with too many risks. Calia was no fighter, and they would have to protect her as they tried to escape into a city where it was becoming clear they didn't know who to trust. Not to mention the fact that if they fought their way through and it ended up being a group of d'Maxilae's men, it would create enemies where there didn't need to be any. Felix would understand, but his underlings might not. All it took was one man with a grudge, and they might find themselves waking up with a knife between the ribs.

The best thing to do would be to gather as much information as they could and try to talk their way out of this. Akos tried to push away the thought that their lives hung on the flip of a coin, but the nagging idea wouldn't go away. Instead, he tried to put on his most amiable face and leaned back against the bar, taking the mug of ale in one hand.

"Relax," Akos told the other two. "Let's see what they want."

The women both gave him an incredulous look. They were still staring at him in disbelief when the doors swung open and a pair of men stepped through. Each of them had the look of hired muscle. Both stood a head taller than Akos, with arms as big around as his thighs and swirling tattoos covering every inch of exposed skin. Akos had seen their type in every realm.

They sized up the trio in the bar with dull, unthinking eyes. Akos could tell that these two could only think in terms of threat assessment. And even that seemed to be lacking, as they relaxed after looking them over. Either one of them could probably outlast Akos in a fair fight, but they were sorely mistaken if they thought that he would fight fair, and underestimating Valesa would prove lethal.

"What do we have here?" a reedy voice asked from outside the tavern.

The man walked in slowly, looking about as if he owned the place. This one was so skinny that Akos wondered how he walked without his legs snapping under the strain. His head was almost comically large one so small a frame. Bulging eyes looked the trio over, clearly coming to the same conclusion that his muscle had.

While the recruiters were eyeballing them, Akos was looking for any clue that might tell him which crew these men belonged to. Felix was a man of ever-evolving style, and any colors or items of clothing that Akos might have used to mark one of his men would no doubt be hopelessly out of date. Still, Akos looked them up and down to see if there were any tattoos, colors, or symbols that he might recognize.

His search came up empty, however. Akos took a sip of ale to buy time while he continued to study the recruiters over the rim of the mug. The thin one seemed to be very fixated on Calia, ignoring the clear warning signs in the murderous glare that Valesa was giving him. Akos cleared his throat to forestall any immediate violence.

"Can we help you gentlemen?" Akos asked.

"No, but might be that you can help us."

"And how is that?"

The skinny man stalked closer, stopping just out of arm's reach.

"You look like you can handle yourself in a scrape," the man said.

Akos bit back a threatening retort. "I would hope so; I've been through enough of them," he said instead. "Who are you?"

"My name's Fleabite."

"I'm sorry."

Fleabite cocked his head and looked genuinely confused. "Why?"

"How about you cut to the quick, Fleabite, and tell us what you and your muscle are doing here?"

"Our boss has a proposition for you," Fleabite said, spreading his hands wide as if offering a gift. "See, our boss had something stolen from him, and he means to get it back."

"Sounds like a problem for the constables."

Fleabite snorted. "You aren't from around here, are you? No, the boss needs fighting men, men who can handle a blade, to help him take back what's his."

"And say I agree to come with you? I'd like to know who I'm working for."

"Why, the scourge of five realms. The man who strikes fear in the hearts of merchants and trembling in the loins of women in all of the known worlds. The man who—"

"Has slain a thousand men and replaced them all with his bastards. The man who subdued a kraken with his dashing good looks, and stole the pride of the Vanocian navy out from under their very noses!" Akos rolled his eyes and glanced at Calia and Valesa. "Felixianus Gessaul Julainda d'Maxilae."

"Uh . . . yeah," Fleabite said.

"Good, that's who we came here to see." Akos slammed the mug of ale down on the bar and stood. "Let's go meet him."

"Well, that's not exactly how things work—"

Akos ignored Fleabite as he strode forward. He swept Fleabite into his stride, one arm wrapped around the slender man's shoulder like he was an old friend. He'd have to bathe for at least a week and possibly burn this jacket afterwards, but he needed to convince the man that there was nothing threatening about him. The muscle tensed, but Akos ignored them and continued to walk toward the exit.

"Fleabite," Akos explained, "I've known Felix since we were green hands. He was my executive officer when I first became a captain. If you don't believe me, run along to him and tell him that Captain Akos of the *Mist Stalker* is in town and wants to have a drink with his old friend. He might have you all beaten for not bringing me straight to him, but that's just the risk you'll have to run if you don't want to bring us along."

Fleabite swallowed hard, weighing his options. Akos hoped that he would buy his act. Unless Felix had gone down a completely different path than the one he'd been on when Akos last saw him, he wouldn't have a subordinate beaten for verifying something before taking the word of a stranger. Akos was hoping that Fleabite was too far down on the chain of command, and too new to the crew, to know that.

"Right then." Fleabite motioned to the muscle. "Send a runner ahead to let the boss know we're coming. You three follow me. But keep a hand close to those weapons. If we run into Garot's boys, they might give us trouble."

Akos smiled, patting the man heartily enough on the back that he was worried the frail man might fall over.

"Lead the way."

Chapter 10

The city of Tersun was nothing like Calia had expected. Rather than the impressive and orderly buildings she'd come to know in Geralis, the streets were winding, the buildings poorly built and dilapidated, and little to no effort was put into decorating their exterior. Coming from a place where outward appearance was everything and the common man wouldn't even think to use a butcher whose facility was unkempt, it was quite the shock.

The people were of a different breed as well. Perhaps it had been Akos's crew, well-disciplined to the point they would not have been out of place in any of the major navies of the realms, that had given her the notion that all pirates would be like that. Perhaps there was a bigger difference between privateers and pirates than she'd originally believed. Or perhaps Akos held his own to a higher standard than the average.

Men and women stood in the streets conversing or plying their wares. Ragged clothes and blades were prominent on all of them. Even the women rolling dough and serving ale at outdoor tables were armed with at least one blade, and most carried a pistol as well. Despite that, they didn't see any violence as they made their way through the maze of streets to meet Felix.

Calia thought back to what Akos had told them about the man they had come all this way to seek help from. He'd described him as an old friend, a dependable man who would help him at a moment's notice. Calia imagined someone like Leo, or even Vibius, waiting for them inside the tavern that Fleabite led them to. But another part of her remembered the way that Vibia had reacted to hearing the name and had to wonder what the man was like. Akos had warned them that Felix had a flair for the dramatic, and that it was best to just play along.

Their guide took them deep into the heart of Tersun. They'd walked for the last hour, Fleabite casting nervous glances all around them with every step as hired muscle crowded around them. It was clear that they'd walked into some kind of fight, and she wondered what kind of fight that was. The way that the hired men referred to Felix as "boss" was curious, but Calia put it down to the idiosyncrasies of different sailing crews. The crew of the *Mist Stalker* always referred to Akos as "captain;" it was possible Felix's crew had a different honorific for their captain.

"Here we are," Fleabite said, relief obvious in his voice.

Calia looked at the tavern and wondered whether this was some sort of practical joke. The tavern was as dilapidated as the rest of the town, but with the addition of rather large holes through the wood planking that made up the walls. At least one of the windows along the shop front was shattered, with nothing to keep out the wind but a thin sheet. A sign hung on one hook, the paint so faded that it was no longer legible.

"Felix has done some work on the place," Akos said dryly.

"It's been a tough couple of months, alright?" Fleabite said. "Garot and his boys know that the boss isn't about to give this place up without a fight, and they've tried to burn it down a few times."

"Is that what the smell is?" Valesa asked.

Calia wasn't sure what smell Valesa was talking about. The general odor of the city was one of refuse and unwashed bodies. Her nose couldn't detect anything that smelled any better or worse through that pungent pall. Fleabite looked as though he wanted to retort, but a glance at Valesa silenced him.

"Why are we wasting time outside?" Akos asked. He stepped around their guide and started toward the door. "We didn't come here to admire the architecture."

"Hold on now." Fleabite did his best to interpose himself between the door and Akos, but it was to little avail. He was far too small to so much as slow down Akos. "The captain's still sleeping, and he doesn't like to be disturbed."

"Trust me when I say that I don't care." Akos smiled. "He'll want to see me."

Dragging a still-protesting Fleabite inside, the group entered the tavern. Calia blinked as her eyes did their best to adjust to the dim common room. Embers smoldered in one corner, and the only other source of light was a lamp set up on a bar. A dozen men snored in the common room, lying about the floor in a ragged mass of humanity. Akos began to pick his way through them to the back door, an apoplectic-looking Fleabite tailing behind him muttering protests. Calia looked over to Valesa, who gave a half-hearted shrug and motioned for Calia to go first.

After picking their way through the sleeping group of men, they arrived at a door that Akos pushed through without a second thought. Calia pondered for a brief moment whether they should go inside, but curiosity got the best of her. She ducked into the room, moving aside to make room for Valesa to follow along behind her.

As she did so, Calia's foot knocked over several empty bottles of varying shapes. Her gaze shot down, but the noise didn't seem to disturb any of the snoring men in the room behind them. Calia looked around the see that the bottles were covering virtually every flat surface in the room, and more than a few were piled up against the walls.

In fact, the only places devoid of liquor bottles were a cupboard, its glass front so covered in dust and smoke that the contents were inscrutable, and a bed. Akos stood at the foot of the bed with his hands on his hips, looking down at the snoring pair there. Calia edged closer so that she could see what was going on.

Akos kicked the footboard of the bed hard enough to shake the entire thing. The man, lying on his face on the out-of-place, opulent pillows that covered the bed, snorted but continued to snore. The woman underneath his arm started awake, trying to blink some of the sleep out of her eyes. When she finally noticed the group of people standing at the foot of the bed she bolted upright, snatching up the blanket to cover her chest.

Akos hooked a thumb toward the door, and the woman dragged the blanket off the bed in a scramble to get out of the room. Calia and Valesa parted, creating a path for her, and she left, scooping up various items of clothing as she did. The man on the bed, finding the room to be a tad breezier, finally lifted his head and groggily cast about.

"Who the hell . . ." the man started in a thick Vanocian accent.

"Wake up, Felix," Akos said.

Felix squinted at Akos as though he was trying to look through a thick haze of smoke. Akos crossed his arms over his chest and waited patiently. Calia took the opportunity to study the person they had come to Tersun to find.

She wasn't impressed. Long, golden blonde hair trailed halfway down his back, held in a loose ponytail by a black ribbon. His pointed jaw was covered by a knife-sharp goatee, or at least Calia imagined that it would be when it wasn't smashed flat by a pillow.

Understanding dawned on Felix, and like a musket shot he was standing on the bed with his arms spread wide in greeting and nothing left to the imagination. Calia felt her cheeks redden as her gaze snapped away. All grogginess was gone from Felix's voice now.

"My brother!" Felix exclaimed, hopping off the bed and trying to embrace Akos. Akos caught him in the chest with an outstretched hand.

"Put some pants on first, dammit," Akos said.

"Ah, of course. I'll meet you in the common room."

The group made their way out of the room to allow Felix to dress. It didn't take long for the man to emerge from his room, wearing trousers and a captain's long coat. He'd at least made a pass at straightening his beard. This time Akos met his embrace, and the two hugged like brothers who'd been too long apart.

"It's good to see you, Felix," Akos said.

"And you as well," Felix said. "When I heard that Leodysus and Vibia were in town, I knew that you would not be far behind."

"Where are they anyway?"

Felix turned away, but for a moment, Calia thought she saw a mixture of fear and anger on his face. Instead of answering immediately, Felix strode back behind the bar, shooing the barman out of the way. He began to thump bottles and glasses down on the bar. He started trying to work the cork out of a thick green bottle, but Akos slammed the cork back home just before Felix had it free.

"Felix," Akos said. There was a note of warning in his tone.

Felix looked him in the eye as long as he could, but eventually his gaze fell to the table and his shoulders sagged. He placed his hands on the bar and leaned into it, looking away as though searching for a good answer. Giving up on his hunt, Felix finally turned back to Akos.

"Garot got to them first."

"That's the second time I've heard that name," Akos said. "And I don't have any more idea who the hell that is than the first time I heard it."

"Let me uncork the bottle. This is a story best told with rum in hand."

For a moment, Calia thought that Akos would refuse, but he took his hand off the top of the bottle. Felix popped the cork and took a deep swig straight out of the bottle. And then kept going. After drinking far more than Calia would have guessed the bottle even contained, Felix slammed the jug down.

"Forgive my manners," Felix said. "Would anyone else like some?"

"Get to it Felix," Akos said.

"Right, right. It's a simple story really. Since I've owned the Crimson Cannon, I've come to become something of a figure in the community."

"You don't say?" Akos asked dryly.

"As shocking to me as it is to you, I assure you. Nevertheless, the Crimson Cannon has flourished where others have failed, and I have gained a reputation for being an honest and fair man. Which is why when a stranded captain by the name of Garot came into my establishment and talked me into a game of cards, and then accused *me* of cheating, I lost my temper. Little did I know that his antics were a shroud thrown up to keep me from finding out that his men were busy capturing *my* ship."

"They stole the *Golden Wing*?"

"No. I'd sold the *Golden Wing* to pay for the Crimson Cannon by that point."

"Which is a different ship?"

"What? No. That's the tavern. Didn't you see the sign?"

"The sign is hanging off the building and illegible," Calia offered.

"What? Is it?" Felix looked genuinely shocked. "That bastard Garot probably knocked it down on his way out just for spite."

"Focus," Akos cut in. "What ship did he steal?"

"Ah, yes. Well, I'm sure you've heard the rumors that I managed to steal the *Pride of Vanocia* from the navy?"

"You stole a ship of the line?!"

"Ah yes, you *have* heard the rumors. There you see my frustration."

Akos sank down onto a barstool and laid his head against the bar. Calia could hardly believe her ears. She'd half expected the rumors to be false and for all of this to be a useless endeavor. But not only had Felix managed to steal one of the premier ships of the line in the entire realm of man, but he'd had it stolen from him in turn.

For his part, Felix reached under the bar and retrieved another jug of alcohol. He had almost wiggled the cork out of that one when Akos raised his head and took notice of it. He reached up and slapped the bottle, sending it crashing off the bar and shattering on the floor. Several of the snoring men around them snorted and started, but none of them actually woke up. In any other situation, Calia might have commended them for their commitment to sleep.

Felix glared down at the shattered glass, slowly swinging his gaze back to Akos. The pair's eyes met, and for a brief moment Calia thought they might come to blows. Then Felix grinned and leaned in.

"I own a bar now, Akos," Felix whispered. "I have more."

"Get me a glass this time," Akos growled. "And while you're at it, explain to me what any of this has to do with my crew."

"Oh yes, that's what we were talking about." Felix began to retrieve a new bottle and slid a trio of glasses in front of them. Calia tried to refuse it, but the man ignored her.

"Well, when I went to his inn to tell him to return it, things went a little . . . sideways. One thing led to another, one of my men killed one of his men, and he swore a blood feud."

Akos filled in the rest. "He set up shop on one side of town and you set up here. You've been scheming on how to get your ship back without having a broadside turn your entire crew into splinters and viscera, all while having a street war with his crew."

Felix looked to the ceiling as if tracking Akos's logic, then looked back down with a smile and a nod.

"That about sums it up, yes. Lucky for me there are so many buildings between here and the harbor or he would have levelled this place a month ago."

"And Leo and Vibia were taken by Garot?" Calia guessed.

"Unfortunately yes," Felix said. "They used my name before they knew that it wasn't safe, and Garot's boys got to them first. Fortunately, he knows they are good friends of mine, and he's using them to try to bargain with me."

Felix seemed to finally notice that there were people other than Akos listening to him speak. He glanced at Valesa, but her back was turned to the bar, examining the patrons behind them. He then blinked at Calia and leaned in. Calia leaned back as he got closer.

"You're not Anastasia," Felix stated.

"No," Calia replied.

"What are you doing with another woman, Akos? Has the great and honorable Captain Akos finally besmirched himself by taking another lover?"

"Gods no," Akos, Calia, and Valesa said in unison.

"Oh. Well forgive me for not introducing myself. I am Felix d' Maxilae! Former privateer extraordinaire and current owner of the Crimson Cannon."

"I'd gathered as much," Calia said, taking his offered hand and allowing him to kiss the back of her hand.

Valesa did not offer her hand or turn around, and Felix turned back toward Akos. As Akos made their introductions, Calia wondered why they had ever bothered to come here. Felix certainly seemed to be an old friend; he might even be willing to do anything within his power to help Akos and Vibius. But the extent of his power seemed to be very limited. And if the main thing they had come to ask him for was in the hands of another man, what could they do? Calia could not help but feel they were wasting time here.

"Say," Felix said after Akos finished introducing them. "Where is Vibius? Surely you did not leave him on the ship?"

"It might be your turn to sit down, Felix," Akos said. "We have a lot to discuss."

Calia waited as Akos relayed their story. The men around them started rousing about halfway through the telling, but Felix stayed focused on Akos. The story that Calia had once thought too unbelievable to be taken seriously had gotten easier to tell with repetition, and Felix didn't seem like he was brushing them off as insane. In fact, he seemed riveted in place, not even reaching for the rum that he'd been so intent on mere moments ago.

Once Akos finished, Felix leaned back, looking at him with questioning eyes. Several times his mouth opened as if to ask a question before closing again without uttering a word. Calia glanced at Valesa, but she seemed more intent on watching the small crowd that was forming at the bar than she was with the conversation going on behind her.

"I have one critique of your story," Felix said.

"It's not open to critique—" Akos said.

"Your tale is almost believable," Felix continued despite Akos's protestations. "But the idea of some great beast being controlled by a man who calls himself a god is a little too far-fetched."

"Everything that I just told you is the truth, Felix. Whether you choose to believe it or not."

"It cannot be true. Because if it were, that would mean that our brother is trapped in the void with no one to keep him company but some maniac with an army of murderous monsters at his beck and call."

"That about sums up our predicament," Calia agreed.

Felix glanced at her for a moment before turning his gaze back at Akos. All of the levity that Calia had felt emanating off the man from the first moment they met was gone. The smile hadn't left his gaunt face, but the warmth was gone from it. For the first time, Calia thought she was seeing the true face of the man that Akos called his brother.

"Well, in that case," Felix said, "we have no time to waste. Let us win a war and go save our friends."

Chapter 11

Despite the appearance that he projected to the world, Akos knew that Felix was, at his heart, an organizer. Perhaps not when it came to his personal belongings, or even the material that it would require to wage a war against another pirate captain. But he was an organizer of men without compare. The man had a talent for reading people, for drawing out the best of their talents. *Not their best*, Akos reminded himself. *The talents that best served his purposes.*

Within an hour of introducing Felix to Calia and Valesa, Felix had already introduced the group to a half dozen of his lieutenants. Each of them had a different mission in the war, from actually leading the gaggle of pirates that followed Felix in fights against Garot's boys to recruiting new muscle to help with the efforts. There was even a man in charge of making sure each man had enough rum when their day was over and it was time to recoup for the next day's efforts.

It was an impressive feat for a man who could hardly remember where he'd left his sword belt the night before. But Akos had never employed Felix for his memory. It shouldn't have been a surprise that he'd been unable to keep ahold of a prize as valuable as the *Pride of Vanocia*. Felix had always been far better at making a conquest than he was at knowing what to do with it afterward.

It seemed that Felix had at the very least earned the loyalty of someone who did have an idea of how to think about that. Akos glanced around at the various maps of Tersun that hung on the walls of the back room of the Crimson Cannon. For the most part, he remembered the layout of the city, but some of the maps included things such as the blueprints for some of the larger structures. One in particular was front and center.

"As you can see, Garot has taken city hall," Felix said as they crowded around the table.

"Why did the local governor give up such an important structure?" Calia asked.

"The governor of Tersun hasn't been in the city in generations. City hall was a haven for the few dozen men who actually tried to enforce some kind of law, or worse, collect taxes. But as soon as they got word that Garot was moving on the hall, they packed up their things and got out of town."

Akos moved closer to study the map. Someone had been marking on the blueprints with a pencil. The building was long and wide, with dozens of interconnected offices in wings extending from a central domed atrium. A small audience chamber extended from the center, perpendicular to the offices.

"What does this line mean?" Akos asked.

"Garot's had his boys digging a dry moat around the building. He's turning it into a fortress."

"Then these must be ravelins?" Calia asked, stepping forward to point at another handful of lines.

Both men looked over at her with curious eyes.

"I studied military history for a semester," Calia explained with a shrug.

Akos shrugged and turned back to Felix, who was still looking at the woman with an evaluating eye. After a moment, Felix snapped back to the present, nodding his head.

"Yes, they are," Felix said. "He's been raising earthworks and putting in gun emplacements here, here, and here."

"What, exactly, has been your plan?" Akos asked.

"Well, I'm glad you asked. In fact, I thought that if I held out for long enough, the military would notice that he was fortifying a hold on the city and they would be forced to end his little tyranny."

"Your plan has been to wait until someone else handled the problem for you?"

Felix looked for a second as if he wanted to disagree. Instead, he burst into a grin and nodded vigorously. Akos rolled his eyes at his friend. Despite knowing that his pride would never allow him to take the same route, Akos had to admit to the efficacy of Felix's plan. If Garot continued to act as he had, even the absentee governor of Tersun would be forced to call in the military, and no fortifications would save the man from that. All Felix had to do was survive until then, and with the network of foot soldiers and spies that he'd built up, it wouldn't be impossible.

"But . . ." Felix held a finger up to forestall any commentary. "Conditions have changed. Now we must move much more quickly."

"Where is he keeping my crew?" Akos asked.

"By my best guess, here." Felix tapped a finger against the audience chamber behind the central dome. "It has only one entrance, and the windows are too high to jump from. If you could even reach one."

"Of course, they could also be in the basement." Felix pointed to a small section of the map that had only one note written on it. The note said "guns?" with a small skull and crossbones drawn next to it. "Of course, if that were the case, I don't know where they would store their gunpowder."

Akos studied the map alongside Calia while Felix sat and watched them. The others drifted away, going about their daily tasks. For over an hour, the two sat and pored over the map, looking for any sign of weakness that could be gleaned from crude drawings on old blueprints. Akos felt his frustration rising as he could see no way in, at least not one that wasn't covered by several layers of defense.

"This is a textbook fortification," Calia said after a while. "The fields of fire overlap perfectly. How many men does Garot have?"

"On land, I'd say a hundred or so," Felix responded.

"And how many do you have?"

"About the same."

"You said on land," Akos said. "Where are the rest of them?"

"Well, I did mention that he stole my ship," Felix said. "I'd say he's running it with a skeleton crew, enough to sail her around the bay and run some of the guns if needed."

"What, exactly, does he use it for?" Calia asked.

"Intimidation mostly." Felix shrugged. "Whenever one of my crews roughs up a few of his boys, he has the *Pride* sail around the bay with her teeth out to remind us who is in charge."

"He bombards the city?"

"No. Well, not yet anyway. He knows better than to indiscriminately bombard Tersun. If he did that, the entire town would turn against him, and he has to get his food and rum from someone. But without it there is no reason for anyone to fear him. He'd be another street thug with a gang trying to extort the locals. And the locals in Tersun know how to handle themselves."

"But if we attacked him outright," Akos said, "he would be able to send a runner to them to start the bombardment."

"Well, yes. He is a petty and vindictive bastard if I've ever met one."

Akos let the thought hang in the air for a moment. It seemed that Garot had set himself up in the perfect position, with the hammer of the *Pride* poised to smash against the anvil that he had made out of town hall. Any move made against one would be met with a response from the other. Akos like to deal with his problems one at a time, but it didn't look like that would be an option here.

After reflecting a bit further, Akos realized that this very predicament had been what paralyzed Felix in the first place. Akos's old friend was not known for his hesitation, but given a situation like this, he would be forced to wait it out. If they couldn't think of a way to handle both the ship and the town hall at the same time, any move against one of them would be an almost certain defeat.

"Have you tried negotiating with Garot?" Calia asked.

Felix snorted and looked at her with mirth in his eyes. Akos knew that she was serious though, and couldn't help but admit that she had a point. That was one of the few things that no one else in this room was likely to consider as a serious option. Felix's gaze switched from her face to Akos's, and when he realized that she didn't mean it as a joke, he laughed. His laugh evolved from a chuckle to a full-blown belly laugh, and it was a minute before it slowed.

The pair waited as the man's laugh dried up, and then for several moments more as Felix caught his breath.

"No," Felix stated simply.

"Why not?" Akos asked.

"He wants the Crimson Cannon!" Felix said with genuine indignation in his voice.

"What if I offered you a spot as my executive officer on the trip of a lifetime?" Akos said. "A trip into the void to kill a mad warlord and save an old friend?"

"You know that I will do anything to help Vibius. But it's the principle of the thing. I will not allow some jumped-up interloper to wander into Tersun and claim what is rightfully mine. Besides, I've asked these men to fight and die for me, and what kind of man would I be if I left them all here to fend for themselves against a man whose fight was with me?"

"I'll need a larger crew to sail back to the realm of behemoths. You can bring any man who wants to join. But I will need a ship."

"If we can get Garot to trade the *Pride of Vanocia* for the Crimson Cannon, will you be willing to leave this fight behind?" Calia asked. "For your brother?"

"Where did you find this woman?" Felix asked. "One that knows how to twist the dagger just so? Fine. If Garot will trade your crew and the *Pride* for the Cannon, he shall have it. *If.* I would not count on this plan working. But I think I will enjoy seeing the look on Garot's face when you make the offer."

"Good," Akos said. "we'll leave at once for town hall."

"I hope you know what you're doing, Akos," Felix said with a sigh.

***

The town hall was even more unimpressive to look at up close. The building was nothing when compared to the public places in Geralis. Rather than smooth polished stone, the building was composed of an assortment of different woods. It looked as though they'd cobbled the thing together out of whatever material they'd had nearby when constructing it. Rough-hewn redwood planks rested next to smooth ashen-colored panels.

Calia wasn't expecting anything so grand as the Governor's Hall in Geralis, but she had been expecting something more than this. The earthen ramparts that had been erected around it were almost more impressive and uniform than the building. At the very least, the dirt was all the same color. Calia noted that Felix hadn't yet drawn the spiked palisade that was being driven into the ground right outside the dry moat on his map at the tavern.

The ravelins that had been neat triangles drawn onto the blueprints in the Crimson Cannon were imposing earthen towers now that she was standing beneath them. Each of them bristled with men, and each of them were glaring down at their approaching group.

Sweat that had nothing to do with the warmer climes of Tersun trickled down her spine. Calia was beginning to wonder whether this meeting would end in disaster. When she'd proposed a meeting, she had imagined it to be a peaceful one, with each side respecting the law of a truce. She was beginning to think that she'd fooled herself into thinking that Akos's own brand of personal honor was a universal thing amongst men in his profession. In fact, as the men scrambled up into firing positions along the ramparts they'd constructed, she knew that she'd misjudged their opponent.

Still, they weren't firing on their party, and that was always a plus. Felix had thrown together a white flag of truce, though it had required the shirt of largest man in the inn's common room, and to call it white was a stretch. Still, the intent to peacefully parlay was apparent. At least, as apparent as it could be with a group of over twenty armed men walking down the street toward the fortress of their foe.

Whether it was shock that their enemy would come straight to them or the fact that Garot's men were probably still as hung over as Felix's group, so far nothing was happening. There was a lot of yelling, but other than that there was no sign of action behind the fortifications of the town hall. The ramparts had settled into a waiting position, watching with weapons held ready to see what the intruders wanted.

"Tell Garot to come out," Felix yelled up at them once they were in shouting distance. "I've come to parlay with him."

"Who goes there?" an unseen voice called back.

"Watch your tone!" Fleabite's shrill voice cried. "You're addressing the great Felix d'Maxilae!"

Everyone on the ramparts, and everyone in the group below, swiveled their heads to look at the slender man. He shrank back under their gazes.

"Thank you, Bedbug," Felix said. "I'll handle this one."

"It's Fleabite, sir."

"I'm sure it is."

As they waited for any kind of reply, whisperings could be heard drifting down from the wall. Calia couldn't help but wonder what they were debating up there. Clearly they weren't going to open fire, but they didn't seem to be sending anyone to fetch Garot either. Annoyance began to creep into the back of her mind. If this ploy wasn't going to work, they needed to know sooner rather than later so they could figure something else out. Vibius didn't have time for them to be wasting it fooling around with the local politics in Tersun.

The thought gave her pause, and she forced the feeling back down. Vibius also did not have time for them to lose his sister, or his friends, to the hands of some pirate who fancied himself king because they got in too much of a hurry to properly deal with him. Calia knew that she would not get the annoyance to go away, but she could avoid letting it influence her actions. Garot was already likely to be adversarial; the least she could do was avoid making the situation worse by letting her anger get the best of her.

Calia's eyes were drawn by that thought to Akos. In profile, he appeared to be serene, almost bored—the same expression she'd seen on his face before they had translated into the void for the first time. Hopefully he could maintain that mask and avoid another outburst like the one at Lord Galith's mansion. If he couldn't control his emotions, Calia couldn't imagine that this parlay would end well.

After waiting long enough that the sweat on her forehead was from the heat rather than nervousness, something began to happen. The whispers that had ceased several minutes before returned, and Calia could see the tops of heads turning back toward the town hall to look at something. The hall was built on a slight hill, and from her place Calia could see that the doors had opened, and that a small group had exited the building. The anxiety that had been killed by boredom was resurrected, and her heart began to pound in her chest.

Why are you *nervous?* Calia asked herself. She had already agreed that she would let Akos and Felix do all the talking. She was just there because, really, there was nowhere else for her to be. Valesa wanted to hide her away in some room and lock the door, but Calia wouldn't allow herself to be treated like a child anymore. She didn't need to be coddled and hidden from danger. If there was any violence, she was confident in Valesa's ability to protect her.

After several more agonizing moments, the ramshackle gate at the center of the uneven palisade flew open. Several men stepped through cautiously, casting to either side as if looking for a possible ambush. When no one came rushing toward them out of the shadows, they came fully through the gate and took up positions on either side.

The man that followed them must have been Garot. He looked to be her height, and his shoulders appeared to be at least as wide as he was tall. His face was covered in small scars, with a heavy brow and deep-set eyes. He had the look of a boxer, thick with muscle and dripping with confidence. He wore a captain's jacket of light brown, and he swept it back to place his hands on his hips as he looked at the group arrayed before him. Calia couldn't help but notice that the hands on his hips rested uncomfortably close to the brace of pistols there.

"I don't know what to think," Garot boomed. "Should I take this as a sign of courage or stupidity? Or maybe desperation?"

"I'm afraid it is none of the above," Felix said. "Just a shifting of priorities."

"Ready to give up that rundown inn and skip town? I must admit, I thought you had a little more spine than this. But I guess I shouldn't expect anything less than a coward. You are a Vanocian, after all."

Calia could see that dig fluster Felix. His mustache twitched, and he swept back his coat to put his hands on his own hips. There was a rattle of swords being drawn and hammers being cocked on muskets in response. Calia resisted the urge to take a step backward, noting that neither Akos nor Valesa had responded to all the weapons that were being readied. Calia couldn't imagine why they shouldn't be running back the way they came at this very moment, but she couldn't think of two better people to take her cues from either.

"We won't be giving you the Cannon," Akos said. "Not for free anyway."

"And who the hell do you think you are?" Garot asked.

"Captain Akos of the *Mist Stalker*."

Garot made a great show of taking one hand and rubbing it along the stubble on his chin with his head turned toward the sky as if wracking his mind for a memory. He turned his finger toward Akos as he feigned recognition.

"Ah, yeah," Garot said. "Name's familiar. I think you're standing on the wrong side of this battlefield, friend. All your boys are on my side."

"That's why I'm here. I'll be needing them back."

"Your crew for the Cannon? Done."

"Not so fast," Felix interjected. "I'll be needing my ship back."

Garot's booming laugh rolled across the street, causing several of the men on each side to flinch. After a moment, some of his men began to join in with their own chuckles. It was clear they didn't know what the joke was, but they didn't want to get caught not laughing at whatever their boss thought was so funny.

Several minutes later, the laughter slowly started to die down. Garot wiped at his cheeks as though the laughter had wrenched actual tears from him. Calia could tell that it was all an act. This man was no nobleman, but he had many similarities to the men she'd known all her life. This was all theater to him. Calia was beginning to get the sinking feeling that nothing they said here was going to matter.

"I'd heard from a bunch of my boys that you had a sense of humor," Garot said. "But I didn't think that you'd be able to catch me off guard with such a stupid joke."

"No joke," Felix spat between gritted teeth. "My ship. His crew."

"See, now I'm beginning to think that you don't understand how negotiating works. We're all men who have done our fair share of negotiating. You should know as well as any of us that the man with the sword to his throat doesn't get to make demands."

"I've hardly got a sword to my throat. More like a small dog growling and barking at my ankles, tugging at a chain that he prays to his gods will not snap."

Calia saw Akos tense at that, and any hint of joviality fled from Garot's face. It looked like the jabs at Felix had found their home, and he had chosen to respond in kind. Calia could practically see their chances of reaching a diplomatic solution drifting away in the morning breeze.

"A dog, eh?" Garot asked. "I'll warn you, Maxi, this dog's got more than just a bark."

"Does it have any sense?" Felix asked. "If it did, it would know better than to insult two of the greatest captains this town has ever played host to."

"Oh? The great Felix d'Maxilae, seducer of desperate women and thief of unguarded ships? And Akos Freedman, the slave turned pirate so scared of a straight fight that he hides in the ways to hunt his prey? A fine and intimidating pair you make."

Both men bristled at that. Valesa slid a half step in front of Calia, shielding her with her body. Calia craned her neck to see over her shoulder. She knew that she was letting her curiosity override her good sense again, but she needed to know what was happening.

"Your time is over," Garot continued. "It ended when I took the *Pride*. But I'm a generous man. Get the hell out of Tersun. Once you've left, I'll let your crew do whatever they want, even pay for them to catch up to you if they so desire. But the *Pride* is mine, and you'll not be getting it back while I still draw breath."

Calia wondered what was going through the minds of the three captains as they stared at each other across the street. *Surely they cannot be considering attacking him here*, Calia thought. They wouldn't stand a chance. Felix had brought a score of men with pistols and swords. Garot had a fortress full of men armed with muskets. Calia could even see cannons facing their direction, surely loaded with grapeshot that would turn the entire street they'd come down into a charnel house.

I have witnessed one of these men charge through a melee without any regard for his own life to close with a foe, Calia reminded herself. Perhaps she should have stayed behind at the inn and let the men come on their own. Valesa would do anything she could to keep her safe, but there was nothing she could do to protect her from cannon shot.

"Perhaps another agreement could be reached."

The entire crowd turned toward her, and it took Calia a moment to realize that the voice speaking was her own. She didn't know quite how that had happened. *Nothing for it now save to press on*, Calia mused. She took a step around Valesa so that she could see the proceedings a little easier.

"Who the hell are you?" Garot asked.

"Calia Hailko, a pleasure. What if we offered to buy the *Pride* from you?"

Another round of chuckles followed her question, but with nowhere near the enthusiasm as before. Calia didn't know whether the men were all too shocked that she had stepped forward to say anything, but it seemed that she'd caught them off guard. Maybe that was an advantage that she could press.

Calia cut their laughter short. "I've hired these two to complete a task for me, a time sensitive one. I don't have time to wait out this little war. Name a price for your ship, and I'm sure we can come to some kind of agreement."

"You don't have the money," Garot said with a chuckle.

There was something behind his eyes that Calia hoped meant that Garot didn't believe himself. *Or perhaps*, Calia thought, *he wants to be wrong.* Surely if Garot was smart enough to assemble this defense, to create a plan to steal a ship right out from under Felix's nose, he wouldn't be so delusional to think that the rightful owners of Tersun would just let him have the town. If Calia could tempt him with a way out that left him with his person intact and his purse fatter, she might have a way in.

"I come from an old family in Geralis," Calia said. "My ancestors helped to build the town, in fact. We've more money than the gods. Name a price."

Some of the pirates started to chuckle again, but Garot waved them down. He studied her as if looking for some kind of a tell. Calia did her best to hold her back straight and her chin high, looking down her nose at him ever so slightly the way she'd seen her peers do back when she'd lived in the high society of Geralis. As the words hung in the air for what felt like far too long, Calia ignored the beads of sweat tickling their way down her back and held her pose.

"I want the Crimson Cannon," Garot said, ticking his list off on his fingers. "Ten thousand golden crowns, and a vow that neither Felix nor Akos will ever return to Tersun."

Calia tilted her head as if to consider the idea. The last thing she wanted Garot to realize was that she had only half that amount. Galith had been generous, but there was only so much he could do from his personal vaults. Calia fumed internally. Ten thousand gold crowns was a prince's ransom, but it would have been no difficulty if her brother hadn't squandered their fortune.

Calia risked a glance at Akos and realized he'd had at least that much saved up as well before he'd been forced to post bail. If he was angry, he wasn't letting it show. He still had the air of cool detachment that Calia was seeking to mimic.

"I think you overvalue your ship's worth," Calia said.

"It ain't about the ship's worth, it's about how bad you need it," Garot stated.

"You are definitely overvaluing my need."

"I don't think I am."

Calia bit back a harsh reply. Garot was right. If she'd had the money, she wouldn't have hesitated. Was this pirate such an excellent judge of character that he read her so easily?

"I need some time to consider your offer and make arrangements," Calia said.

"You have a day," Garot said. "After that, everything said here is off the table. Meet back here at noon tomorrow if you have the gold; otherwise don't bother. After this, there will be no more parleys and no more truces. If you come back without the money, d'Maxilae, you'd better come with cannons instead."

Garot turned to make his way back to his stronghold, but thought better of it and spun on his heel.

"Oh, and Akos, you'd better hope your employer is good for it. Because if the money isn't here, I'll start taking it out of your men's hides. I've held my crew in check because I figured yours would be more valuable to me whole and healthy. But that all changes tomorrow at noon."

Without another word, Garot turned around and swept back through the gate. The group watched until the doors had slammed shut behind him. Then, at a signal from Felix, they turned and began to walk away. Calia hurried to keep up, sparing a glance over to Valesa. She wasn't sure what was going on in her mind, but whatever else Valesa was thinking, she wasn't happy.

"I think that went well," Fleabite offered as they made their way back to the Crimson Cannon. "All we have to do is pay up and we'll have the *Pride* back."

"We don't have that kind of money," Akos said.

"Even if we did, I would not throw a single copper at that man," Felix said through gritted teeth.

"Then what are we going to do?" Fleabite asked.

"Think of a new plan," Akos said.

CHAPTER 12

Cold darkness surrounded Vibius for all eternity. No matter which way he turned he could see nothing but empty void. There was a horizon, if he could call it that, but it eluded his perception no matter how hard he strained his senses toward it. Vibius was beginning to wonder whether it truly existed at all, or if it was a figment of his broken mind, his subconscious giving his waking mind something to strive toward.

If he was even awake at all. Vibius could no longer tell. He'd thought the first few weeks had been bad, with days and nights dragging into each other in the eternal darkness. This was something else though. The boundary between his conscious thoughts and subconscious sleep was blurring. At any given moment Vibius had no idea whether he was standing in the center of his cell flexing his mental muscles to try to reach his gift or dreaming of doing so while slumped against the uneven stone wall of his cell.

Regardless of which it was right now, Vibius felt that he was making good progress. Sure, his wayfarer's sight still eluded him, but at least he had managed to stand for a full shift without collapsing. Or had he? It was an interesting question to Vibius's addled mind. He pressed down with a foot, the sudden shifting of weight threatening to topple him.

Vibius cursed himself. The sudden surprise had forced him to focus on something other than the horizon, and it shifted away from him again. Vibius tried to drag it back, but nothing happened. His concentration was broken. Vibius let out a roar of frustration as he collapsed to his knees. The sound of his voice reverberated through the empty dungeon and echoed back to him.

Drained by the disappointment of losing all his progress, Vibius fell forward onto his hands. He balled them into fists and shook with rage. He drew himself back up into a kneeling position, trying his best to control the anger that was building in his chest.

"Akos wouldn't let his anger get the best of him," Vibius whispered to himself.

"Of course I would," Akos said. "Why else do you think you're here?"

Vibius spun his head to see Akos lounging in the corner of the cell next to him. He would have rubbed his eyes, but that would send a wave of agony through him. That thought reminded him that whatever he was currently *seeing* was nothing more than a figment of his own shattered mind. He could no longer see anything, much less a friend that was a realm away.

"I let my anger get the best of me in that fight with Anson," Akos continued. "I should have directed the fight, or at least noticed that there was a behemoth there."

"And if you had?" Vibius snapped back. "What would it have changed?"

Some small part of Vibius's mind realized that he was arguing with a person that wasn't there. The rest of him didn't care. He wouldn't have a friend's name dragged through the mud by his own subconscious. Even if that subconscious was taking the form of said friend.

"I might have been able to direct the crew to overwhelm the creature," Akos said.

"Or, it would have killed everyone else and left me in this exact same predicament," Vibius countered. "Now off with you, specter. I've work to get back to."

"Oh, I'm sorry. Am I distracting you from your busy schedule of rotting to nothingness in a cell?"

Vibius ignored him and stood up, bracing himself against the wall. It took a moment to regain his feet. A growl from his stomach forced him to wonder how long it had been since the guards had bothered to remember to bring him food. Perhaps the next time they came he could talk them into bringing Akos a plate as well. Then he could have double.

The thought wrung a chuckle from him, and the chuckle devolved into an unstoppable belly laugh. Vibius had to throw an arm against the wall to keep from keeling back over onto the ground, but his hand slipped off the wall and he crashed down anyway. He lay with his back to the rough stone wall, laughing until there was no more air in his lungs and tears streamed down his face. A figure moved in front of him and squatted down. Vibius refused to look up at the figment that wore his friend's face, no matter how close it got to him.

"Pathetic," Akos said. "It's no wonder you can't find your gift. It *is* a wonder that the gods bothered to give it to you in the first place."

"Shut up," Vibius croaked. He was still having trouble getting air to go into his lungs without immediately laughing it back out.

Akos's specter ignored his mirth. "You've always been nothing. You just managed to hide it behind those golden eyes. Did they make you feel special when you were a kid? Knowing that through nothing but dumb luck you were blessed with a gift that most children would kill for?

"Did it make you feel like you were better than me? When you helped me gain my freedom, did it make you feel like you were some gracious rescuer gifting me a station that I could never reach on my own?"

"Now I know that you're a figment of my subconscious," Vibius said. "The real Akos knows better than that."

"You're right. I'm not Akos. I'm you."

Vibius finally looked up to see a mirror image of himself towering over him. He forced himself up onto his seat and stared upwards at his double. Unlike the tattered rags that he was dressed in, his double wore the finest clothes that Vibius had ever seen. Vibius's face flushed and he could feel anger welling up in his chest when their eyes met. Staring back into the ragged empty sockets that Anson had left him with were the golden eyes that he had been so proud of.

"I know you better than anyone else," the double told him. "I know that you did think that you were better than all your peers in Geromia. I know that you looked down on everyone around you, that you thought yourself smarter than them, better because of the gift given to you by fate. I know that you always looked down on Akos."

"No," Vibius growled. He let the rage flooding through him give him the strength to rise to his feet. He met his double's gaze unflinchingly.

"I always respected Akos. Looked up to him even. Because everything he was, he made for himself. And everything I am is a result of nothing but luck."

"I'm glad you realize it," the double said with a smirk. "Now that you finally realize that you are nothing, you can give up this fruitless attempt at reclaiming your gift."

"I am Vibius Antonius, wayfarer of the *Mist Stalker*. And I will be fit to return to those duties when I am called to do so."

The specter continued to berate him, trying to distract him, but Vibius pushed past him and resumed his post in the center of the room. He had dealt with distractions when trying to ply the ways in the past, and he had always been able to tune them out. This would be no different.

***

The horizon continued to appear at the edge of Vibius's sight, always tantalizingly close and agonizingly out of reach. At this point he didn't even expect to be able to do anything if he did see it. But he needed to know that he still could. If he couldn't, then he didn't know what he would do if he ever did manage to get out of this cage. It wasn't as though there was much use for a blind nobleman on a sailing vessel.

Vibius found himself holding onto that impossible hope that, somehow, he would end up getting released from this dungeon. He could dream a dozen different scenarios of how that might happen, from a rival god conquering Logathia to Akos returning with a fleet and freeing him by force. None of them seemed particularly likely, but Vibius didn't allow himself to dwell on the implausibility of his plans. If he did that, there would be no reason to do anything but curl up in the corner and refuse to eat his gruel until madness overtook him or he wasted away.

Instead, Vibius reached with his mind, straining it ever further, trying to catch a glimpse of the ways. His imaginary double still lounged in the corner, glaring at him with hate-filled eyes as he grasped at his visions. Vibius wondered if his mind had cracked, never to be the same again, or if the figment was a product of his isolation. He'd heard tales of marooned men who had all but gone insane in their solitude, only to return to their full faculties once they reentered society.

Vibius was desperately hoping for the latter.

As he strained his mind, the horizon wavered ever closer. Vibius stretched toward it, gritting his teeth against the effort. It was like trying to climb a sheer wall to reach a window for just a peek outside. All he needed was a glimpse, a sliver of a flash of the ways, and he would know that he could still reach them. Desperation fueled his concentration as he forced his mind further out than he ever had before in search of that glimpse.

Something popped in Vibius's mind, and his senses were overwhelmed. Light seemed to surround him, bathing him in radiance the likes of which he had never known. Vibius shrank back, trying to cover his eyes, but it was no use. The light was not physical, but instead shining inside his wayfarer's senses.

The way the light clawed at his mind, demanding to be let in, was all too familiar to Vibius. He had to imagine that it would be a common sensation among any who had the wayfarer's gifts. It was almost like the madness that came over wayfarers when they sailed too close to a realm. Vibius had never felt it so strong before, even when they had been approaching the void. It threatened to overwhelm him and leave him a gibbering madman writhing on the floor.

No, Vibius thought. *I've come too far to be reduced to madness by my own gift.* The only way to stave off the proximity madness, in Vibius' experience, was to turn directly toward or away from it. But there was nothing to turn away from here. Usually there was a solid presence, a weight that Vibius could feel that let him know that a realm was there. There was nothing like that here.

With nothing to physically turn away from, Vibius swung his mind's gaze directly toward the source.

The attempt lessened the clawing somewhat, but it was not gone entirely. Vibius could understand why. Just as there was nothing solid to turn away from, there was nothing to turn directly toward either. At least now he could think without feeling as though his mind were going to be torn apart. He realized that his heart was threatening to pound its way out of his chest, and he took a slow and ragged breath to try to calm it.

Vibius took another slow breath and began to send his senses forth again. It was dangerous. He could feel the threat of gibbering madness waiting for him if he pressed too hard. Vibius supposed that he could close his wayfarer's sight altogether. Something inside him urged him to keep going. After all, it wasn't as if he had anything to lose.

With that cheerfully nihilistic thought in mind, Vibius pressed forward rather than shrinking back. It was almost as if he were glimpsing the ways, but there were far too many of them, stretching out in all directions. The ways were twisting and complex, but they were all on the same plane as the realms. That was one of the fundamentals of wayfaring.

The light around him stretched out like tree roots, branching out every which way. Some extended out flat along the plane that he was used to. Others twisted upward and downward, or even reversed themselves halfway through and plunged up or down. As Vibius began to plot some of the nearest ones in his mind, he began to feel the familiar pull of a realm at the end of them. As he sensed them out, the clawing at the back of his mind faded away.

Vibius felt his knees give out and his body collapse to the ground. A strange sound filled the air around him, and he realized that he was once again laughing. It was a rasping and ugly sound, but he knew it for what it was.

In his attempt to prove that he still had his gift, Vibius had stumbled across a world of new possibilities. What he wouldn't give to have Calia here to talk about this. She wouldn't believe it. After all, everyone knew that there were only five realms, six if you counted the void. From the few moments of mental exploring he'd done, he'd counted at least a dozen, with a dozen more unexplored routes to go.

If you were looking for a reason to stay alive, Vibius told himself, *you found one.* Someone had to bring this news to the world. And as far as he knew, he was the only one who could.

CHAPTER 13

The mood in the Crimson Cannon was tense. Even Calia could feel it hanging in the air. Or perhaps it was just their group that was feeling the pressure of the situation. Felix's men seemed to be having the party of their lives in the next room over.

Not that Calia could blame them. It wasn't as if their situation had changed at all. They were still at war with Garot's men, and unless their commanders came up with something drastic in the next few hours, that wouldn't change. Still, Calia wished that they would keep it down so that she could think. The cacophony was almost impressive in a way. If she didn't know better, Calia would have thought they'd brought in an entire orchestra which only employed instruments that were off-key and players that didn't know how to play them.

That's just an excuse for why you can't think of anything, and you know it, Calia told herself. Not that anyone else in the group seemed to be doing much better. They hadn't spoken since they'd returned from their parley with Garot. Felix had immediately started swigging his way through what seemed like a small barrel of rum, while Akos had taken up position in front of the map of town hall. Every so often he would make a mark somewhere, though Calia could not discern their purpose from across the room. Valesa had sat down next to the door, ensuring that they had the privacy to think. Even Felix's top men were hesitant to attempt to make their way past her once she'd made it clear that interruptions would not be welcome.

Though she couldn't be sure of the reason for the others' silence, Calia knew that she hadn't thought of a single idea worth bringing to their attention since they'd sat down. They couldn't pay the price that Garot had demanded, and his ultimatum hadn't left much room for further negotiation. She doubted that he would allow her to extend him a line of credit. *Oh sure*, Calia mused, *tell the pirate to go to Geralis and collect the difference from Halis.* That would go over swimmingly she was sure.

She was mad enough at her brother to try anyway. As if having Akos imprisoned wasn't bad enough, having Lusalin attempt to kill him was a step too far. She'd always known there was more than a superficial difference between them. Since they were children, she'd known that their father had failed to instill the same ideals in her brother that he had managed to ingrain in her. But never would Calia have thought that he was capable of something like that. To be fair, Calia never would have believed that she'd be capable of intervening in a pirate parley a year ago. It seemed that they'd both harbored surprises.

Calia shook her head to clear it. She was thinking of her brother to avoid thinking of the problem at hand. Perhaps a different vantage would help her clear her head. She rose from the table and went to join Akos at the map. He gave no indication that he had any idea she was there. Akos seemed to be deep in thought, so Calia didn't say anything to break his concentration. Instead, she turned her attention to the little marks he had been making on the map.

Despite the lack of a key for the symbols, they were easy enough to decipher. Whoever had drawn the map must have fancied themself something of an artist. Little pirate figures marked the routes of patrols, with cannons dotting the crenellations. Having seen the place in person, Calia thought that the hand-drawn wooden palisade was spot on.

Akos's symbols were a little more difficult to make out. They were plain x's, drawn at various points along the perimeter and against the walls of the town hall itself. As Calia watched, Akos reached out with the charcoal pencil and scratched another x along the wall near a window. He looked at it for a moment and frowned.

"Do you remember if that window was boarded up?" Akos asked.

The question came so suddenly after their long silence that it made Calia jump. She cast her thoughts back, trying to remember if she had seen the window he was referring to. It was the farthest from the door along the front face of the building. Calia hadn't paid much attention to the windows, focusing on the muskets and cannons instead.

"I don't remember," Calia answered. "I didn't look at the windows."

"I couldn't quite see the farthest wings of the building from where we were. But if they aren't boarded up, I think that might be my best way in."

"What do you mean? Surely you don't intend to try to storm the town hall by force?"

"Of course not. The moment we try to mount an attack, he will have the crew put to the sword. I'm going to sneak in and let the crew out so that we have more time to figure out what we're going to do about a ship."

"That's insane."

"Have you thought of something better?"

Calia wanted to argue with him, but he was right. They were running out of time, and they weren't any closer to a plan than when they'd started. Still, this would be suicide. Calia knew that Akos was a capable man, but she could also see that he was still slowed by the injuries he'd sustained in his battle with Anson. Krallek had confided in her that he might never recover the same, and that even once he was confident everything was set, it would take months, if not years, of work to regain his former strength.

"Garot has done a fair job of securing the town hall itself, but he hasn't bothered to trim back the buildings around it," Akos explained. "I noticed several buildings with roofs that almost overhang the palisade. It would be an easy jump across and onto the walls. Then it would be a matter of dodging the patrols and finding an entryway into the hall itself."

"And once you're inside? Do you plan to check every room until you find the crew?"

"If that's what it takes."

Calia pursed her lips as she looked up at him. There was defiance in his eyes, and she wondered if he was trying to prove to himself that he still could. She had never considered Akos lacking for pride, after all.

But there was something else there. It only took a few moments for Calia to realize that it was responsibility. Akos held himself responsible for Vibius's loss; he hadn't tried to hide that at all. She could only imagine that he now felt culpable for the rest of his crew being in captivity as well. *He must think that he sent them straight into the mouth of the beast*, Calia thought. Though there was no way he could have known what was happening, Calia knew that Akos would never accept that as an excuse.

At this point, there was probably no stopping him. If he'd decided that this was the course, there was nothing she could do to change his mind. Especially when she had nothing better to offer him. If only she could come up with a better plan, she might be able to dissuade him. But Calia still couldn't think of anything.

Instead of challenging Akos, Calia turned back toward the map hanging on the wall. She began to study it as intensely as any theoretical manuscript she might have read front to back at the university. If she couldn't give Akos a better option, Calia could at least make sure the one plan they had might succeed. She cast her mind back to the fortress Garot had made of the town hall and began to mark weak spots of her own.

"It would be best if there were a distraction," Calia mumbled to herself as she thought.

"Perhaps I could help with that," Felix said. "After all, I have all these pirates with no ship to sail on and an enemy to fight a few hundred yards away."

"I'm not going to ask you to assault a fortified position so that I can sneak in and find my crew," Akos said.

"You don't have to. My boys are so riled up by that asshole's demands that they might go without the order anyway. At least if I direct them, they might stand a chance."

"If you had the strength and will to storm the town hall, you'd have done so before it was a fortress," Calia said.

Felix shrugged. "I do not think we will succeed at actually taking the building from him. But we do not have to take the building to threaten it. And his men are no more disciplined soldiers than mine. Chances are if we scream loud enough at the front, they won't notice you slipping through into the back."

The room went silent for a few moments as everyone seemed to consider it. Calia couldn't stand the idea of any more blood being shed for her cause, unless it was Anson's of course. But it didn't seem they would be able to avoid it. They needed the crew and they needed a ship. Garot wasn't going to give them either for just a please and thank-you.

Calia cast a glance over to Valesa to see if she had any opinion. If she did, she was keeping her face from showing it. Calia couldn't glean a single thing of her thoughts, which was odd. Normally she could read Valesa like an open book. With nowhere else to look for outward opinions, Calia turned her mind inward and tried to do what she did best and reason through what information she had.

If Felix was right and his men might attack the fortress regardless of him giving a command, then there was no reason to waste their assault when it could be used to further their own ends. Akos might not be strong enough yet to do what needed to be done though, but she wasn't the best judge of that. Only he could decide what he was able to do. And she didn't think that he would even broach the subject if he had any doubts. At least, not when the fate of his crew was on the line.

Still, something felt wrong about this. It felt rushed. It *was* rushed. Garot had left them with no other options but to cobble together a plan. If they didn't act fast, they might as well not act at all. They may as well pray that it was a bluff and wait for the Tersun military to return and lay siege to the town hall.

Vibius might not have that kind of time. Could Calia live with herself if she stayed safe at the Crimson Cannon waiting through the days and nights while he remained in the hands of a madman like Anson? *No*, Calia realized. She couldn't. And she would not be able to live with the weight of the rest of the crew being killed for her outburst at the parley either. If no other path presented itself, they would have to tread the one laid out before them.

"I don't think we have any other choice," Calia said. "At least if we have the crew with us we can make a plan that doesn't involve an ultimatum."

Akos looked between them for a moment, arms crossed over his chest. Akos sighed. "Volunteers only. I'll not have you drafting people to charge to their deaths on my behalf."

Felix grinned and swept the jug of rum off the table as he rose to his feet. Calia was almost impressed. Despite the lack of liquid left in the massive bottle, Felix didn't waver on his feet whatsoever.

"I'll go see who is up for a little fun."

Felix swept out of the room, and Calia saw Akos shaking his head a little.

"Where did you ever find him?" Calia asked.

"He was my first executive officer," Akos said. "When we were both little more than kids. He's the son of some Vanocian count or something like that, but he got bored with his life and read one too many pirate novels. Sometimes I think this is all some grand game to him, but other times he can be deadly serious."

"I can't even imagine that."

"It's hard to picture, even for someone who's known him as long as I have. Well, I'm going to get some rest for tonight. If you will, please keep studying the map and see if there is anything else you can think of that might help."

Calia continued to do just that, going over and over the map wondering if there were any hidden gems that she might be able to uncover that would help with their task. It wasn't until several minutes after Akos left that she noticed Valesa had joined her. She leaned against the table, brow furrowed in thought.

"Is something bothering you?" Calia asked after a moment.

"Not really," Valesa said.

The words came quick enough, but there was no feeling behind them. This was something new. Calia was used to Valesa acting as her confidant, helping her to make sense of her own emotions and plotting a course of action. The role had never been reversed, but it was clear that Valesa was facing some kind of dilemma. Calia owed it to her to help sort through it if she could.

"Then what has you so distant?" Calia asked.

Valesa chewed on her lip for a moment, doing her best to pretend that she was studying the map rather than trying to avoid meeting Calia's eyes.

"At Duke Galith's estate, with Lusalin, something odd happened," Valesa said.

Things were beginning to click together in Calia's mind, but she decided that the best thing she could do at the moment was hear her maidservant out rather than interject with her own thoughts. Valesa was taking her time, thinking hard about each word before speaking it aloud. Calia had never seen such indecision from her before.

"When he attacked Akos, I didn't think twice. Akos was with us, Lusalin was a shadow with a sword. I bought Akos more than enough time to escape."

Calia tilted her head as she listened. This wasn't going the way she'd thought it would. She didn't know much about the mysterious academy that had trained the Hailko family's closest servants, but she knew that it was unforgiving. Calia had assumed that the conversation would turn toward regret, or even a discussion of the morality of Valesa's actions.

"He ran, I fought. It's what I've been trained to do my whole life. I didn't think anything of it at the time. Since then, I haven't been able to think of anything else."

"What have you been thinking of?" Calia asked.

"Why did he come back? There was no reason for it. All ties to us were gone. I was convinced the only reason he bothered to include us in his prison break plans from Logathia was because he needed you for your money. But we haven't got the money to help him with his rescue. Once he'd escaped, he could have come all the way to Tersun on his own and there was nothing I would have been able to do to stop him."

Calia considered that thought. Lusalin would have returned them to the Hailko estate, and Calia would have never had the opportunity to continue with her plans to rescue Vibius. Akos would have continued with his own rescue plans, but Calia would likely have never known whether he was successful or not.

"But he came back. With a fresh healed arm and a blunt sword he still launched himself at a man that would have outclassed him in a fair fight. Without him, Lusalin would have killed me. I just can't understand why a pirate would put himself in harm's way like that."

"I think you already know the answer to that," Calia stated.

"I think I do too. He has proven that he is no mere pirate. Perhaps I am too slow to trust."

"To be fair," Calia interjected, "that is part of your job. And I think you are missing a point that might help you understand Akos."

"What is that?"

"He would do anything for his crew. He's the only captain in the history of seafaring that has managed to sail out of the void, and he's willing to plunge right back in for his friend."

"What does that have to do with him helping me?"

"You must have missed it. To be completely honest, I don't know when it happened myself. But at some point we became a part of his crew."

Valesa considered that point for a long moment. She sighed, and Calia could tell that there was one more thing bothering her that she hadn't said yet. Rather than press her for it, Calia decided to take a page out of Valesa's own book and wait until she dragged it out of herself.

"I . . . I have a dilemma," Valesa admitted.

"What is it?" Calia asked.

"I think that this"—Valesa gestured at the map"—is a suicide mission. Even if Akos is capable of making it over the wall without getting caught, there's no way he can free fifty some odd men from Garot without help."

"And what is conflicting about that?"

"I want to go with him. I owe it to him. He saved my life, and I'm sure that if the worst comes to pass, I can hit him over the head with something and drag him back over the wall. But I can't bring myself to leave you here unguarded and alone with no one but a rum-soaked pirate to keep you safe."

In that moment, Calia's heart and mind were torn in two different directions. Her mind knew that the best chance for Akos's success came with Valesa at his side. But her heart pointed out that she hadn't been without Valesa by her side since she was a child. Calia didn't know what she would do if something happened while her maidservant wasn't there to help her.

Just the thought of it sent a shiver down her spine. Calia knew that she was a competent woman when it came to the world she was familiar with. But that world included universities, high society, and conflicts that took place entirely with whispered words and pointed rumors.

This world was nothing like that. Here, pointed words were substituted with edged weapons. And Calia was out of her depth. She would be helpless if a conflict broke out and Valesa weren't around to help. That thought terrified her.

Just as she had on Logathia, Calia refused to allow that terror to control her. She'd decided then that she would do whatever it took to take agency in her life. In the void, it meant discarding propriety in favor of pragmatism, and now it meant discarding a sense of safety for the necessity of getting things done. If that's what it took, then Calia would do it. Regardless of the way her heart pounded at the thought.

"I'll be fine," Calia lied. "You'll only be gone a few hours. I get the feeling that Felix wouldn't do anything to get on Akos's bad side, and he knows that includes letting anything happen to me."

"I think so too," Valesa agreed. "It's the only thing that makes me consider leaving. But you'll have to promise me that you'll not put yourself in any danger before I'll go."

"Oh, you have nothing to worry about there. You go help save our friends, and I'll wait here."

Chapter 14

Akos couldn't help but feel a growing sense of trepidation as the sun ducked behind the low skyline of Tersun. It was close to how he'd felt when he captained the *Mist Stalker* through the ways toward an unsuspecting target. Only rather than a relatively harmless and unsuspecting merchantman, Akos was about to test a fully aware and heavily guarded compound that he knew next to nothing about.

That was where the trepidation was coming from, Akos was sure of it. When he'd been preparing to raid ships in the ways, he'd felt a sense of anxiousness, true, but it had been filled with excitement. Akos couldn't wait to sink his teeth into another prize. In those moments, he was sure he knew how a wolf felt as it circled unsuspecting prey.

It was the sense of control that allowed that feeling to prosper. Akos had picked the time, the place, and the approach. Night was the only feasible time to try to sneak into the town hall, and it was the time that a good guard detail would be at its most wary. The place was fixed. The only thing that he felt any control over was the approach, and even that was limited to a half dozen high roofs they could access.

As Akos scanned for any sign of guard patrols, he made room for Valesa to crawl up next to him to help him look. He had to admit, he'd been shocked when she'd asked if she could come along. *Well, less asked and more informed*, Akos thought. Still, he was grateful for the help. The idea of going into a hostile environment with no one to watch his back was not a happy one. With Valesa's help, he was sure that his odds of success had shot up drastically.

Akos had been too shocked to ask what Calia was going to do while they were on their mission. She'd informed him that she would be accompanying Felix to oversee the assault on the front gates. That had surprised him almost as much as Valesa's determination to accompany him.

If it had been anyone but Felix, he might have tried to talk her out of it. But Akos knew that Felix would do whatever it took to keep her safe. The man didn't shy away from danger—Akos wouldn't have respected him much if he did—but he didn't go out of his way to face it either. As long as she stayed close to him, Calia would be far safer than she would if she remained at the Crimson Cannon where no one he trusted would be able to keep an eye on her.

Despite their brief time together, Akos was still a little unnerved to see her walk away without Valesa. The pair had been all but inseparable since he'd met them. It hadn't been hard to see the nerves below the surface on Calia's face as they'd informed him of their plans. Her eyes had twitched this way and that, as if already looking for masked assassins to spring from every shadow. But there had been iron hard resolve there as well.

Valesa nudged his elbow and pointed. The guards positioned along this side of the wall had all turned at a faint shout from farther down. Akos didn't need any help to notice the loud boom as Felix's men began the assault.

It turned out that the Crimson Cannon was more than a name. Parked behind the building had been an old artillery piece. It was small and ancient, cast from bronze rather than iron like the carronades that Akos was used to from naval combat. Still, it would pack more than enough punch to hammer at the palisade that Garot had thrown up. And true to the name, the carriage and wheels had been painted a flaking and faded crimson red.

The snap and pop of distant small arms fire erupted in wake of the cannon shot. It wasn't long until the shout to take up arms had circulated around the walls. Akos and Valesa waited with as much patience as they could muster as the guards posted around the wall turned and began to rush toward the action. Akos could see the silhouettes of men spilling from the various doors around the main building as well. They were flickering shadows against the distant and dim lanterns that lit the exterior, but Akos did his best to count them as they passed the entrance.

Two dozen, maybe a few more. Nothing like the army he'd feared. Akos was beginning to feel more hopeful for their mission with every passing second. Akos and Valesa held their ground until they heard the cannon fire for a second time. This time, there was a reply from the keep. Akos wondered how long they would be able to keep up the assault. Enraged pirates weren't famous for their discipline. Akos could only hope that Felix could exhort them to keep up a running fight with Garot's men long enough for them to sneak in and find the crew.

After checking one last time, Akos bid his heart to stop hammering so hard at his rib cage and then rose without a word. Valesa stood with him, and they stalked as swiftly as they could along the roof of the house they were positioned on.

It was slow going. They had been forced to stay several houses back due to the threat of guards noticing them. The roof they'd chosen didn't quite overhang the wall, but it wouldn't be a long jump either. That wasn't the part that worried Akos.

Tersun was not known for the sturdiness of its architecture. Roof tiles slipped beneath their feet as they stalked toward their destination. Akos cursed silently as he settled his weight on one only for it to skitter away from underneath him and clatter to the ground with a sound that he was sure was loud enough to rouse the rest of the guard. A furtive glance at the walls told him that wasn't true. He supposed it made sense. The crack of a musket would make him ignore the sound of a breaking tile too.

Guided by nothing but the light of distant lanterns, Akos and Valesa picked their way across the uneven roofs. More than once they had to stop and find a different way due to holes and even outright gaps in the roofs they crossed. Termite-worn timbers threatened to give way beneath them as they approached their goal. Ominous creaking filled the air as they edged out toward the end of the roof where it neared the palisade walls.

From where they stood, Akos couldn't see the other side of the wall. The guards had to be standing on something, though, as they patrolled the wall. There had to be some kind of firing step on the other side that they could safely hop onto. Otherwise, it would be an eight-foot drop on the other side. Probably not fatal, but not pleasant either. A broken leg would be as lethal as any blade in this situation.

Akos glanced over at Valesa. She spotted the motion and looked back at him. With a sense of confidence that he did not feel in the slightest, Akos nodded. Then he turned back toward the wall and leapt.

Akos was able to reach out and use the logs to vault him over. That was almost a mistake, as he skidded to the very edge of the firing step Garot's men had assembled. Dust tumbled down the steep ledge. They'd shored up the palisade by piling the dirt they'd been digging out to sink the timbers into the ground up behind it, making a crude platform for guards to use to look over the wall. Akos used every inch of it to stop his momentum. Valesa touched down next to him with all the grace of a cat leaping up onto a table. Akos didn't even hear her feet touch the ground.

Ignoring his companion for a moment, Akos turned his gaze toward the revelins that dotted the interior of the palisade. The bore of a cannon stared back at him, and Akos waited with bated breath for it to roar its annoyance at their intrusion. But after a half dozen heartbeats of it doing nothing but glinting lantern light into the darkness, Akos was confident that the men manning it had gone to join the main fight on the other side of the town hall.

Valesa motioned for him to follow, and Akos did. They found a set of steep stairs carved in the dirt mound under them. From there they were in the trenches between the raised bastions. Akos and Valesa crept their way through the earthworks, checking each corner and turn carefully for any sign of activity. With any luck, Garot's crew was an unruly bunch and had all rushed toward the sound of combat. A disciplined soldier or guard would know that any attack might be a diversion to allow another to thrive and would remain at his post until called for.

But empty corridors followed one after another, and soon enough the town hall rose up before them. Akos and Valesa waited several seconds to make sure that all the guards had gone toward the sounds of fighting before making their way to any of the entryways. The window that Akos had marked on the map as a possible entrance was boarded up far too well for them to attempt to use.

Long minutes crept by as the pair made their way down the wall, checking each window to see if it could be used. Each one was solidly boarded, leaving room for a musket to poke out and not much more. A cool bead of sweat began to drip down the center of Akos's back that had nothing to do with the balmy Tersun nights. Their best advantage at this point was darkness. So far it seemed that the pirates in control of the town hall hadn't bothered to light any of the many lanterns that dotted the side of the building. But that would change as they approached the door.

Just as Akos thought that they would be forced to go all the way to the grand entrance, Valesa pressed on a board that gave way. Akos snatched the other end before it could clatter to the ground, and they lowered it to the dirt outside. It provided enough space for them to slither and scrape through. Akos gave Valesa a boost through before hoisting himself up onto the window ledge and squeezing through the small space in the planking.

Akos had to blink several times and throw his hand over his mouth to prevent a cough from escaping his lips as they entered the pirate's den. The air was thick with pipe smoke, and lingering behind it he could detect the distinct scent of xheiat smoke. With any luck, those few pirates who hadn't made their way to the wall were too drunk or high to know what was going on around them. Once they were certain that they hadn't been spotted coming in, Valesa and Akos poked their way out into the hall.

Lanterns dotted the walls of the main hall, doing their best to penetrate the thick pall of smoke. Fortunately they were doing little more than providing glowing waypoints in the haze. It was a double-edged sword. It would be almost impossible for someone to spot the pair until they were almost completely on top of them, but it also made finding their friends that much more difficult.

"Which way?" Valesa whispered.

"They're most likely in the meeting chambers behind the main atrium," Akos answered. "If they aren't there, then they must be somewhere in the basement."

Akos peered down the length of the hall, squinting in an effort to pierce the haze and watch for patrols. He called the map of the place to mind, thinking of the best route to get to the main atrium and the private meeting room behind it. It was the most logical place to keep prisoners. The room looked to be large enough for the whole crew, had no windows, and only a single entrance. Akos hoped they were there; otherwise they would have to search through the labyrinthine basement. That might take until daylight, and he could only imagine they would not be welcome guests once Garot's crew got back from their fight with Felix.

Akos led the way as the pair began to make their way to the atrium. The more time passed, the less Akos felt much need for stealth. The building seemed to have emptied out every last man to fight against Felix. Akos was surprised that Felix hadn't attacked before, if only to test the response. It hadn't been difficult for Akos and Valesa to climb over the walls, and it wouldn't have been difficult for Felix to get a dozen or so men in while a diversionary attack was launched.

A dozen men might not be enough to turn the tide of a battle, but they could easily turn one of Garot's cannons on the backs of his unsuspecting crew. The death and panic that caused would be significant, the type of thing a battle hinged on. Akos wondered how complacent his friend had gotten to not even consider the option.

A door burst open in front of them, so close that Akos almost ran into it before he managed to stop himself. His heart skipped a beat as a pair of men tumbled out. Akos could smell the harsh stench of bad liquor pouring off them even as they rolled about on the ground in some drunken approximation of a fight. Beside him, Valesa's had already started to draw her blade from its sheath, but Akos put a hand out to forestall her.

"You two!" Akos put a lifetime's worth of command behind the words.

Despite the fact that their blood was probably flammable, the two men shoved away from each other and scrambled to their feet. Well, one man did. The other got halfway up and then lost his balance and slumped face-first into the wall. There was a crunch that made Akos wince as the man's nose broke, and then the man slid, face against the wall, all the way to the floor. Akos looked at him for a moment before turning his full attention to the other man.

"What are you doing, lad?" Akos asked. He didn't wait for the drunken response. "Haven't you heard there's a fight over at the east wall? Get out there!"

The man snapped a hasty salute before turning on his heel and stumbling away. Akos stepped aside to let him past, not seeing any point in mentioning that he was heading the wrong way. After the man had gotten a good ten paces away, Akos motioned for Valesa and they resumed moving toward their goal.

No more drunken pirates emerged from their slumber to accost the pair as they made their way into the atrium. They checked every room in their path, just in case, but it hadn't yielded any results. Akos hadn't expected anything, but there was no harm in checking. If he'd taken a good measure of Garot in their short meeting yesterday, the man was no fool. Arrogant, yes, but even an arrogant man could be a capable commander.

As they entered the massive atrium, Akos was struck by how much it reminded him of Anson's self-aggrandizing. Rather than an entire wall, the domed ceiling was painted with scenes from Tersun's past, highlighting the glories of the local lords, Akos was sure. It was impressive in a technical way. It must have taken hundreds of hours to paint that tableau, not to mention the engineers that had likely spent weeks crafting the scaffolding and pulley rigs that would allow someone to even begin a project of that scale.

Still, it was not to Akos's tastes. He'd never been a fan of the arts. He'd always figured it was something that rich people used to show off their wealth to their equally rich friends. He'd assumed that Anastasia would take care of decorating their estate when they got married.

The thought drove a cold dagger into Akos's gut. He shook his head and silently scolded himself for allowing himself to be distracted while there was so much at stake. Vibia needed him here, not hundreds of miles away in the arms of a woman who didn't want him. *Where is this coming from?* Akos wondered.

The pull of his thoughts was so distracting that Akos almost didn't notice Valesa hissing at him. He glanced at her, and she directed a pointed glance at the massive double door at the end of the hall. It was beginning to swing open from the inside. Valesa ducked behind a column, and Akos followed suit. The columns were wide enough, and the room dark enough, that they should go unnoticed. Akos's hand wrapped around the hilt of the dagger tucked through his belt regardless.

"I've been waiting on Felix to snap," Garot said from the doors. "I've been doing my best to tempt him for a month."

Heavy boots stomped down the marbled floors as a pair of men strode out toward the fighting. Garot and his second in command, if Akos had to guess. He urged them to keep walking straight out the front door and toward the fight.

Instead of honoring his wishes, the pair slowed for a moment. Akos resisted the urge to sneak a peek around the edge of the column. There was no way Garot and his men would be able to see them if he held his place. The urge to act was strong, but Akos's willpower was stronger. He kept his back pressed to the cool stone of the column, doing his best to keep his breathing even and low.

"What the hell?" Garot asked.

The stomping footsteps turned toward Akos and Valesa. The pair exchanged a furtive glance. Valesa shrugged, but it turned into a pointed chin as she spotted whatever had drawn Garot's interest. Akos's heart skipped a beat as the footsteps got louder with every stride. He turned his head to see what Valesa was pointing to. His grip tightened on the hilt of his dagger. He'd have the element of surprise, but Garot had the look of an experienced fighter. Akos would have to be fast. Garot was a big man; he wouldn't be stopped with just one stab. Akos would have to get as many in as he could before the man could react.

Finally, Akos's eyes settled on the hallway. A pirate was still stumbling out of it, the same one that Akos had accosted in the hallway. The pirate did his best to pull himself straight and salute his captain, but he barely had enough sobriety to stand. In the gloom, Akos had a hard time seeing the man. The haze of alcohol combined with the haze of smoke and darkness would make it impossible for him to see the pair hugging the masonry in the darkness.

"What the hell are you doing?" Garot growled.

"Trying to get to the fight, sir," the man slurred.

"What? What the hell have you been doing?"

"Er . . ."

Garot didn't wait for an answer. Just outside of view he must have pulled a pistol, because a shot shattered the relative serenity of the hall. The flash of the pistol blinded Akos for a moment. The man slumped over, blood pouring from his chest onto the floor. Akos's heart raced, and he held his breath against a gasp that had almost escaped him unbidden.

Leather creaked as Garot shoved the pistol back through its loop on his belt and snorted.

"I told the crew to be ready tonight," Garot said.

"Aye, sir," the second man said. "That you did."

"Don't need crew who can't listen to orders."

"Nay, sir, you don't."

"Come along, Kilnare. Time to see what d'Maxilae has for us."

With that, their march resumed. Akos didn't dare breathe until he heard the front door open and close. Then he let his shoulders sag and his hand unclench. He sucked in a deep breath, casting one glance back for the pirate lying dead on the floor before turning his gaze to Valesa. She appeared to be in much the same state as him.

"Well," Akos whispered. "I'd wager the chambers are clear now."

"Should we take a look?" Valesa asked. "If Garot's in there, the crew probably isn't."

"This man could be an enemy for a while. I don't think that it would hurt to have a look at what he keeps in his closet."

A stiff nod was all he got in return. Akos turned his attention back to the atrium. They'd come too far to start taking things for granted. Akos took his time sliding back around the column, making sure that they were alone the entire time. Once he was satisfied that there were no hidden guards or any other people there, he quickly made his way over to the meeting chambers.

Valesa cracked the door enough for the two of them to squeeze through. Fortunately, Garot had left a lantern burning for them. Otherwise, the room would have been pitch-dark. The lack of windows or skylights that made Akos so sure that any prisoners would be held here made the room far darker than it should have been.

A quick glance told him that no one else was there. It wasn't until after they had closed the door behind them that Akos wondered what he would have done if there had been someone inside. Of course, if it had been an enemy crewman, he wouldn't have hesitated to kill them before they could raise an alarm. But his mind flashed back to opening the door to the back of the Crimson Cannon and finding Felix with a woman he was sure had nothing to do with this feud. He didn't know if he could bring himself to kill an innocent person on the chance that they would try to raise an alarm.

A glance at Valesa sliding her dagger back into its sheath reminded him that she might not share that same hesitancy. There was nothing he could do to stop her if she did decide to do something like that. She was more than a match to him in a fight when he was at one hundred percent, and even more so now. It wasn't as if she had any allegiance to him that would cause her to follow his commands. And Akos wasn't sure at this point that was a bad thing. If she could make the decisions that he didn't want to and sleep well at night, that was one less thing he had to deal with.

That's not quite true though, is it? Akos questioned himself. It wasn't. He would feel guilty for her actions as surely as if he had guided the blade himself. This wasn't the time for him to try to talk to her about what he was alright with a member of his crew doing though, so he would have to shelf that thought for later and hope they didn't run into anyone that wasn't involved.

"What, exactly, are we looking for?" Valesa asked.

"Anything useful," Akos said.

"Thank you so much."

"I don't know. Maps, lists, logbooks—"

"Something like this?"

Akos turned to see that Valesa had a worn leather-bound journal in her hands. She flipped it open and skimmed the pages as he walked over. Akos had to admit that beyond the pure practical application of gaining intelligence on an adversary, he was more than a little curious about what someone like Garot thought important enough to write down. Akos didn't want to stand there on tiptoe trying to read over Valesa's shoulder, so he continued past her and checked the dresser that had been shoved up against the railing separating the main audience chamber from the councilors' seats.

There was nothing much in it. Trousers, undergarments, shirts. At the bottom of one drawer Akos felt something wiry. Pulling it out, he realized that Garot was most likely a nickname. He wondered how many men he'd silenced with the thick curl of cable before they started calling him that. *Might make a good souvenir*, Akos mused, *if I make it out of here alive of course.* Akos pocketed the weapon.

"I've seen several mentions of the *Pride*," Valesa said, "along with times and dates. I think it's a crew rotation."

"Take it," Akos said. "We might be able to use it to get to the ship."

"What now?"

Akos sighed as he took a last look around Garot's appropriated stateroom. It would have been too easy for his crew to be locked up here. Then they could make their way out of the wing that they knew was unoccupied and over the palisade to safety. Relative safety, anyway.

"The only thing we can do," Akos said. "Head downstairs and check the basement."

CHAPTER 15

The fight was nothing like what Calia had been expecting. When she'd agreed to observe the battle, she had been thinking that it would be something akin to what she'd witnessed aboard the *Mist Stalker*. That had been a formless melee, men fighting whoever happened to be in front of them on the close confines of a ship deck.

This was much more organized. Felix shouted orders above the din of screaming men and cracking muskets. They were far enough back that they wouldn't be hit by a stray musket shot or cannonball. At least, that was what they kept telling her. Calia happened to know from her studies that modern artillery had an effective range far beyond where they would be able to see the fight through the dense city of Tersun.

But so far no shots had been directed their way. They were watching from the balcony of a house that Felix had requisitioned for the night, sending directions through runners to various knots of pirates that were scrambling along the outside of the wall. Calia could only see faint silhouettes in the darkness, and those were obscured by gun smoke. The worst was when the cannon fired.

Their own artillery bellowed great clouds of stinking smoke every few minutes. Felix had the crew of the weapon pacing themselves and aiming each shot before firing. They only had so much cannon shot, he explained, and the thing ate powder like no other weapon they possessed. The crewmen could fire at will all night and he wouldn't run through his stockpiles, but that beast would eat through their entire stores in no time. Calia flinched as the cannon roared once more, watching for the ball to strike home.

It did so spectacularly. A ravelin behind the front wall was lit by a fireball that must have spanned a dozen yards. As quick as the blaze went up, it was gone, leaving Calia blinking in the darkness that followed. The only thing she could think of capable of causing such a massive explosion was if the shot landed amongst the powder reserves for a battery of cannons.

Calia lifted the spyglass that Felix had loaned her to watch the battle to her eye. It brought the fight into much sharper focus. She watched a handful of men moving behind buildings at the base of the wall. Every so often, one or two would pop out from their cover to aim a shot toward the men firing down at them from the palisade. None of them were so foolish as to try to rush the wooden barricade and storm the wall.

Panning the glass around, Calia spotted a figure emerging from the front of the town hall. She couldn't see more than a silhouette, but from his size there was only one man she could think it to be. Garot had finally come out to observe their fight as well. Calia wondered whether his men would fight harder now that he had joined them. Or perhaps they would be better directed. Either way, his appearance wouldn't be good for them unless they managed to skip a cannonball straight through him.

The intensity of that thought sent a wave of guilt through her. Calia snatched the glass away from her eye. What was becoming of her that she could so casually wish for the death of another human being? She had never hated easily. Even those she disliked she generally wished the best for. In fact, the only person in her life she could say she truly hated with no hesitation was Anson. What she had seen him do to the poor people of Sanctuary, and what he had wanted to do to all the realms, was unforgivable.

Yet, here she was hoping for a man to be ripped apart by artillery fire. Calia didn't know when this change had started to happen. Perhaps it had been during their captivity. Anson might have opened a floodgate to an area of her heart that only knew how to hate.

And was it a bad thing? Calia had learned well enough that there were evil people in the world that did unspeakable things for no reason other than the fact that they could. Was it wrong to hate those men?

She raised the glass once more, searching Garot out against the smoke and confusion that the battle was raising. The man stalked along behind his men, shouting and waving at them. Men began to move with renewed purpose. It must have been her imagination, but Calia thought she saw fear amongst them as they moved. They were much too far for her to make out something like that though, so she put it down to an overactive imagination.

Seeing the man move filled Calia's heart with rage. But it wasn't the same kind of white-hot vitriol that filled her when she thought of Anson. It was a dull anger, colder. It was, she realized, the same kind of anger she would feel when she'd run out of sources to verify a thesis before she felt she was finished with it. It was the anger she'd direct toward an obstacle in her path.

Garot was no more than a roadblock in the way of her quest to rescue Vibius. Calia realized that she'd used that logic to dehumanize him. But Felix had filled her in on some of the things Garot had done, and in the short time he had been in Tersun, he'd done more than enough to dehumanize himself.

The revelation did nothing to drive the anger from Calia's heart. She pursed her lips as she thought about that. She supposed that the best she could do was make sure that if she hated someone, it was for good reasons.

Calia watched as the man waved and pointed, disappearing behind a column of smoke as several cannons fired around him. Tired of watching Garot, Calia began to trace the outline of the wall with her spyglass. No one knew how long it would take Akos and Valesa to find their friends, so Felix had resolved to keep the assault up all night if he could.

That might hit a snag, Calia thought, *if Garot comes out to meet us.* Calia watched men gather behind the palisade, disappearing from sight as they grouped up. She could only imagine that they were gathering for a sally against them. Akos's plan would only work if Garot's men were occupied for a while. If they sallied forth to meet Felix's forces, the fight would be over far too soon. Felix seemed to think they would not be able to take Garot's forces in open combat.

"Damn," Felix said.

Clearly they were thinking the same thing. A quick glance told Calia that the man was deep in thought, stroking the dagger of a beard that he wore on his chin. Calia didn't know that there was anything they could do. If they let Garot charge them, they might be overrun. If they didn't stand and fight, the crew within the town hall would return and catch Akos and Valesa before they had time to get everyone out.

There had to be a way they could help their friends, or at least warn them, before the town hall was crawling with Garot's crew. They hadn't had time to set up signals, and Calia hadn't even thought to do something like that until now. There wasn't much they could do to be noticed inside the hall without Garot also being aware.

The cannon roared again next to her. A ball screamed through the air, blasting into the palisade and splintering the wood. The crack reverberated through the empty streets. Calia waved the pungent smoke away from her face as it drifted up toward them.

An idea jolted through her like a lightning bolt. Calia strode forward and tapped Felix on the shoulder. He ignored her for a moment, continuing to give orders to the men around him. Calia looked back toward the palisade and saw that even more men had disappeared from the firing step, joining with the party preparing to charge out and meet them. With no time to waste, Calia grabbed Felix's shoulder and jerked as hard as she could.

The man spun around, anger flashing in his eyes. This was a side of him that Calia hadn't seen before, and it threatened to stagger her. Felix didn't say a word, fixing her with blue eyes that demanded an answer for her approach. Calia did her best to put authority behind what she was sure would be an uncertain voice.

"Fire the cannon at the main building."

"Why in the hell would we do that?" Felix snapped. "Akos is in there!"

"I know that. But Garot doesn't."

It took several seconds, but Calia could see understanding overtaking the anger in Felix's eyes. Akos knew that Felix knew that he was there. If he heard the building being hit, he would wonder why. Calia was confident the captain was smart enough to figure out they were trying to warn him of the impending arrival of Garot's forces. But to Garot it would look like nothing more than a petty shot taken at the symbol of his dominance over the city.

"Do it," Felix snapped at a nearby runner.

The man fired off a quick salute and took off to alert the cannon crew.

"After this shot, inform the men to pull back. We've stirred this hornet's nest up enough for one evening."

The other runner sprinted off to carry out his orders. Calia noted with some trepidation that they were now alone on the balcony, and Felix hadn't taken his gaze away from her. A prickle went down her spine as silence hung over the pair.

"If you need something again," Felix said, his voice low, "ask. I'll excuse this once since you are friends with Akos, but I have a reputation to uphold and it won't be damaged by some noble wench who thinks she knows better than everyone else putting hands on me."

"Pay attention next time and I won't have to."

The corner of Felix's mouth jerked up, and he finally broke the gaze.

"I see why Akos has kept you around," Felix said. His voice had lost the menace it held only moments before. "He's always appreciated people with some spine and a defiant streak."

The abrupt change in tone made Calia wonder if she'd properly heard him before. But the memory of his eyes boring into hers reminded her that it had happened. There was no mistaking the implicit threat behind them.

Calia did her best to keep her knees from shaking. Physical confrontation was Valesa's specialty, not hers. But she wouldn't allow him the pleasure of seeing that he'd gotten to her. Calia had survived Anson and his behemoths. She wouldn't be cowed by Felix.

Calia's train of thought was broken by the final firing of the cannon. A shot arced through the air, blasting a hole through the wall of the town hall. Masonry and wood flew away from the iron shot. Dust rose to obscure their view, and Felix turned away from the balcony.

"Well, I suppose we had best go to meet the troops and rally them to defend the Crimson Cannon," Felix said. "I'm certain that Garot will not let this attack go unpunished."

Calia turned to go with him as he strode back into the house She spared one last look over her shoulder at the town hall. She hoped that

Akos and Valesa had heard the shot and that they understood what it meant. Otherwise they might have company before they were ready to make their escape.

***

Dust drifted down from the ceiling as Akos and Valesa made their way through the basement of the town hall. The pair glanced at each other as the building shook, and Akos heard the familiar sound of timber shattering before a cannonball. Felix knew better than to fire wildly into the building, and it wasn't as if it would be difficult for them to hit the palisade. These men were used to putting shot on moving targets from a moving platform; they would have no trouble with an immobile wall.

"Accident?" Valesa whispered.

"I think we'd better hurry," Akos said.

They'd cleared half the basement already. Most of the rooms were still filled with nothing but cabinets full of paperwork. The smell of musty parchment filled the air, mixing with the greasy smell of lantern smoke. There were only a few more rooms to check. The crew had to be in one of them.

Abandoning all subterfuge, Akos kicked in the next door. The wood cracked and fell away, revealing nothing but more cabinets. Valesa repeated the process one door down, grunting with effort as she did so. She shook her head as Akos went past, looking for another door to bash in.

One room they knocked open had no lanterns burning. Instead, it was filled with barrel after barrel marked with crude explosions in bright red paint. This must be the powder reserve for Garot's forces. Akos noted that it wasn't nearly as much as it could have been; about half of the room was empty. It made much more sense now why Garot's crew hadn't tried to engage Felix's forces wherever they were. They didn't have the powder to get into any extended engagements.

If Akos had to guess, the majority of the powder was probably dedicated to the cannons on the *Pride*. A beast her size would need countless barrels to feed her cannons for anything more than a single salvo. Garot was probably planning for the day when he had to abandon the hall to the local military and flee aboard his flagship.

None of that mattered now, though. Akos turned away from the powder storage and continued his path down the basement hallway. There were only a few doors left, but if the shot above was any kind of signal, they would need to be moving now. They had well over fifty people to evacuate, and that would be tough to do if they had to wade through a crowd of armed and angry pirates.

Akos kicked in another door and was immediately floored by a plank of wood to the chest. The air fled his lungs as he hit the ground hard. Valesa immediately stepped over him, dagger drawn, ready to face whatever foe emerged. Instead of an angry pirate, Gasci emerged from the entrance. He dropped the plank of wood he'd been wielding as soon as he realized who it was he'd struck.

"Captain!"

The call ran through the room, and soon enough a group had formed trying to push their way through the door and into the hallway. Several hands grasped at him and pulled him to his feet. Akos was still doing his best to catch his breath. With one hand braced on his knee, the other explored his ribs and back, making sure that nothing had been broken in the fall. Fortunately, it felt as if any new damage was just bruising.

"I'm sorry, Captain," Gasci said.

"No, it was a good swing," Akos wheezed.

"We thought that Garot would be sending men after us once we heard the attack upstairs."

"Speaking of which," Valesa said. "We need to leave. Now."

Akos nodded and counted heads. They were short. His heart dropped from his chest as he tried to determine who was missing. Gasci must have realized what he was looking for, because his face dropped.

"They separated us," Gasci said. "There was nothing we could do."

"Are the others here?" Akos asked.

"I've heard the guards say they took them to the *Pride*."

There was nothing they could do. Akos pushed the guilt and anger building in his gut to the side. Most of the crew was here, and they needed him to be his usual self. Akos did his best to arrange his features in a look of detached disdain for the danger around them and then turned back to the crew.

"We're getting out of here, boys," Akos said. "Follow us and be ready. We don't know how many are left in here. If anyone gets in the way, take care of them. We're going up and over the palisade."

The group began to move, and Akos led the way back upstairs. His head was swimming, but he tried to keep it in the present. Leo, Krallek, Vibia. None of them were there. They were trapped on the *Pride*. No matter how hard he pressed himself to keep his mind on the situation at hand, it kept straying to them. Once again, Akos cursed himself for allowing any of this to happen in the first place.

As they emerged from the staircase, a group of men was straggled into the hallway. Akos could see all the familiar signs of battle on their faces. Fatigue mixed with elation that they'd live to see another night. Jittery movements that told of the tail end of an adrenaline rush.

He also saw the confusion in their eyes as they were rushed by five times their number of men. Confusion turned to realization far too slowly. Some of them died without understanding what was happening. Akos looked into the eyes of the man beneath him, his dagger in his neck and his hand clamped across his mouth, and he knew the man had no idea who they were or where they'd come from.

There was no time for pity. Akos stripped the dead man of his pistols and tossed them to his men. Without a word, they continued on.

They made their way outside and into the trenches that surrounded the hall without further incident. After their last escape attempt, Akos refused to allow himself to relax until they were safe on the other side of the wall. He doubted that Garot had any clue what was going on, but he'd underestimated Anson and it had cost him Vibius. He wouldn't allow another misestimation to cost any more of his crew.

But the trenches gave way to the palisades. Akos turned back to keep watch as his men lowered their fellows to the other side before turning to be lowered down themselves. Akos could see the silhouettes of men making their way back into the town hall. It wouldn't be long before their handiwork was uncovered and the alarm was raised.

As if on cue, men began to dash back out the front of the hall. Akos could distantly hear them shouting into the night that something was wrong. There were dead men everywhere. The men bunched up in front of the building, looking outward for any sign of Felix's men emerging from the darkness around them. Akos smiled to himself as he realized that they thought Felix had snuck a death squad into their fortress while he'd distracted them from it with his assault.

Akos was still smiling when Valesa tapped him on the shoulder. They were the only two left on the wall. Akos sheathed his dagger and grasped her forearm, lowering her into the waiting arms of his men. He took one last look at the town hall before flipping over the parapets and down to the street.

Garot stood outside the door, waving his arms and exhorting his men back into the hall. Despite the dark and the distance, Akos thought that he could see genuine surprise and anger on the man's face. His head turned this way and that, looking alongside the rest of his men for an enemy that wasn't there. He looked directly at Akos before his silhouette disappeared behind the palisade. Akos wasn't about to wait around to figure out if he had actually spotted them. He turned and led his men silently through the streets toward the relative safety of the Crimson Cannon.

It wasn't until they were blocks away with no sounds of pursuit that Akos let his stomach unclench. There was no relief there, though, only a pang of fear as he realized that now they had to do it all over again. Akos was careful not to let his mask slip as he cursed inwardly. His men needed to think that he had everything under control. They needed the confidence that he didn't feel.

CHAPTER 16

Vibius threw himself to a seat as he heard the door to the dungeon squeal open. He wondered for a split second what the guards would do if they caught him feeling out the ways around the realm of behemoths. They likely wouldn't know what he was doing at all. Vibius had been told that when he was using his gift, his eyes glowed with a faint golden light. A wry grin perked the corner of Vibius's lips as he realized that wouldn't be a giveaway any longer.

Still, he didn't want it getting back to Lord Anson that he was doing anything strange at all. If the man thought that his prisoner had resigned himself to his fate, he was less likely to get suspicious. Despite his newfound resolve, Vibius was not keen on the idea of losing any more appendages. From the recent mutterings of the guards when they delivered his daily gruel, Vibius could gather that Anson had become enamored with dismemberment as of late.

Vibius waited for the all too familiar clatter of a wooden bowl hitting the stone and spilling half its contents to the floor. It never came. Instead, shock ran through him as he heard the clatter of keys and the scrape of metal on metal. The door swung open and two pairs of boots stomped forward. Vibius tensed up before two pair of hands roughly hauled him to his feet.

"What's going on?" Vibius demanded.

"Lord Anson demands your presence."

Vibius had a dozen more questions to ask, but the guard's tone told him that none of them would be answered anyway, so he held his tongue. His mind raced as they half led, half dragged him through the corridors of the dungeon. Anson had given him no indication that his sentence to waste away in the dark would be anything but permanent.

He could only imagine what the man could want to see him for now, especially if he was going as mad as his men seemed to believe he was.

The first indication that they had exited the dungeon was the rising heat. Vibius felt sweat bead on his forehead and begin began to dribble down. Fortunately his wounds had healed enough that the salt didn't sting as it trailed down to drip off his chin. Still, it tickled, and he wished that the guards would let him have one of his hands to wipe it away. It didn't seem that they were going to give him the chance. Instead, Vibius practiced his newfound mental discipline and managed not to shout at them to let him go.

Being down in the cool of the dungeon had forced Vibius to forget how warm Logathia was. It wasn't quite tropical, but it was close. His body had acclimated to the chill so much that Vibius thought dragging him back into the humid heat of Anson's keep was as effective a torture as taking his eyes had been. *Well,* Vibius silently admitted, *that might be exaggerating a bit.*

Still, it was fortunate that the guards were dragging him since the heat had robbed him of any strength he might have possessed. Whatever Anson wanted him for, Vibius hoped it wouldn't involve much standing. A week ago, he might not have feared what the lord might do to him for his insolence, but now that he had something to live for, he found the fear had returned. Vibius could have explained his hammering heart away as a result of the unexpected and unprepared for physical activity, but it would have been a lie.

If Anson had pulled him from his dungeon home to finish the job that he had started with Vibius's eyes, Vibius would never get a chance to speak to Calia again. He wanted to hear her voice and have the opportunity to tell her he knew what caused the extreme proximity madness around the realm of behemoths. He knew she would be ecstatic to learn the reason her theory had been correct.

None of that would happen if Anson had decided it was time to dispose of his unwilling guest. If that were the case, Vibius would have to do his best to talk him out of it. Now that flight was no longer an option, it might be easier to convince the lord that he had no intention of fleeing.

Doors slammed open and Vibius was deposited in a chair. The rough hands of the guards unclamped from around his arms, and he took the opportunity to scrub the sweat away from his face. He leaned back in the chair, reveling in the comfort. He'd begun to forget what it was like to sit on something with even a little bit of padding. He'd grown accustomed to the hard stone floor of his dungeon. Considering that he was probably going right back after this, Vibius reminded himself that it would be best not to fall any further in love with the luxury.

The sound of feet shuffling across the floor brought Vibius out of his reverie. He straightened as best he could, trying to project something akin to strength. Vibius knew he was failing miserably, but he wanted to at least pretend in his own mind that he could carry himself with some pride despite everything he had been through.

Voices followed the feet. Vibius strained his ears to hear what was being said. He didn't recognize the first man speaking, but the second was Anson. Vibius felt himself tense. All it took was the man's voice to send a shiver of fear straight down his spine. He couldn't make out any of the words yet, but the voices were getting louder as the men approached the room he was in. The doors swung open once more, and two sets of footsteps strode in.

"And here he is," Lord Anson said.

"My lord," the second man said. "If you were hoping to convince me he wasn't mad, you should have bathed him first."

"I assure you; this wayfarer is quite sane."

Lord Anson sounded well composed. Vibius wondered if all the talk was mere hearsay—rumors concocted by men with little else to do but speak of things they knew very little about. Still, as Vibius well knew, appearances could be deceiving. Anson had played the part of gracious host for as long as it suited him before. Vibius could only imagine he would be able to manage it again.

"Wayfarer Antonius." Lord Anson's voice was in front of him now. "Tell Lord Laran that you are, in fact, sane and still able to perform your gift."

Vibius opened his mouth to speak, but then closed it again as he considered how best to answer. He'd never been asked to prove that he was sane before. How did a man go about proving that he wasn't crazy?

Vibius imagined that a crazy man would say the same things as a sane one when trying to prove that point.

"Well?" Anson prodded. Vibius could hear an edge creeping into his voice.

"I'm not quite sure how to prove that I'm not lost to the madness," Vibius admitted.

Vibius heard footsteps approach and stop a few feet away. He could only imagine the other man was leaning forward and staring at him, examining him up and down. For a long moment, no one said a word.

As the men examined him, Vibius realized something. Anson had introduced this man as "Lord Laran." As far as Vibius knew, that could only mean one of two things: Laran could be a lord in the sense of the lords of Logathia, the men that Anson called princes and counts that he used to keep his slave population in line. Or he could be a lord in the sense that Anson himself was, ruling his own island as god-king through the use of eternal life and control of the monstrous behemoths. And Vibius doubted Anson had any lords who wouldn't have already heard of him.

"An interesting trick," Laran said.

His voice was smooth and soft. Laran sounded much younger than Anson. A slight footstep sounded as Laran stepped back, probably shifting his attention from Vibius to Anson.

"Trick?" Anson asked.

"You've clearly taught him some words to repeat."

"Then ask him anything you'd like."

"Very well, let's begin with your name."

"Vibius Antonius," Vibius responded. "Please, call me Vibius."

"What happened to your eyes?"

Vibius flinched as he asked. Just thinking about it made his mouth go dry and sweat begin to bead on his back. Flashes of phantom pain strobed through his mind, but he ignored all that to answer the question.

"Lord Anson took them to 'keep me from looking for an escape' from Logathia."

There was a long pause, and Vibius could only imagine a questioning eyebrow from Laran and a shrug from Anson. The pause dragged on as Laran considered his next question. For his part, Vibius felt that he was performing admirably considering the circumstances. His friends excluded, he'd not met many madmen during his life. Those few he had met seemed to be ravening lunatics foaming at the mouth, though he had heard of men that appeared sane until you looked deeper into what they said.

"Do you know where you are?" Laran asked finally.

"Do you mean in the keep?" Vibius asked in response. "I'm afraid they dragged me straight from the dungeons, so no. If you meant that more generally, then I am in Logathia. If you meant more generally than that, I am in the void, though I suppose they will rename it the realm of behemoths once the news of its existence breaks."

"What do you mean by that?"

The tone had shifted. Doubt was gone, replaced by a sharp curiosity. Vibius swore he could almost feel the man's gaze boring into him, but he shook it off as a product of the same overactive imagination that had forced him to hallucinate his friends in the darkness.

"That is one of the reasons I wanted to speak to you," Anson interrupted before Vibius could respond. "The situation of the realm has shifted, and our situation along with it."

"And what could you possibly mean by that?" Laran asked.

"Come, we will discuss it over lunch."

"And what of your wayfarer?"

Vibius did his best to not look terrified. He had no idea if he was succeeding or not. If he were to place a wager, he would put his money on not. Despite all the brave words he'd told himself in the cold, cramped dungeon, he had no real desire to go back. The same deep, maddening, and utterly terrifying sense of helplessness he'd first felt after being discarded by Anson's torturers began to creep back into his heart.

"That would depend on him," Anson answered after some consideration. "If he has learned his lesson, then he may join us. Though I would warn him that should he try to escape again, I will be forced to take something to keep him from attempting to run."

Despite himself, Vibius considered the idea. The implications were clear enough. Step back into the fold and be rewarded with a small bit of comfort or stay the course he'd set months ago and keep losing bits of himself until there was nothing left. As much as Vibius didn't want to go back on his ideals, he really didn't want to lose his legs.

Perhaps it was time to change tactics. After all, Akos hadn't walked up to Anson and declared his intention to betray him and escape. Of course, Anson would now be well aware of that possibility. Vibius could only imagine that the penalty for betraying him again would be a steep one.

Still, there was nothing he could do from the dungeon. He still had no intention of actually helping the madman overtake the realm of man. But he could pretend for as long as it took. And if nothing else, he might be able to get Anson to accompany him onto a boat into the ways. If that happened, it would be very tempting to let go of the ways and drift into whatever eternal nothingness awaited them, content with the knowledge that he had taken a great evil along with him.

"I have learned my lesson," Vibius declared.

"Very well," Anson said. "I'll have my servants lay out the meal at once."

***

The moment the scent of food was in the air, Vibius's mouth began to water. He couldn't tell what it was, and he decided that he didn't actually care. As long as it was more appetizing than the gruel he had been eating, it would be a feast. Vibius wasn't sure exactly how long it had been since he'd eaten something other than the questionable stew. Regardless of the circumstances, this would be a welcome change.

The lords exchanged small talk as they waited for the meal to be served. Vibius only half listened. They didn't seem to be saying anything of consequence. Vibius had listened to dozens of conversations between nobles in his life and had found that they were almost never worth hearing.

The food was nothing special, some kind of beef with a handful of fruits and vegetables. It could have been a meal fit for the gods as far as

Vibius cared. He relished every bite. It wasn't guaranteed that he would ever get another chance at a meal like this.

His stomach packed fit to bursting, Vibius leaned back into his chair to relax. It was a simple padded dining chair, but relative to his cell it was the height of luxury. It was taking everything he had not to fall asleep right there. He wouldn't have bothered fighting it at all if he weren't sure the lords would eventually discuss something worth hearing.

The men were taking their time eating. *Perhaps they weren't as hungry*, Vibius thought. Eventually he heard the distinctive sound of silverware being set against a plate. It seemed they were finally done. Vibius did his best to look uninterested, though he was sure he was failing. There was nothing he could do if they forced him to leave, but he did want to know what it was they were planning.

"I'll ask," Lord Laran said finally. "Why have you brought me here, Lord Anson? Just to show me that you have the capability to leave the realm?"

"Of course not," Lord Anson replied. "That would be rude."

"Then please explain. I'll admit I am driving myself mad trying to think through the implications."

Lord Anson's chair scraped the ground and Vibius could hear him step over to the window that dominated the far wall. He wondered how long it had taken Anson to replace it after the behemoth had crashed through. The thought brought a smirk to his face that he wiped away with his napkin.

"I've made it no secret that I intend to rule this realm, and the rest of them as well," Anson said.

"I'd say so," Laran agreed. "Your declaration made you something of a laughingstock amongst the other gods."

"Perhaps my declaration was . . . premature."

"As I recall, you said that you would 'Rule this realm alone over a pile of all our corpses.' Do you remember?"

"Yes, I remember well enough, thank you."

Laran chuckled as his own chair scraped away from the table and he joined Anson at the window. Vibius was content to stay right where he was and swirl his wine, listening without injecting himself into the conversation.

"I never took it personally," Laran assured him. "Plara is excellent at getting under everyone's skin. She'd been working you for a solid week at that point."

"Regardless of the circumstances, I misspoke. We specifically set up our current system so that no single god or goddess could take the realm for themselves."

"I feel that you are about to ask me to join a coalition."

"That is exactly what I am going to do."

"You know that is too dangerous. There are fourteen gods. Unless you plan on getting another five of us to sign on, the others will coalesce against you."

"Oh come now, don't be coy. I know that you have not followed the accords."

There was a long moment of silence. Vibius had heard the accords mentioned in passing before, but he had never stopped to think of what might be in them.

"Don't act surprised," Anson said. "My spies are everywhere."

"And what do you plan to do with this information?"

"Nothing at all. In fact, I'll share a secret with you. I have not bothered to follow the accords either."

This time the silence stretched into minutes. Vibius couldn't help but hold his breath as he waited for the men to speak. Whatever the accords were, they were serious business. Serious enough that it would give Laran pause to learn that he was not the only one breaking them. Curiosity was threatening to overwhelm Vibius as he sat there. What could possibly be detailed in this agreement that would cause two men to think they could stand a chance against five times their number?

"I see," Laran said at last.

"Do you?" Anson asked. "With our powers combined, the others would be forced to either join us or be swept away."

"You assume that none of them have broken the accords as well."

"I don't have to assume. I know. I mentioned that my spies are everywhere, didn't I? Would you like to see their reports?"

"Even with that card up our sleeves, there is no guarantee that we could subjugate enough of them quickly enough to keep them from overwhelming us with pure numbers. Even with our advantage in behemoths."

"You're missing the grander picture, my friend."

"And what is that?"

"Sitting at that table is an opportunity. How long have you been stuck here? And your master before that? Since the first ships were wrecked here, we have longed for a way out, and now we finally have one. The outside world has no possible way to be prepared for us. If we can gain enough support, there is no way that the fractious realm of men could stop us. We could rule every realm. This is finally the time to throw caution to the wind and take our chance."

"And if we can't garner enough support?"

"Then we put people who will support us in power. Just announcing a coalition will encourage others to join us, and with a wayfarer in our grasp, there will be those who do so immediately. With enough surprise on our side, we can take the rest with ease."

"You're putting a lot of faith in unknowable factors. You can't know how many of our peers will be open to joining your faction, and you can't know that we would be able to overwhelm our foes."

"Maybe not, but I do have some secrets up my sleeves."

"Oh?"

"This wayfarer is a remnant of the crew that brought him here. The rest of them seem to have escaped the realm somehow, though I'm not sure how unless they had a secret second wayfarer. Before they left, their captain designed me a new breed of ship. Though we do not have the technology yet to fully take advantage of its capabilities, we have repurposed some of the ideas present in them to our own ends."

"Such as?"

"A vessel that requires half as many crewmen as a behemoth barge that can cover distance in half the time. We'll be able to strike our foes, leave, and strike a new target before our enemies have begun to react to the first attack."

"I . . . I'll have to think about this, Lord Anson."

"Of course. Take all the time that you want. But know that every moment you delay is another moment that we could be moving toward our freedom."

Lord Laran dismissed himself, retreating down the hallway. Vibius listened as his footsteps faded in the distance, leaving him alone with Anson. Neither man spoke for a time. Vibius wondered whether Anson was observing something happening outside the window or if the lord was staring right at him. The hair on the back of his neck rose as he considered the thought. Vibius felt around for his wine glass and took a heavy sip.

"I assume that you listened to all of that," Anson said.

"Ah …" Vibius tried to think of an answer that wouldn't set his captor off.

"Oh, just speak plain. I know you aren't a stupid man, and only a fool wouldn't be interested in the events unfolding around him. Especially when they so intimately involve him."

"Well, I did catch a few things."

Anson snorted, and Vibius listened as he strode back over to his chair and sat down heavily on it. There was an edge of weariness in his voice when he spoke again.

"What I am attempting to do has been done before," Anson said. "Several times, in fact. None have been successful. I have joined coalitions against uppity lords who thought they were fit to rule the realm on more than one occasion."

Anson paused, but Vibius didn't dare interject any of his own thoughts. Anson was speaking with the cadence and weight of a man recalling the past, and Vibius didn't have anything to add. It wasn't as if he would be quick to comfort his captor even if he thought that was what the man was after.

"I'm only telling you this to let you know that if it is not me attempting to use your gift for their own gain, it will be someone else," Anson admitted. "I know that we have had some trouble seeing eye to— Well, we've had our differences. None of it was personal. I intended to honor my bargain with Captain Akos before he betrayed me, and I intend to honor my bargain with you. Provided, of course, that you will honor your end of it. If you do not, I will be forced to kill you."

"Why is that?"

"To keep you from falling into the hands of one of my rivals, of course."

"You're so petty that you'd ruin the best chance anyone has ever had to get out of this realm just to spite them?"

Vibius realized too late that he'd spoken aloud. Too much time in utter isolation must have ruined his ability to keep his thoughts in his head. He braced himself for harsh words, or even a physical assault, but Anson merely chuckled.

"When you've been around as long as I have, you learn that spite is as good a motivation as anything else."

Vibius considered his options. It was clear that Anson was asking him if he would help with his plan or not. Vibius considered telling him then and there to stick a behemoth up his ass, but he didn't think that would be very productive. As satisfying as it would be to damage Anson's plans, he had his own life to think about.

At the very least, he had to survive to tell Calia his theory about the various realms surrounding this one. Just the thought of her made him want to agree to whatever Anson asked of him. Anything to get one more chance to see her. But he knew that if he were to come to her as Anson's willing puppet, she would lose any love she might have had for him. Still, he had to find some way back to her.

And even if he did help Anson back to the realm of men—if he could without the xheiat tea—it wasn't as if he would win the ensuing war. Behemoths were terrifying, and he was sure they could do a great deal of damage to an unsuspecting military unit. But surprise only lasted so long. Eventually the militaries of the realm would figure out the creatures' capabilities, and they would develop their own tactics to fight them. He'd seen one hurt before by a tribesman's spear on Sanctuary, and if a crude steel spear could pierce its hide, a bullet would punch through it easily enough.

Do you believe all that, Vibius asked himself, *or are you telling yourself pleasant things to make it easier to do what you want to do anyway?*

Vibius didn't know if he had an honest answer for that yet. But even if he agreed to Anson's plan, he wouldn't have to act immediately. There would still be time to figure something out while Anson made his play for rule of the realm.

"I'll agree to help you," Vibius stated.

"Excellent." Anson clapped once as he spoke.

"There are some conditions."

"I'll honor the same deal that we made before."

"Power, wealth, and women, I remember. I think you'll be unsurprised to learn that I lied about wanting those things."

"I suspected."

"Then here are my new terms. When we return to the realm of men, I want to know that my friends will be unharmed."

"I cannot allow the insolence and disobedience that Captain Akos showed to go unpunished."

"Punish him then, but allow the others to go free. They had no choice in the matter."

Anson considered that. Vibius was sure he would refuse and have him taken back to the dungeon. Seconds stretched into minutes, and after an agonizing eternity, Anson gave his response.

"Very well. I will spare the rest of the crew when we eventually return. They will receive full pardons for their treason."

"Then it looks like we have a deal," Vibius said.

CHAPTER 17

Calia stood behind the bar of the Crimson Cannon and did her best to pretend that it was a podium at the university. Most of Felix's men were still sleeping off the victory party from the night before, but their commanders had managed to drag themselves out of their stupor. At least, those she cared about had. Felix was facedown on the bar, snoring and accruing a pool of drool that would add to the mystery stains that covered the wood.

Akos and Valesa were awake enough to pay attention. Calia rubbed at the fatigue building in the corners of her own eyes. She might not have spent the night leaping fortifications and sneaking through mansions, but she hadn't slept at all. She'd been too busy burning her way through Garot's journal, hunting for any information that could help them.

Calia glanced down at said journal in her hands, placing it on the bar and opening it to the first of the marks she'd made. It wasn't as though she needed to reread what she'd gone over the night before, but she'd learned in academia that the exact verbiage of a passage could dramatically change the meaning of it. It wouldn't hurt to have it open in case she needed to reference Garot's exact wording.

Not that most of it meant anything. It was a logistical journal, detailing the movement of men, food, and supplies back and forth between the various caches that Garot had set up throughout the city. If she turned it over to Felix, assuming the man could read, he would be able to use it to seize tons of powder, weapons, and possibly turn this little turf war on its head.

She didn't plan to do that unless Akos asked her to. Calia didn't much care how a criminal dispute over territory played out, not in the long run. What she cared about was getting to the *Pride* so they could sail to save Vibius. The rest was irrelevant. After Felix's threats the night before, she wasn't sure she wanted him to win anyway.

The memory of her rooftop conversation with Felix caused her to shoot a guilty glance at Valesa. Calia cursed herself for the lack of self-control, but fortunately it seemed that Valesa was too tired to notice. She hadn't told her maidservant of the conversation, and she didn't intend to. They needed allies in their endeavors, and it wouldn't do to have her bodyguard murdering one of the few they had.

"Did you get a chance to read the journal?" Akos asked.

The question snapped her attention back to the present, and Calia focused back on the task at hand. She smoothed out the pages before speaking, gathering her thoughts. She'd developed a plan, but she'd decided to let Akos sleep off the events of the night before bringing it to him for his thoughts. While Calia was sure that she was intellectually smarter than Akos, the man had a depth of experience that she could not hope to rival.

"I have," Calia said.

"That's a pretty thick journal. Did you get through the whole thing?"

Valesa scoffed, and Calia couldn't help but smile.

"Compared to cramming for an exam at the university, this was nothing."

"What did you find out?"

"I've got locations on all, or at least most, of Garot's stashes of supplies and weaponry. It also has a schedule for when and where they resupply the *Pride*."

Akos sat up straight at that. Calia had to admit she'd been so engrossed in devouring the words the night before that she hadn't immediately understood the implications they held. It was clear that Akos had no such delay. Though to be fair, he hadn't had to trawl through the entire journal to find the information either.

"The more important thing might be what I didn't find in the journal." Calia paused as she would in a lecture.

"Which was?" Akos leaned in.

"I didn't see a signal system that would allow them to warn the *Pride* to not dock here."

Akos leaned back on his stool, crossing his arms as his brow furrowed in thought. Calia let him chew through whatever was on his mind for a moment. She didn't want to plant any of her own ideas in his mind; she'd rather see what he thought up on his own before she introduced her plan. It was always better to have two unique perspectives on the problem.

"You think we could intercept the *Pride* on the docks and take her from under Garot's nose?" Akos asked.

"That is precisely what I think we can do."

"There is one issue with that plan."

"What's that?"

"Garot will notice that missing journal sooner or later. When he does, he will have an army waiting on the docks for us to show up for just such an attempt."

Now it was Calia's turn to work through the problem. In her excitement the night before, she hadn't considered that nuance. Akos was right; the next resupply was a week away. Garot would have plenty of time to notice his missing journal between now and then. He'd proven that he was a capable commander of men, and whether he was smart or just cunning, he would almost certainly be able to realize what they were planning to do.

They could always try to brute force their way onto the ship, but even if that route were successful, it would carry too high a cost. Casualties would be numerous. And there was always the possibility that the men on the ship were under standing orders to kill their captives if anyone tried to storm their ship. Calia wouldn't put it past Garot to issue such a petty order.

Surprise wouldn't be an option either. Garot would plan on them making an attempt. Calia wracked her brain, trying to think back to her military history classes. Unfortunately, they had all revolved around campaigns and politics. She knew battles were won with clever tactics all the time. They'd accomplished their mission the night before thanks to misdirection and subterfuge. But she couldn't think of anything off the top of her head that might help them here.

"You're right, but it is either take that ship now or risk losing it forever," Calia said. "If I were Garot, I would pack my men into that ship and sail away from this godforsaken town. He'll lose the fight in the long term, and he knows it."

"I would too. So, we have to do something the next time they dock."

"We can't take a direct approach." Calia tapped a finger against the pages while she thought. "It's too bad we have to come from the city side."

"Why do we have to do that?"

"Well, we don't have any ships."

Akos turned and looked pointedly over his shoulder. Calia followed his gaze. At first she didn't understand what he was driving at. Then she realized that the entire common room of the bar was filled with snoring privateers and pirates.

"Well, I still don't know how we would get close enough to the *Pride* to get aboard without someone taking drastic action," Calia said.

"Following that line of thought, I've got an idea."

Akos looked around and grabbed several of the empty bottles that littered the floor. The clink of glass as he set them on the bar threatened to wake Felix, but instead he muttered something about rum and promptly returned to snoring. Akos arranged the bottles on the bar, taking a look at them for a moment before nodding to himself and continuing to speak.

"The jug is the *Pride*." Akos motioned toward the largest of the bottles. "We commandeer two vessels and sail them out at night. Then when the *Pride* is coming in to dock, we spring our trap."

"Won't the *Pride* be able to demolish any vessel we can bring to bear on her?" Valesa asked.

Akos held up a finger and pointed to the first of their two bottle-ships.

"Yes, they can. But the first ship won't be manned. In fact, what we'll do is lock her rudder in place and cover her deck with pitch and firewood . . ."

"A fireship?" Calia whispered, starting to grasp his plan.

"Good, you're familiar with the concept. We sail that one straight into the docks."

"How does that benefit us?"

"We sail in on the second ship, trailing behind in the smoke cloud until we are close enough to get to them without taking too much damage."

"What's to stop them from killing all our friends the moment they see the fireship?" Valesa asked.

"Garot knows we have their schedule," Calia answered for Akos, "but he didn't set up any way to inform his men of that. Garot might know it's a ruse, but they won't."

"Precisely. They'll think they are coming in for a standard resupply. By the time they realize that it isn't an accident, we'll be aboard."

Akos didn't say it, but Calia was sure there was supposed to be an "I hope" at the end of that sentence. He was placing a lot of faith in the idea that Garot didn't have any way to warn his men that something might be coming. It wasn't in his journal, but it could be something they'd had set up for so long he hadn't bothered to include it.

Calia sighed as she realized there would never be a perfect answer. They would have to assume some things in their plan. This plan was better than anything she'd thought up on her own.

"What do you think?" Akos asked.

"Well, fireships were used to great effect in the battles of . . ." Calia realized that Akos's eyes were already beginning to glaze over. "The theory behind your idea is solid."

"We'll plan on this then. I'll need to go down to the docks later and scout for a good pair of ships to commandeer. For now, Krallek said he needs to check my ribs and collarbone. If you'll excuse me."

Calia watched the man push away from the bar and step over sailors on his way to find the surgeon. She looked back at the bottles that covered the bar. Calia tried to picture them as ships in her head. She pictured their crew swarming over the railing of the bottle onto the jug, taking it without a single wound.

Then her mind flashed to visions of the jug unleashing a broadside into their poor bottle, blasting it to bits before it could get within a hundred yards. She pictured in her mind, so vivid it was startling, the crew of the *Mist Stalker* being blasted apart with it. She closed her eyes and shook away the image.

Sleep, Calia decided, was long overdue.

***

Despite his short stature, Krallek had fingers like belaying pins. Currently he was using those pins to test Akos's ribs. If they weren't still broken, Akos was sure they would be by the end of this checkup.

Neither man spoke as Krallek went about his work. Akos responded to his grunts and points by raising or lowering his arms, turning side to side, and allowing Krallek to do what he needed to do. Truth be told, Akos was a little afraid to speak. By now Krallek would have heard what Akos had done to help them escape, as well as what he'd done to get to Tersun in the first place. The dwarf would be incensed that his strict instructions as to how much Akos could exercise in a day were not being followed.

As far as his healing went, Akos was feeling remarkably well. His ribs still ached, and his shoulder hurt when he overworked it, but nowhere near as bad as it had right after the injury. Whatever Krallek had done in the aftermath of the injury had worked wonders. Still, Krallek was not known for his optimism or good humor.

Akos jumped when Krallek finally did speak.

"It seems to me," Krallek said, "that our lives have become much more dangerous since we picked up our latest passengers."

"Oh, I don't know about that," Akos replied.

"Chasing ships through the mist never felt half so dangerous as this."

"We were lucky. There was always the chance that we came out of the mists and pounced on the one ship that was ready."

"Sure, but there is more than a chance that men will die when we attempt to storm the *Pride*."

"We could get lucky again."

"Not likely."

"You're right. But I'm not ordering anyone along. Any man who wants to stay may do so."

Krallek scoffed as he settled on a nearby stool.

"That won't stop a single man from following behind you. They already followed you into the void. What makes you think they won't follow you into the teeth of Garot's power as well?"

Akos pulled his shirt back on as Krallek began to clean out his pipe. He regarded the dwarf with curious eyes. Krallek had never been one to worry about the danger of anything. In fact, this was the first time that Akos could remember him raising a concern about anything other than the state of his supply cabinet.

"It's their choice," Akos said.

"The hell it is. You know that when you speak, they listen. You know that when you order, they do. And you know that when you ask, they agree."

"And what would you have me do? I won't leave Vibius in the void to fend for himself."

"You don't need the *Pride* to rescue him. Not unless you are planning to take the entire realm by storm."

"I'll not leave Felix to fend against Garot for himself either."

"Why not? He'd leave it all to you."

"No, he wouldn't."

Krallek pulled a match from his pocket and struck it, taking several heavy draws on the pipe. Each man's eyes never wavered from the other's. Akos wasn't one to back down from a staring match. He felt his annoyance at Krallek's words turning to anger, but he managed to hold it back, at least until he found out what the dwarf was driving at.

"Felix doesn't give a damn about helping anyone but himself," Krallek stated. "He'd have let us rot in that basement until the world ended."

"I'm sure that he would have done something about it if he could."

"Would he now? Are you so sure about that? I've heard what his plan was. He was going to wait for someone else to take care of his problem for him. The only thing that changed about his plan was the face of the man pulling his ass out of the fire for him."

"Felix wouldn't use us like that."

"You're letting your friendship blind you, Akos. Felix will let you solve his problems for him. He will even help you out so long as it doesn't place him in any real danger. He might even accompany us to the void just for the novelty of it. But the moment your interests stray from his, he will betray you without a second thought."

"You're out of line, Krallek."

"You're not thinking clearly. I should've checked your head rather than your ribs."

"That's enough."

"Fine. You're healed. At least as much as you're ever going to be. I'd say don't go climbing any ratlines, but I know you'd just ignore my advice anyway, so take it slow. Build your strength back up before you bet your life on it."

"Thank you, surgeon."

"Aye, Captain. You may not have liked what you heard today, but give it some thought. You would never betray someone you considered a friend. But Felix isn't you."

Chapter 18

Tersun's docks should have been crowded. It was one of the largest ports in the world, and one of the only ones that didn't impose massive taxes on top of the usual fees. It was a place to offload cargos that could not be sold anywhere else, a place for less than reputable men to find work with unscrupulous captains.

Instead, they were empty. Akos looked out over the scene from the window of a nearby inn. Felix had assured him this one was a friendly establishment. Perhaps he had meant that a little too literally though, as he was in the next room over taking advantage of the hospitality of one of the working girls. Akos knew as soon as they arrived that he would be making this decision alone. Something about the shoving match that the women had taken part in to get to Felix first had informed him he would be on his own with this one.

That was fine with him for now. There were only a half dozen ships in the harbor for him to ponder over anyway. They would have to choose two of them, and so far he was liking a pair of barges that looked as though they would be perfect for his intentions.

But that wasn't the real reason he was appreciative of the alone time. Akos needed to think about what Krallek had said now that the moment had passed and his anger had faded. He encouraged his men to bring anything to him, regardless of what they assumed he might think about it, and not fear the repercussions. He couldn't put forth that idea with one hand if he were going to punish them for doing what he'd encouraged with the other.

That didn't change the fact that Akos felt almost personally attacked by Krallek's allegations. He would have felt the same way about any of his friends, but Felix was in a tier that few had achieved. Vibius and Vibia had been the first people he'd called friends, with Leo and Felix being third and fourth. The man had been with him through more scrapes than he could count, and had been the cause of more good times than he could remember. The only people he trusted more were the Antonius twins and Leo.

Akos sighed and forced himself to set his personal feelings aside. He knew that Krallek wasn't challenging his ability to judge people or calling him out for befriending Felix in the first place. He was trying to get him to look at something from an angle that he might not otherwise be able to consider.

So he tried. Akos couldn't imagine a scenario in which Felix betrayed him, or even didn't follow his orders. Sure they had parted some years ago, but it wasn't because of any bad blood between them. Felix had outgrown his role on the *Mist Stalker*. There was only room for one captain aboard a ship, after all, and Akos wasn't about to give up his place to allow the man the opportunity to prove himself. He'd even lent Felix the seed money for his own vessel, knowing full well that he would never see a cent of it back.

Felix had even dropped everything and offered to help the moment he learned that Vibius was in danger. Sure, he had let the rest of the crew sit in the basement of his enemy's fortress, but there wasn't a lot he could have done about that. Try as he might, Akos couldn't fault his strategy of waiting out his opponent. It was the least risky path, both for him and for the prisoners in Garot's hands.

Krallek was a smart dwarf and the best surgeon that Akos had ever met. But it was possible that he was jumping at shadows. Krallek had never liked Felix's boisterous personality. Akos didn't think that the surgeon would make an accusation like that to discredit someone he didn't like. But Akos had learned that when a man was already disinclined to like another, he tended to see the worst possible motivations behind everything that man did.

"I'd offer a coin for your thoughts," Felix said from the doorway, "but we both know that they aren't worth that much."

Akos glanced back to see the man leaning against the door with the working girl leaning on his chest. They both looked more than pleased with themselves. Akos raised an eyebrow, and Felix winked at him. Akos rolled his eyes and turned back toward the port.

After a moment, Felix joined him. He was absentmindedly rubbing at the distinct red imprint of lips on his neck.

"I see you're familiar with the local girls," Akos stated.

"Ah, yes." Felix sighed. "I get to spend far too little time here lately between my duties at the Cannon and this business with Garot."

"The girls seem to share that opinion."

"What can I say? I'm as generous a tipper as I am a lover."

Akos snorted out a laugh.

"Speaking of which," Felix said, "I'm sure they'd be more than willing to give you my rate if one of them caught your eye."

"Not interested, but thank you."

"Still holding out for Anastasia I see. When are you going to see that she is playing you for a fool?"

It was an old joke. Akos should have been expecting it, but for some reason he hadn't seen it coming. Pain flooded his chest, no less than when Anastasia had first torn it in two.

Felix looked at him, and Akos's face must have betrayed his heart. Felix's smile wavered and fled, and all levity was gone. The man reached up and placed a firm hand on Akos's shoulder, squeezing firmly.

"What happened?" Felix asked.

"I asked her to run away with me. She declined."

Felix didn't say anything. Akos was thankful for that. He didn't think he could handle any of Felix's jokes at the moment. And he certainly didn't need to hear an "I told you so."

"I don't understand what happened. The last time I saw her before that, Anastasia begged me to stay. She was acting like she couldn't wait for our wedding."

"How much was she planning to spend on that wedding?" Felix asked.

"I don't know. Do you truly believe that it was all about the money?"

Once again, Felix said nothing. Akos knew the answer in his heart though. Anastasia had always talked of their future together, and it would have required every cent of the fortune Akos had managed to acquire over the years.

"I think that I knew that all along," Akos admitted. "But I didn't want to believe it. I thought that maybe she'd felt she wasn't the first priority in my life, or that I was going to put her in danger to save a friend."

"If she'd truly loved you, she would have come along anyway," Felix said.

"I suppose you're right."

"Don't worry, love makes fools out of the smartest men. And if it can do it to the smartest, it can damn sure do it to you."

Despite himself, Akos cracked a smile at that. The pain in his chest had not receded, but it had dulled somewhat. Acknowledging his pain in front of someone else, someone who knew how much of his life had been dedicated to Anastasia, helped immensely.

"Back on task." Akos turned back toward the window and pointed at the ships he'd selected. "I think those two would serve our purposes well enough."

The first was a barge, designed for coastal waters and not much more. It was low, fat, and heavy. Plenty of deck space for a nice raging bonfire. Provided the wind was right, it would be able to put up a massive smoke screen that they could hide behind. It was lightly armed too, which meant they wouldn't have to move massive powder stores out of it to make sure that the fire didn't send the whole thing up in a ball of flame.

The second was a caravel. Built in the Gelleritian style, it had a short, stubby deck nestled in between massive fore and aft castles. Popular back before firearms were easily available and still widely used as transports and messengers, it was designed to allow men to board other vessels easily. Though it was nothing compared to the modern design of the *Pride*, it would allow them to board from deck to deck without requiring a large amount of time to scale ropes and ladders.

"A fine pair of choices," Felix said. "Do you think the owners will give them up for the promise of their safe return?"

"Unlikely, but neither seems to have a large crew. My men should be able to overwhelm them and get them out to sea."

"Well, let's hope they don't put up too much of a fight. When do you want to move on them?"

"Dusk. We'll be able to move without worrying as much about being intercepted by Garot's men, and we can take them out far enough to carry out our preparations unnoticed."

"When did your girl say that the *Pride* was scheduled for its next resupply?"

"Calia said that it should be tomorrow, midmorning."

"Not much time to prepare a fireship."

"No, it isn't. We'll have to work fast. Let's get back to the Cannon and make sure everyone knows what they need to do."

***

The last rays of the sun were beginning to fade over the top of the Tersun skyline as Akos moved out onto the docks. There were still a few dozen men out and about, unloading ships or taking care of the myriad other tasks that needed doing on a dock. That number more than doubled as Akos and his crew stepped into the crowd, doing their best to stay unnoticed.

Akos glanced over to make sure the ships he'd targeted were still at their quays. Fortunately, they were. He stepped onto the wooden planking of the wharfs and toward his target. Only a few men moved on the wharfs themselves, wheeling carts full of supplies back and forth. He noted the turned heads and curious gazes of the workers as they passed by and quickened his pace.

As he approached his target, the barge named *Buyer's Remorse*, he sent a silent thanks to whatever gods were listening. They were in the middle of unloading and their gangway was still attached. The men were so busy bustling about making sure that everything was in order that they didn't notice the two dozen armed men approaching them until they were practically among them.

The only person who did notice their approach was the boss of the crew of teamsters, who wisely stepped out of the way and hollered at his men to clear the space. They were laborers, not soldiers. It seemed that their crew leader had decided they had no business getting in the middle of whatever was going on here. Akos nodded to him as he strode past.

Akos's heart sped up as he approached the gangway. They needed to do this quickly but, almost as importantly, quietly. If they gave Garot any indication they were up to something tricky, they would blow their main advantage. They could, and would, make some noise. But they needed to do this without a full-scale battle breaking out aboard either ship. Rumors of a pair of ships being stolen in the night would make it to Garot eventually, but news of a gunfight at the docks would run through the town like wildfire.

Akos had discovered early in his life that if you acted like you belonged somewhere, people who might otherwise say something let you go. So rather than challenge the crew from the wharf, Akos turned and jogged up the gangway. It wasn't until several of his men had managed to make it up behind him that anyone bothered to challenge them.

"Hey, who goes there?" a portly man with a curling mustache asked. "We've not given permission to come aboard."

Rather than answer him, Akos drew his pistol and cocked back the hammer, pointing it directly at the portly man's chest. He continued striding forward, allowing his men room to spring aboard and level their own weapons. The portly man sputtered as Akos pushed him backwards with the barrel of his pistol, motioning for him to go to the center of the ship.

"I am Captain Akos. Your ship is being commandeered. We do not wish to hurt anyone, but we will not hesitate."

"We've already paid our taxes and our fees!" the portly man said, his face growing red.

"What's your name?"

"Issan Kep, captain of the *Buyer's Remorse.*"

"Well, Captain Kep, I am not with the port authority. Nor am I with the local government. I am a man in need of a ship."

"You're a bloody pirate!"

"Welcome to Tersun."

Akos left his men to gather up the crew of the vessel. The barge was already lightly armed, and the men had been caught unaware. A small pile of knives and hatchets was being collected, with a single pistol here and there. Akos was confident they'd surprised their vessel well enough to have avoided a fight. Now he had to worry about the other one.

He made his way to the railing and peered out, trying to catch a glimpse of the Gelleritian caravel through the deepening darkness. He could see the outlines of a half dozen vessels and the silhouettes of figures moving about on all of them.

Akos waited with bated breath for the bark of a pistol or the scream of a man being cut down. Both parties had departed for their vessels at the same time. Seconds stretched into minutes as Akos drummed his fingers against the railing. Just when he thought he would have to go and check on Felix's progress, he saw a lantern light on the back end of the vessel he believed was the right one.

The light winked once, then twice. Akos let out a sigh of relief. That was the signal he'd instructed Felix to give once they had secured their ship.

"Gasci, signal Felix that we are secure as well," Akos ordered. "Everyone else make ready to sail."

As Akos walked back toward the center of the ship, he paused at the gangway long enough to offer Calia a hand down onto the deck. She graciously accepted and dropped down to the deck, Valesa close on her heels. The bodyguard scanned the gathered prisoners, searching for any weapons that his crew might have missed.

"I'd much prefer that you were aboard the other ship," Akos told Calia. "This is the one we plan on turning into the fireship."

"I'd rather be here," Calia replied. "I've never seen a fireship, and I might never get the chance again."

"With any luck it will only ever be once."

"And you'd have me miss my chance to see such a once-in-a-lifetime occurrence for a shred of extra safety?"

"Of course, how foolish of me."

Akos was once again struck by Calia's bravery. At first he'd believed her to be a pampered noblewoman like most others he'd met in his life. But she had put her own life on the line when they first entered the void rather than having someone else do it for her. There was a steel spine there that was belied by her soft appearance. Akos could see once again why Vibius had fallen so hard for her.

Still, Akos wished that Calia would be a little safer. Of course, considering their situation there was no such thing as true safety. But she could do things to minimize the danger she was putting herself in.

Akos didn't think he'd be able to look Vibius in the eyes if he rescued him only to have to tell him that he'd allowed the love of his life to be killed on the way there.

Akos supposed that he could always order her to do what he wanted. Not that she would listen to him. Technically, she wasn't a part of his crew. Akos might have to change that so he could feel a little better about giving her orders. As it was, she had no reason to obey unless it was already what she wanted to do. It probably wouldn't work the way he hoped it would, but it wouldn't hurt to give it further thought.

"Captain, we're ready to make sail," Gasci said.

"Very well." Akos turned back to the ship. "Cast off and take us out of the harbor. The moment we are clear of the docks I want the crews to start making the ship ready."

Akos started for his place by the helm, manned by Old Haroln. Calia followed him. They stood shoulder to shoulder next to Haroln as he guided the vessel out of the harbor. Akos stood with his hands clasped behind his back and his feet planted, his face fixed in a look of indifference. Calia wrung her hands nervously and glanced at everything going on around her.

"Something troubling you, Ms. Hailko?" Akos asked.

"Do you think that this will work?" Calia asked.

"The plan is solid. I would never have thought of it if you hadn't mentioned being able to attack from the sea. I doubt Garot will consider it either. We will have the element of surprise on our side."

"We are risking a lot on this."

Akos shrugged. "We would have risked a lot no matter what."

"Still, if this fails . . ."

"If this fails, we'll probably all be dead." Akos picked up where she'd trailed off. "In which case I can't imagine we'll care too much about it one way or another."

"How can you be so nonchalant about death?"

"Don't worry, I've still got too much to do in this life to run to my death. But one thing you learn on the seas is that you can't fear death. That fear will paralyze you. The man who fears death is guaranteed to meet him in the worst way possible. You have to let the fear wash past you or you won't be able to do what you have to do to make sure you stay alive."

166

"An odd paradox."

"The life of a sailor is full of those."

"So in order to live and save Vibius, I have to be unafraid to die in the attempt?"

"Precisely, we'll make a sailor out of you yet. Speaking of which, how would you feel about being an officer?"

"More than three decades of experience on her and she still makes officer before me," Haroln muttered aloud. "I should be insulted."

Chapter 19

A warm dusk breeze wafted through the window of Vibius's tower cell. It had only been a day or so since they'd returned him to this room rather than the dungeon, and he was still unsure if it was a dream. It felt real, but the ghosts he'd seen in his cell had seemed real as well.

Anson had been nice enough to send a barber by. He'd trimmed his unruly hair and shaved his face. Vibius had no idea if he looked good, but at least he didn't feel like a wild man anymore. He ran a hand over his chin and was happy to find not even a hint of stubble. He'd tried to wear a beard once and Akos and Vibia had both teased him endlessly for it.

Still, if this was all real, then it meant his deal with Anson was real as well. And if that was real, then Anson's dealings with Lord Laran were real. And if those were real, then the realms were in danger.

Perhaps not anytime soon, but Anson or another god would try to make a move on the realms outside of the void. As long as Vibius was alive, of course. He could find some way to remedy that now he was as free as he could be.

But his resolve to survive and tell Calia what he'd discovered had not waivered. One way or another, he had to find his way back to her. Vibius was the only person in all the realms who knew about all the other realms. He couldn't afford to end his own life while that was true, and he sure as hell wasn't going to tell Anson.

There was a brief knock on the door before it swung open. Vibius turned away from his window and did his best to face where he believed the door to be. He was still getting used to locating things based on sound rather than by sight, but he felt he was getting better at it.

"Come in," Vibius said as though the door weren't already wide open.

"You've a visitor," the door guard said. "Lord Laran here to see you."

All the tension that Vibius had managed to shed in his brief respite from the dungeon flooded back. Vibius still didn't know everything that was going on, but he was sure that Lord Laran coming to see him wasn't a good thing. Or perhaps it was. Vibius cursed his lack of knowledge. It would be nice to know who was an enemy and who was a potential ally for once.

"Is Lord Anson here as well?"

"No, I'm afraid he isn't," Lord Laran stated. "He did give me permission to speak with you in hopes that you could further convince me to join his cause."

"Ah, I see. Please, take a seat."

Vibius strode over to where he was sure the chairs were and spread his hands out. Once he'd found one, he managed to cautiously sit down. He heard Lord Laran make his way to the chair across from him and sit as well. The man regarded him without speaking for an uncomfortable amount of time. Vibius decided to break the silence himself.

"I'm not sure how well I can convince you," Vibius explained. "I haven't been keeping fully abreast of local politics."

"I'd thought as much. I'm not particularly sure what Anson thought you might be able to say to convince me either. But that isn't the real reason I leapt at the chance to speak to you alone."

"And what might the real reason be?"

"To convince you to join me instead."

Vibius was instantly wary, though he tried his best not to show it. He wouldn't put it past Anson to throw this together as a test of his loyalty. The man might be looking for any reason to distrust him, and if he found out he couldn't, he would either throw him in the dungeon and forget him there or have him killed out of hand.

"I think you have it backwards, Lord Laran," Vibius said. "We need you to join us so that we may conquer the realm together."

"And in exchange for your help, what has he offered you?" Laran asked. "Money, power, women, everlasting life, and the secret to his famous roast duck recipe?"

"Well, now that you mention it, he didn't offer that last thing. I knew I should've driven a harder bargain."

"Enough joking, Antonius. All men have a price. Most would leap at any one of the things that a god can offer. But eternal life is the one that the old gods always throw into their deals that sets it over the top."

"That does seem to be the one that carries the most weight."

"Has he ever told you the secret to his eternal life? Of course he hasn't. The old gods guard that secret with their lives, as though anyone could take it from them."

Vibius didn't respond. Lord Laran seemed in the mood to monologue, and the longer he could keep the man talking without having to give up anything himself, the better.

"Did you ever see the golden fruit he has at every meal?" Laran asked.

"Yes."

"It's more than just a delicacy. That fruit is the secret to eternal life. So far as I know, only one tree grows per island, and those trees are sacred secrets that only a few know about. And only the gods know the true effect of the fruit."

"Is that what gives you control over the behemoths?"

"No. That is an innate trait. Only a few dozen with the gift are born each generation, and they are hunted down by the gods of their islands ruthlessly. It wouldn't do to have competition for supremacy."

"I see."

Vibius's mind raced. This was more information than any he had ever read in Anson's library, or that had ever been told to him. How a fruit could bestow everlasting life was beyond him, but how a person could be born with a gift of magic was something he understood well. He could only imagine it was like his own gift of wayfaring.

As he was pondering it, Vibius felt Laran grab his wrist and pull his hand closer. He resisted the motion at first, then he felt a finger jab into the palm of his hand. Laran began to trace on it. Vibius thought about calling out for the guards, but then he realized that Laran was writing letters on his palm.

DO YOU UNDERSTAND

Vibius nodded hesitantly.

KEEP TALKING THEY ARE LISTENING

"You said that I should join you," Vibius said. "And yet you offer so much less than Anson did."

"I offered you the truth as a token of my goodwill," Laran corrected. "I imagine it is more truth than you've been told since you arrived here." When Vibius didn't respond, he continued. "Anson is an old god. He views all of the younger gods with contempt."

"Younger?"

"Less than a millenium."

I DO NOT WANT TO CONQUER ALL REALMS

"Arrogant or not, it still doesn't explain why I should join you rather than him. Nor does it explain what you plan to do differently."

"Anson looks to conquer this realm before looking outward. I will gain allies outside of the realm before returning to conquer it."

I AM ONLY INTERESTED IN CONTROLLING THIS REALM

It was an interesting proposition. There was no way to know for sure if it was the truth either. But if it were, that would mean that Vibius might have a potential ally against Anson, one that he could trust not to turn his attention outward as soon as he got the opportunity.

"I'm afraid I don't think that will work," Vibius stated.

"And why is that?" Laran asked.

"Because you don't have a wayfarer to help you."

NOD IF YOU MEAN THAT

The words hung in the air. Vibius didn't know what to do. All of this was happening far too fast, and he didn't know whether he could trust this man. Laran was an unknown. And he was a god. In Vibius's admittedly limited experience, the gods of this realm weren't inherently honest. Still, he didn't want to close any doors just yet. If Laran were telling the truth, then he would be at least marginally better to work with than Anson. Vibius shook his head.

"You're making a mistake," Laran growled. "Anson will use you to his own ends and then discard you."

"Whereas I'm sure that you will use me and then treat me like a prince for the rest of my life."

"I will!"

"I've the same guarantee from Anson. And since you came to me, a blind prisoner, for aid against him, I'm certain you know you cannot defeat him."

"Of course I can. I do not need your help defeating one god. I can defeat any one god. I need help when the others inevitably form together against me."

"Then join Anson. Do as he says, and you will have your victory."

"You're nothing but a brainwashed fool. I can't believe I wasted my time on this."

WE WILL SPEAK AGAIN WHEN WE CAN

Laran stood from his chair, scraping it against the stone of the floor. He strode over to the door and banged on it hard. The guards opened it and let him leave. Before it shut, Vibius called after him.

"Can I assume that I can give Anson your answer?" Vibius asked.

"You'll do no such thing," Laran said. "I'll give my own answer once I've had time to discuss the matter with my advisors."

The door slammed and Vibius was once again left alone with his thoughts. He would have to approach this carefully. If he told Anson about this conversation and Laran denied it, who would Anson believe? If Laran went straight down and told Anson that his wayfarer had cost him any chance at an alliance, how would he react? There were too many variables for Vibius to settle on a course of action. His hesitation might already have marked him as a dead man.

***

"I should have known that little snake would try something like this," Anson hissed. "The young gods have no respect for the wisdom of their elders. They think they can do everything for themselves. They've no idea what it takes to hold their position for a thousand years."

"What are you going to do about it?" Vibius asked.

"Nothing for now. Let him consult his advisors. If he returns and joins my cause then this will all be put behind us, and if he does not, then I will simply crush him for his treachery."

"Wouldn't it be better to strike now, before he leaves?"

"No. This alliance is important. If I killed every scheming member, I would have to slay every single person involved."

"And if he doesn't return to give his answer?"

"Then he will be my first target. I smash his armies and burn his home to the ground."

Vibius sipped the wine that was put before him and thought for a moment. The vintage wasn't to his liking, but he wasn't about to complain. It was a few thousand leagues above the gruel he had been eating for the last few months. Not to mention the food. It was almost good enough to take his mind off the murderous dinner conversation and the maniac that he was having it with.

It seemed that Laran had at least been correct in his assumption that Anson had his men listening in on their conversation. Vibius mentioned that Laran had come to talk to him and that he had proposed that Vibius go with him. Anson had informed him that he'd already known about the subject of their conversation. Hopefully that had garnered him some points of trust with the god, even if he hadn't disclosed the full conversation.

"Has he already left?" Vibius asked.

"He has. He left this afternoon. He told me that he would take some months to decide whether he would join me or not."

"Is that not worrisome?"

"Gods take a long time to make major decisions. It is the one commodity that we have in no short supply. He'll gather as much information on our potential enemies as he can, as well as information on me. And when he is confident that he has all the intelligence that he needs, he will make his decision."

"So now we wait?"

"Yes. Now we wait."

Vibius had never been very good at waiting, but maybe all his time in the dungeon had improved that ability. They would find out. He didn't need to draw any unnecessary attention to himself in the meantime. Vibius would be as patient as he could. At least now he had a new project to focus on while he waited.

One of the first things he'd done when he reached his new room was confirm that he could still sense the other realms. If all of his findings had been nothing but the delusions of a mind deprived of light, sound, and company, he would have given up. Instead, he'd found that his discoveries held up to the changed conditions. Now that he had discovered them, it seemed he could always find them, the same way he had with the realms everyone was familiar with.

Vibius would keep practicing seeking them out to make sure his senses didn't dull, but he had something else he wanted to try. Laran's words had awoken a familiar curiosity in him. He'd stated the magic that allowed the gods to control the behemoths was an inborn one. Vibius had intuited that it was similar to what allowed him to move ships through the ways.

But what if it was the same ability? What if, instead of possible rivals being born a few dozen to each generation, the magically gifted being born were nascent wayfarers? It would explain why, in the thousands of years since the realm had been settled, no wayfarers had been born to try to escape. And if they were all hunted down and killed by fearful rulers, it would explain why there were so few of them born in every generation.

No one had ever been able to pinpoint the exact cause, but the gift of wayfaring did tend to run down familial lines. Sure, a child whose family had no history of the gift could be randomly born with it. But the gift seemed much more likely to be inherited. If the gods exterminated every line that contained the trait, they would be ensuring that fewer and fewer of them were born with every passing year.

Vibius listened for the telltale scratching of claws on stone. He had to listen very closely, past the sound of footsteps as servers moved about and the clank of silverware on plates. He pretended to be contemplating his wine as he strained his hearing for even a hint of one of the beast's presence. Vibius knew that Anson kept at least one close ever since Akos's surprise attack at dinner.

Finally he heard it. A behemoth was in the room, shifting its weight from foot to foot and dragging its claws against the ground.

Once he was sure the creature was there, he extended his wayfaring senses outward.

The world around him faded away as his mind was filled with the images that always accompanied his gift. Rather than look to the ways as he always did, he tried his best to block them out and focus on the realm he was in. It was a difficult task, one he had never bothered to practice before. Why would he? A wayfarer could not see anything within the realms themselves, only outside of them. There was no use in trying. At least, there hadn't been a use for it before.

Vibius did his best to focus his mind on the exact point where he knew a behemoth to be. He focused until he was sure he was being obvious, looking for anything that could give him a hint that he was correct. Every wayfarer described the ways differently. Vibia had always described the realms as great bells that she could find by following the chimes. For others he'd known, it was a scent they could track like a bloodhound. Vibius had always been able to see a glow given off by each one, and he could follow the light through the ways.

Turning his mind's eye away from the glow of other realms was difficult, but he managed to turn back into the realm he was in. It was like staring directly at the sun. It seared the inside of his mind, but he persisted. Unlike his real eyes, at least when he still had them, he couldn't permanently damage his mind's eye by staring into the light too long. It would hurt, and it would make him want to look away, but it couldn't fry his mind. He hoped.

So he forced himself to stare at the realm until he was sure he knew where he was looking, and then he looked for where he believed the behemoth to be. Vibius stared as long as he was able and saw nothing. Certain that if he kept up his attempt at the dinner table he would give himself away, Vibius was about to silence his gift when he saw it. A brief flicker, something that was not the realm but was connected to it.

Vibius swallowed a shout of excitement and hid his smile with his wine glass. It might have been a trick of his mind, desperate to get away from the light. But it was something he could work on while he waited for something to happen. Just before he let go of his gift, he focused on that flicker and thought, hard, one single word. *Shift.*

The scrape of claws on stone was unmistakable.

Chapter 20

The preparations were complete. Akos looked them over one more time. A nice bonfire had been constructed in the center of the deck, covered in pitch, lamp oil, and other materials that would burn thick and black. The deck was being wetted down so that it wouldn't catch, at least not immediately. It would be a shame if they burned a hole in the bottom of their fireship out in the middle of the harbor where they couldn't use it for cover.

Akos had sent all but a few men across to Felix's caravel on a few longboats. The rest of them were being used by the former crew of the *Buyer's Remorse*. He'd set them adrift with only a pair of paddles. Even if they rowed nonstop from now until dawn, they wouldn't make it back to the harbor in time to warn anyone of what was coming.

The breeze coming off the sea was cool, but Akos felt as though he might break into a sweat anyway. He adjusted the borrowed pistol in his borrowed belt. It felt odd on his hip. It was a stubby little thing, less than half the length of the dueling pistol he usually carried and nowhere near the same weight. But the pistols that Vibius had given him were two of a kind. One of them was in Geralis, most likely in the hands of Halis Hailko, and the other was in Logathia with Anson.

That thought steadied Akos's resolve. He needed to get back to Vibius, and this was the best way to get there. Garot would have no idea they were coming from this angle, and no way to stop them even if he figured it out. They had the element of surprise and a strategy that would keep Garot guessing until the very last moment.

The only thing left to do was implement it. Akos turned to the few men left on the ship, handpicked to help him guide it into the harbor. The only one that stood out of the group was Calia, who was looking at him expectantly with the rest of them. Akos motioned for her to join him.

"How can I help you, Captain?" Calia asked.

"You can help by going to the other ship now," Akos said.

"You're sure that I can't stay? I want to see this through."

"The only thing left to do on this vessel is steer it into harbor and then set it alight. Then abandon it and get aboard the other ship with enough time to still make it to the *Pride*. That is a dangerous enough thing to do without mentioning the fact that we will not be able to slow down to pick up the crew ditching this vessel."

"How, exactly, do you plan to get back aboard Felix's vessel anyway?"

"He'll be coming in behind us. We'll jump overboard and he'll throw out lines as he passes for us to grab and he'll pull us aboard. He'll drop a longboat for anyone who doesn't manage to grab a line, and we'll swing back after we are done with our business at the docks to pick them up."

"Is that safe?"

"Not at all. A thousand things could go wrong. Which is why you aren't going to be one of the people doing it. You're going to go to Felix's ship, go into the cabins, and wait until we've seized the *Pride*."

Valesa had moved close to Calia's shoulder and was nodding as Akos laid out his plan. Calia must have felt her presence because she glanced back and frowned. She turned back to Akos with a defeated look.

"I suppose I have been outvoted," Calia said.

"It certainly looks that way," Akos agreed.

"Just be careful. We'll see you on the other side of this, Captain. Good luck."

"Thank you. I'll come get you once we've won."

With that the pair departed on the last longboat heading to the caravel. Akos handed Valesa his sword belt as she passed by so it would not get soaked when he went overboard. Then he waited until the lantern attached to the back of the longboat had ascended up into the caravel before turning back to the men that were still gathered there, waiting for orders.

"Does anyone have any questions about the plan?" Akos asked.

There was a chorus of "no's" and a round of shaking heads. Akos nodded, looking them over. They were all veterans of the *Mist Stalker*, and he trusted that each of them would do what they needed to do.

"Well then, no more time to waste," Akos said. "Let's get to it."

The men scrambled to assume their positions, and Akos took his place at the helm. Normally he would let someone else handle this for him, but he needed as few people aboard as possible. The men that were left would man the sails so any last-minute adjustments could be made, and he would steer them in. Once he was satisfied with their trajectory, he would lock the rudder and give the order to jump overboard.

Akos settled in and led the vessel through the dark, using the stars and the rising sun to guide his hand. It had been a long time since he'd manned a helm, but it might as well have been the day before. He'd done it long enough to know the trade by heart. For a while there was nothing but the ship, the stars, and a destination. Nothing else in the entire world mattered. Occasionally he would bark an order to the men down on the deck and they would snap to complete his instructions.

As they neared the harbor, Akos glanced back to make sure Felix was in the correct position. With the sun rising behind them, Akos could see the outline of the vessel dotted with lanterns. He nodded his head at no one in particular, drawing in a deep breath to settle his nerves. It was almost time.

"Is it there?" Akos shouted up to the crow's nest.

"Pulling into the harbor now!" the lookout replied.

Akos could try to intercept them before they ever reached the docks. All it would take was an order to his men, a shift in the helm, and they would be on the way. But Akos wanted the *Pride* pinned against the docks where it had less room to maneuver. So he kept his course and prayed they would reach the docks before Garot could tell them to have their weapons ready.

By the time they'd entered the harbor proper and could see the docks, the sun had risen fully over the horizon. Their shadows were still long, and it would be difficult for anyone on shore to make out any details about them, but it would not be long before they reached their target.

"Sir," a voice called to him.

One of his crew offered up a looking glass. Akos extended it to its full length and looked out at the docks. There was some activity there, but not much. Business was probably slow due to the large crowd of pirates lining the docks. Akos could see Garot's men ringing the harbors, inspecting each and every person that was coming or going. The man himself stood in the center, overseeing everything and casting furtive glances out to sea.

Akos turned his glass to find what Garot was looking at. Eventually his gaze settled on the *Pride*. The paint indicating her the name had been chipped away, but it was obvious who she was. There was no mistaking a warship like that.

She sat high and proud in the water, unafraid of any threat. Akos could make out three separate gun decks, with ports closed to keep out the conditions. He wondered if she had her full complement of cannons, or if some of those ports were hiding empty slots. Regardless, she had more than enough teeth to tear through the pitiful barge he was steering and the caravel Felix captained and and still have extra cannons to fire a salute.

This was the type of vessel that every privateer and pirate avoided at all costs. Akos was not ashamed to admit that he'd turned tail and run from several prizes in his career at the mere sight of a ship of the line such as the *Pride*. The *Mist Stalker* could outrun any vessel that she couldn't fight, and fight any vessel she couldn't outrun. The mere sight of the vessel awakened a flight instinct in Akos that he hadn't realized was there, begging him to turn the wheel and abandon his quest.

Instead, Akos steeled his hand and his heart, aiming for a point ahead of where he believed the *Pride* was going to dock. He turned his glass back toward the docks, where the pirates of Garot's crew were preparing for her arrival. If Akos was judging their speeds right, he would arrive at the docks at the same time as the *Pride*, if not a little sooner.

"Make ready!" Akos ordered.

Men scrambled to get into position. Akos kept a firm hand on the wheel, making small adjustments as he guided them to their target. In another few minutes, they'd begin to spring their trap. Until then, it was a race to get into position before Garot realized what was going on.

Akos was used to the tension of an encroaching naval battle. There was nothing for it but patience. There was nothing he could do to speed them along their way, nothing he could do to join the fight any quicker. Any nervous action on his part would be seen and translated by his crew in the worst possible ways. If he paced, drummed his fingers, or fidgeted, they would see it as fear. If they saw him afraid. they would assume it was because he was not confident in their chances. If they didn't think he was confident, they would panic and disobey orders.

So instead of doing any of the things he'd really like to, Akos forced himself to keep his expression neutral, almost bored, and stood stock still. They inched toward their goal, far too slow for his liking. But still, they closed ground. Now Akos could see that they would arrive right before the *Pride*. It was perfect timing. He would cut them off from true support from the docks while still limiting their ability to get back out into the open harbor.

"Light it!" Akos shouted.

The appointed man took the lantern he was holding and threw it into the bonfire they'd prepared. The glass shattered, splashing more oil over the already soaked wood. The small flame took to the oil immediately, washing over the bonfire they'd made. In mere moments it was throwing billowing clouds of black smoke. Luckily the wind was still behind them, blowing the cloud forward, but Akos had his men cover their faces with bandanas to be safe.

"Keep me on target!" Akos shouted to the man in the crow's nest.

"Aye, sir!"

Akos kept a vice grip on the wheel, doing his best to keep from moving it in the slightest. This was the most delicate part. He couldn't see through the cloud he was creating to make sure he didn't accidentally ram the *Pride*. He was sure that his ship would take the worst of it, but he didn't want to spread the fire aboard his vessel to that one. And every day they were forced to waste on repairs was another day Vibius was forced to wait for them.

Akos tried to look at the situation from Garot's eyes. It wouldn't be long now before he noticed the flaming ship coming directly for him, if he hadn't already. Ship fires were a common occurrence, so he probably wouldn't think anything of it. In a usual situation, the sails would burn up long before the ship reached the port and bring it to a harmless standstill out in the harbor, leaving the helpless crew to wait for rescue.

What Garot couldn't know was that they had positioned their bonfire so that it would not reach the sails. They would continue ahead at pace until they rammed into the docks. Akos shifted his hand slightly, following the direction of the man in the crow's nest. His heart pounded in his chest as they drew closer and closer. Noxious black smoke billowed forth, more than enough to shield the caravel behind them from vision. Akos began to let himself hope that their plan might work after all.

"How far?" Akos asked.

"Half a mile!"

Akos wanted to wait as long as he could before setting the rudder and abandoning ship. Any of a thousand things could throw them off course, from a stiffening breeze to a large wave. But if they waited too long, they wouldn't have time for Felix to pick them up before he made his way to engage the *Pride*. Akos refused to let someone else put themselves in danger while he sat in the water and watched from afar.

"Quarter mile!"

"Everyone overboard!"

Akos waited until he'd seen every single one of them jump into the water of the bay. Once the spotter had descended the lines and hopped overboard, he set the rudder and went to the railing. Akos glanced back to make sure that Felix was still trailing them and then took a deep breath. The water was probably cold this morning. Akos hated swimming in cold water.

Without thinking any more about it, he clambered up the railing and dove over it. The water was just as cold as he'd feared it would be. He plunged deep, then kicked to bring himself back up. Akos broke the surface and watched as the *Buyer's Remorse* plodded forward toward the docks. After a moment, he turned to see where Felix was.

Treading water in wet clothes was tiring, so thankfully Felix was not far behind. The line was thrown expertly, and Akos managed to grab on while they pulled him in. Once he was close enough, he clutched the railing and let the men aboard pull him over. Someone offered him dry clothes and he took them, changing while they made their way forward. Someone else cleared their throat and he turned to see Valesa standing there, waiting for him to take his sword belt.

"We're almost on them," Valesa said.

"Good," Akos said. "Can the crow's nest still see them?"

"Yes. They've reported that they have begun to turn toward us to avoid running into the barge."

That was excellent news. That would make it all the easier to pull alongside them before they knew what was happening. Akos made his way to the forecastle of the ship, leaning over the railing to get a better view. Unfortunately, all he could see was a wall of thick smoke and the back end of the *Buyer's Remorse*.

Akos almost jumped backwards when the *Pride* cut through the smoke right ahead of them. She was still turning, and Akos was forced to clutch the railing for balance as Felix threw the vessel in a sharp turn to avoid her. Men readied grappling hooks, pistols, and blades. They were close enough that Akos could see the confused crew of the *Pride* milling about on her deck, trying their best to avoid what they thought was an accident.

The few men that took notice of them didn't look as though they were too concerned. There was a massive crash of timber on stone as the barge rammed into the dock at speed, throwing bits of flaming pitch and wood everywhere. Now a fire really would break out and spread. *Good*, Akos thought. *The more confusion the better.*

The caravel would have sped right past her prey and into the same fate as the barge, but Felix had his men ready. At a barked command, his men cut the sails, allowing them to flap loose in the wind and kill a great deal of their speed. Another order saw an anchor pushed off the back of the vessel, slowing their momentum.

Then they were beside her. Despite the high forecastle of the caravel, they were still a few feet shorter than the *Pride*. The men with grapnels threw and pulled, bringing the two vessels closer together. Akos joined the nearest line, straining to bring the two ships side by side. Men on the ratlines were already attempting to leap across. Akos gritted his teeth and heaved harder. He needed to get aboard, now.

Finally, the ships were close enough that several men brought forth ladders with hooked ends. They slotted them up and over the railing, slamming them down into place so they would be difficult to dislodge. Akos swung onto the nearest ladder, sprinting up as quick as he could. It was only a few feet, so he swung over the side in no time.

Unlike the barge they'd boarded the day before, this ship had been ready for trouble. Clearly they hadn't been expecting anything like what Akos had brought to them, but they at least had real weapons at hand. A man rushed him with a cutlass, attempting to skewer him on the end of it.

Akos sidestepped and pushed out with his hand, forcing the cutlass around him. With his other arm he swung his elbow in a short, sharp arc. The tip of his elbow connected with the man's nose, snapping his head back with a sickening crunch. Akos yanked on his arm hard and levered him up and over the railing, flinging him out into space. He would either land in the small space between the ships and be out of the fight, or he would land on the deck amongst Akos's men, where he would be cut to ribbons or taken prisoner. Either way, he was no longer Akos's problem.

Dwarven steel leapt into his hand as Akos made his way further onto the ship. The long blade was not made for close combat, but there was enough room up on the deck that it would be useable. Akos proved that point as another man launched himself at him. Akos easily turned his blade aside and lashed out with a counterstrike that opened the man's guts. Still he pushed forward, looking for his way into the belly of the ship. That's where they would be keeping his crew members.

Akos spotted a staircase leading down below and raced toward it. He ignored the small knots of fighting around him, confident his men would be able to carry the day. He needed to reach the prisoners before anyone with authority realized that was what they were after. Akos wouldn't put it past Garot to have ordered his men to put them to death if they were attacked. It was exactly the kind of spiteful thing Garot would do.

As he made his way, Akos grabbed the attention of several men who weren't engaged and motioned for them to follow him. Once he had a decent squad ready to go, he sheathed his blade and made his way down into the belly of the ship. One of the men handed him a short-handled boarding ax as he descended. It wasn't his favorite weapon, but it would have to do.

The interior of the ship was lit by nothing but lanterns and what little light spilled around the plugs in the gun ports. Akos blinked as his eyes tried to adjust to the darkness. He thought he saw movement ahead of him, but he couldn't be sure.

"Out of the way, sir!" A sailor pushed him aside.

Akos hit the wall hard, grunting with the impact. The barrel of a pistol extended past him and fired. Magnified by their closed in surroundings, the pistol might as well have deafened him. In the flash of flame that flowered from the barrel, Akos could see a half dozen enemy pirates approaching them from deeper in the gun deck. Akos caught the lead man's ax on his own, shoving him back hard to create space.

"They'll be further down!" Akos shouted over the ringing in his ears.

"We'll take care of this, sir!"

Akos waited until his men had pushed the foe back some before turning toward the second set of stairs and continuing down. He flew through the decks, eventually finding the brig. It was nothing but a set of iron cages set in the cargo deck. His eyes had finally adjusted to the light well enough that he could make out the faces of his friends in the cages. There was a man frantically thumbing through a set of keys, trying to pull Vibia out of her cage. Rage filled Akos's chest as he realized that he planned to use her as a hostage to guarantee his own safety.

The man realized he was there as he strode forward. He dropped the key ring and fumbled for a pistol at his belt. He extended it toward the cage at Vibia. Akos couldn't hear what he was saying, but he could read his lips well enough to know what he was after.

Let me go or I'll kill her.

Akos glanced to the side to make sure Vibia had moved out of the pirate's line of fire. The pirate was so intent on him that he hadn't noticed Vibia was in no real danger. Besides, he hadn't so much as cocked the hammer of his pistol.

In one smooth motion, Akos drew his own stubby pistol and cocked it, firing without a word of warning. The bullet slammed home into the pirate's shoulder, knocking the pistol from his hand as he gasped. Akos was on him before he had time to drop to his knees and beg for his life. The hatchet he'd been given rose and fell, each swing fueled by rage.

A hand wrapped around his wrist, stopping him midswing. Akos spun and tried to rip his hand free from his assailant, but the vice grip did not budge. He realized it was Leodysus reaching through the bars to arrest his swing.

Akos dropped the axe and pistol, picking up the keys and handing them to Leo.

"Can you handle this?" Akos shouted. "There's still a battle going on up there."

"Yes," Leo shouted back. "Go."

Akos scooped up his ax and the pirate's pistol, cocking it before heading back up the stairs.

***

Akos stood on the top deck. He was bloody and tired, but he was victorious. The caravel had been detached and his men now controlled the *Pride*. Though the fight aboard the ship was done, the day was not over yet. There was still the matter of the men on the docks.

The crow's nest had reported that the men on the docks were still trying to fight the fire and that they hadn't fled. Akos realized they didn't know they'd lost their only advantage. The smoke must have covered them more effectively than he'd thought. Either way, he was having the ship come round to present its broadside to the docks.

"Cannon crews," Akos shouted. "Make ready!"

Leo echoed the order down to the gunnery officer's on the first gun deck. They couldn't man all the cannons, but they could man enough of them to make a difference. Akos watched from his place next to the helmsman as they drew parallel to land.

Akos realized he could see Garot. The man was directing traffic, shouting and exhorting his men to greater effort as they tried to put out the fire. Akos watched as Garot glanced in his direction and then back to the fire before realization dawned across his face. Garot turned back toward him, shock written across his features, before turning his blade from the fire toward them. Men raced to reach the dock mounted cannons.

"Cannons ready!" Leo reported.

"Fire."

Grapeshot tore from the barrels of dozens of cannons. Once the roar of the guns subsided, the steel balls buzzed through the air like a swarm of angry bees. The first volley wiped away the men rushing toward the cannons. Akos forced himself to watch as men were reduced to smears of blood and viscera. This was his doing; he couldn't shy away from it now.

"Load!" Akos ordered.

Now it was a frantic race. The stunned pirates on the shore were torn between manning the guns and attempting to make a fight of it or dropping everything and running. That indecision would cost them. Akos knew they had no hope. The entire city of Tersun had fewer cannons than the *Pride*. They would best serve themselves by abandoning their posts and saving themselves.

But the fear of Garot must have been stronger than the fear of the buzzing swarms of steel death. Some men broke and ran, but most continued to make their way to the shore batteries. Garot had disappeared from his perch. Akos caught sight of him, lying bleeding and broken amongst the wreckage of the crate he'd been standing on when the shots had fired. *Too noble a fate for him*, Akos thought to himself.

"Ready!" Leo called.

"Fire!"

The command repeated, over and over. The shore batteries were reduced to rubble by the time they were done. Some of the men stubbornly refused to break, and Akos refused to present them his stern to fire at. It wasn't until the last shoreside gun had been silenced that Akos called off his men.

Smoke drifted from the shore, slowly clearing to reveal the wreckage he'd wrought. The prisoners they'd taken in the fighting were being loaded into a longboat to be put to shore. Akos didn't want them, and now that Garot was dead he didn't care what these men did with their lives. They'd lost a dozen men in the assault, far fewer than they could have lost in such a reckless attack. But it was still far too many for him to sleep easily tonight.

"Captain?" Leo said. "Your orders?"

Akos was happy he could hear Leo without him having to shout anymore. His hearing was finally coming back. Akos took one last look at the docks, taking in the sight of burning, broken, and bloody bodies before turning back to his second.

"Rendezvous with Felix's ship and make for open waters," Akos ordered. "We've won."

A cheer went up from the men. Akos resisted the urge to slump against the railing. Best he could tell, none of the blood that stained his clothes was his. But he was still tired, down to his very bones. He wanted nothing more than to slump into bed, but so did his men, and they had to work. So he would stay right here until they were safely away from this place.

Hours later, the sun had begun to set. Akos finally left his place by the helm, allowing the first shift to take over and the rest of the men to go below decks and sleep. They would take inventory of what they had tomorrow, after they were slightly better rested and once they were sure no one was trying to follow them with retribution in their hearts.

Akos stumbled into the cabins, finding the captain's cabin unlocked. He opened it and went in, seeing that there was someone there. Vibia stood up from where she was sitting at the desk.

Despite the fatigue that plagued every step, Akos rushed forward to hug her. Even though he was covered in other people's blood, Vibia returned the embrace. They stood that way for a long time, neither willing to be the first to break the hug. When Akos finally released her and stepped back, he looked up into her golden eyes.

"I'm glad you're safe," Akos managed.

"Me too," Vibia said. "Now go to sleep."

Akos nodded and stepped past her, falling face-first onto the bed. He fell asleep with a smile on his lips, knowing they'd done it. The next step was to save Vibius. Akos dreamed of blasting apart Anson's keep, brick by brick, with his newfound firepower. It wouldn't be long now before he could make that dream a reality.

***

Vibia winced as Akos fell face-first onto a dirty mattress. Within moments he was snoring, muttering something about bricks and cannons. Vibia couldn't help but roll her eyes and snort, rolling him halfway onto his back so that she could get his sword belt off. She'd hate for him to have risked so much to rescue them, and have been lucky enough lucky to escape injury, only to roll over onto a blade and stab himself.

Once she was certain that Akos wouldn't accidentally harm himself in his sleep, Vibia left the room, making sure to gently close the cabin door behind her. The ship was still a buzz of activity, though the tone had changed. During the battle there had been a sense of naked aggression and desperation. Now that victory had settled in, the mood had changed to one of elation. Men were so joyous to be alive that it infected everything they did, from greeting each other as they carried out their duties to swabbing bloodstains from the deck.

It was a familiar sight. Vibia had seen the aftermath of dozens of battles. It wasn't always like this. Sometimes the cost was so great that a victory felt like a defeat, but today was not one of those days. It seemed that the men had decided that the cost today had been more than worth the victory. Still, there were more than a few men gathered around the coffins being constructed on the deck, saying their final goodbyes.

"There she is," an all too familiar voice called from the helm. "The woman of the hour."

"Oh please, gods, no," Vibia muttered without turning around.

"It has been far too long, my dear," Felix continued.

"I've done nothing to deserve this today."

Footsteps behind her on the steps were the only indication that Felix was approaching. Vibia refused to turn around. Maybe if she never acknowledged him, he would get bored and go away. *It's just as likely that the pig will learn to fly*, Vibia thought.

"Don't you have better things to do than bother me, Felix?" Vibia asked.

"I can clear my schedule." Felix smiled.

With no other options, Vibia turned and looked at him. The man hadn't changed a bit. He wore the same haircut, the same dagger of a beard, and the same lascivious smile. Of all the crew members of the *Mist Stalker* that had left them over the years, Vibia missed Felix least of all.

"I'd really love to stay and chat with you," Vibia said, "but I'd rather be doing anything else."

"Oh, don't be like that. It will be an awful long journey if you spurn me the entire way."

"You're joining us? How . . . lovely."

"As if I had a choice. When I heard that your brother was in danger, there was no other option but to help however I could."

"Wonderful. If you'll excuse me, I need to be sick, and then I need to find Ms. Hailko. There are things we need to discuss."

"Ah, friends with our guest I take it?"

"Oh, what's wrong, Felix? Upset because she refused to sleep with you too?"

"I'll have you know that I have made no such attempt. My eyes are for you and you alone, darling."

"Now I'm definitely going to be sick."

Vibia walked off without allowing him to respond. She'd found over the years that people took much less pleasure in getting the last word when they had to say it to your back. She did need to find Calia and get caught up on what had happened while she'd been in captivity. Then she needed to find out if they had a plan for how to proceed.

Hopefully they had a plan. Vibia hated when they winged it.

Chapter 21

Calia stood on the deck, wrapped in heavy furs. The mist swirled in front of her, marking the edge of the realm of man and the entry into the way between worlds. After what had seemed an eternity, they had finally arrived.

A quick glance back confirmed that Akos was at his position near the helm. Vibia stood next to him. It almost looked as though she were sleeping, eyes closed, her breath slow and even. If Calia had to guess, she was meditating in preparation to use her gift.

It had been several weeks since the battle at the docks of Tersun. Since then, they had only docked once in Illyris to gather supplies for their long journey through the ways. They'd sold the caravel they'd stolen to pay for food, water, and gunpowder. Lots and lots of gunpowder. Akos had packed their arsenal full of the stuff. Whatever their plan was, he wanted to be well prepared.

Now that they were on the cusp of their journey back to the void, the lack of a plan was beginning to worry her. Vibia had mentioned to her that she hated not having a plan, and Calia could see why. It was frustrating not knowing what their next move was going to be, especially when so much rode on them getting everything right. Though to be fair to Akos, Calia hadn't exactly come up with anything groundbreaking either.

Still, she intended to bring it up the next time she had a chance. They couldn't wander blindly into the void and expect everything to turn out alright. They'd done that in Tersun, and it hadn't turned out well at all. Calia would think of something; she just needed to think a little harder.

"All ready?" Akos shouted across the deck.

"Aye, Captain," Leodysus shouted back. As usual, the man wore nothing but his trousers. From her previous experience, Calia knew that the ways were colder than even the deepest winter. How the half-orc first mate could stand the chill was beyond her.

"Make the transition," Akos said.

Calia reached out and gripped the railing firmly. Vibia's eyes snapped open, and the gold in them started to glow. The ship lurched hard enough to shake even the steadiest legs, and then settled. Calia let go of her white-knuckle grip of the railing, determined not to lose her breakfast. This was her fifth transition after all; she should be getting used to it at some point. She watched as one of the crew wobbled to the railing and leaned over, hurling his guts into the water.

Maybe not.

Then the chill struck her. Despite the furs she wore, and having tempered her mind beforehand, Calia was struck by how cold it was. There was no breeze, but it still cut straight through her heavy coat. She rubbed at her arms with thick mittens and shivered.

"I'll never get used to that," Valesa mumbled.

"I'm beginning to worry that I won't either," Calia agreed. "Perhaps we ought to head below deck."

"No argument from me."

The two made their way inside. The best place to be would be the galley, where the nearby cooking stoves would provide a decent amount of heat. They would also be able to listen to the tales that were continuously told as a ship made its way through the ways in an effort to stave off both boredom and ill fortune. Calia enjoyed listening to Old Haroln spin his yarns the first time she'd made her way through the ways. She imagined it might be a good way to kill the time on their journey. At least, until it was time to come up with a plan.

A quick glance backward told her that Akos would not be joining them. Just as he had during their other trips through the ways, he would be staying by their wayfarer until they were done for the day. Calia had never learned whether this was something that only Akos did or if it was common practice for all captains. She had some suspicion that it was due, at least in part, to the fact that both of his wayfarers also happened to be his closest friends.

Calia ducked inside, heat hitting her like a wave. Every man that didn't absolutely have to be above deck was finding something to do here, and their crew had grown considerably. In addition to the freed crew of the *Mist Stalker*, they had taken on many of Felix's men who volunteered to come along. The heat from so many people in such close proximity would normally be stifling, but here it was a welcome reprieve from the frigid air above decks.

The *Pride* was laid out very differently from the *Mist Stalker* and was much larger. Calia frequently found herself heading the wrong way looking for the galley, even though they'd been aboard for over a month. She only had to backtrack once to find it this time, and she counted that as a small victory. Old Haroln was already perched in his usual spot, spinning tales to the other crewmen. Calia grabbed some food from the galley and joined them, passing the hours listening to the yarns unfold while trying her best not to think of the vast nothingness that surrounded them.

Eventually there was a small commotion behind her, and Calia turned to see that a path was being opened for Akos and Vibia. Vibia made no sound as she stomped to the galley and then began to eat before she'd even found a seat. Akos, on the other hand, greeted his men and spoke soft words to each of them on his way to sit next to them.

"How are you, Vibia," Calia tried to ask.

All she got by way of response was a grunt between bites. Vibia hadn't even glanced up from her food. Calia decided that she would wait until after the wayfarer was done before trying to talk to her. Akos set his own plate down and sat with a nod. His face was bright red, though Calia didn't know if it was from the cold outside or from the sudden heat of coming below deck.

"Captain," Calia said. "How was your day?"

"Cold," Akos said. "But I think we are making good time."

"That is good to hear. But it does raise a concern."

Akos looked at her evenly from across the table. Calia met his gaze. They'd had this particular conversation every night since they'd begun to set sail toward the ways. Now that they were on their way to the void proper, Calia couldn't imagine why they would put off making a plan any longer than they already had.

"Agreed," Vibia mumbled.

"Really, that's going to be the first word you speak today?" Akos asked.

"We need a plan," Calia said.

"I have a plan."

"Please, enlighten us. Because I have no idea what we are going to do."

"Men like Anson only understand force and the threat of violence. So we have to show him that we are the stronger force and he will surrender."

"And how do you intend to do that? Sail right up to his keep and start blasting?"

Akos looked down at his plate with a thoughtful expression.

"That is exactly what you were planning, wasn't it?" Calia demanded.

"Yes. It will be the quickest way to show him that we are not to be messed with, and that we can tear down everything he has built without having to get within range of his behemoths."

"You're mad."

Calia looked back and forth between their group. Vibia was once again lost in her dinner, while Valesa seemed to be pondering the ramifications of Akos's plan. Calia was apparently the only one with immediate concerns.

"What happens when you hit Vibius with a stray cannonball?" Calia asked.

"We'll start small, level the wall surrounding his keep. If he continues to hold out, we will level the town of Ferundun. If he continues to play hardball, we will sail around, knocking down his towns and his ports until he has no choice but to give us Vibius."

"Anson is as likely to kill Vibius out of spite as he is to give him back to us if we go around demolishing his kingdom."

Akos shook his head.

"He knows that if he does that then we will burn down everything he has ever built, and then kill him. There will be nothing he can do to stop us, no matter how many behemoths he has. His ships will not be able to do anything to us without cannons, and I doubt his men have puzzled those out yet."

"He could flee into the interior of Logathia. We might be able to destroy anything along the coast, but if he fortifies the interior there will be nothing we can do to reach him. We haven't got the manpower to take on an army of behemoths."

"If that happens then we will have to find a different way to lure him out. But I don't think he'll run. I think he is too proud. And more importantly, what would it tell his nobles if their god ran from mere mortals? They'd turn on him in an instant. He'll realize that surrendering is the only thing he can do to keep his power."

"You're wagering a lot on this gambit," Calia said. "I don't like this plan."

"Feel free to propose something else. I'm always open to suggestions."

Calia wanted to unveil a master strategy that posed no risk to anyone. Something that would free Vibius, keep the entire crew safe, and guarantee their success. Frustration bubbled in her chest as she realized that she couldn't think of anything. *What good is all my learning if I can't use it to help anyone?* Calia asked herself.

The silence stretched on, proving Akos's point. Despite what Akos was saying, none of them could predict Anson's twisted mind. It was as likely that he would kill Vibius and try to kill them as it was that he would realize that he was beat and surrender.

"If something changes, we'll improvise," Akos said. "But until then, I think this plan gives us the best chance of making sure that everyone comes out of this alive."

"Even Anson?" Calia asked.

"If that's what it takes."

The thought of leaving the god alive put a sour taste in Calia's mouth. This entire ordeal had been his doing, and she had hoped that he would get his comeuppance once they returned. But she was forced to agree with Akos's sentiment. If it meant the safe return of Vibius, she supposed they would have to leave Anson alive at the end of it.

"I've yet to hear anyone ask the most obvious question," Felix said from further down the table.

"Felix, not now," Akos warned.

The executive officer showed no sign that he'd heard his captain. Calia could smell the rum on his breath from here, and he was several chairs away. Felix raised his head from the table and looked at them.

"What if Vibius is already dead?"

Calia felt her mouth fall open in shock at the question. If Vibius was already dead, then everything they had done thus far would be for naught. She'd refused to consider the possibility until now. A look at Akos told her that he had put the idea far from his mind as well. Anger warred with fear and sorrow on his face as he glared at Felix. Calia felt a similar mix of emotions in her own heart, but managed to push it aside.

"Then we destroy everything and kill him," Calia stated.

Felix didn't seem to have heard, resting his head back against the table and snoring gently. How the man had come to such a position of prominence was beyond Calia. Instead of wasting any more focus on the drunkard, she turned back toward the group. They were all nodding their agreement with her words.

"Well, it sounds like we have our plan then," Akos said.

Perhaps it was just her, but Calia thought that the captain sounded a little less sure of himself than usual. She hoped it was her imagination. They would need every ounce of confidence they could muster to carry them through the end of this fight.

CHAPTER 22

Vibius's stomach growled. He tried his best to ignore it. It seemed that controlling the behemoths took as much a physical toll as wayfaring, and it activated the same appetite. It had been a delicate balance trying to stuff as much food as he could into his face during meals while trying not to look as though he was eating any more than usual.

Not that Anson was very perceptive as of late. All his attention was focused on worry over whether Laran would accept his offer of allegiance. It was all he talked about; his entire plan revolved around Laran agreeing to it. Not for the first time, Vibius wondered if it was his only option, or if he was unable to explore others because he had fixated on this one.

Vibius certainly didn't know whether there were any other options. Anson had done a good job of keeping him in the dark as much as possible. Vibius still knew next to nothing about the politics that surrounded the gods and their interactions, and he wished there was some way to remedy that. If he was going to have to take a more active role in this realm to ensure his escape, he was going to need to know what was happening.

As Vibius approached the dining room, he heard what was fast becoming a familiar scenario. Some unfortunate cook or server had made a minor mistake, and Anson was threatening to have their entire family line exterminated for it. Vibius wondered what caused the outburst this time: a misplaced fork or maybe an undercooked steak? Whatever it was, Vibius was sure it wouldn't be enough to make a sane man flinch. But there was no such thing as a forgivable mistake in Anson's eyes.

It was the only thing that made Vibius hesitate to ask him for more information. Given their history, he was sure Anson would assume he was only asking to further some escape plot. Anson wanted Vibius as a tool—useful when needed but, most importantly, quiet when not in use.

Ignoring the clatter of the servants tripping over themselves to leave the room, Vibius strode into the dining room. He made sure to bump into the server, eliciting another outburst from Anson. It wasn't that he had anything against the server in particular, but Vibius decided that the less Anson knew about his senses the better. So Vibius had taken to pretending he was much less aware of his surroundings than he actually was.

Vibius found he could navigate the castle without much problem. He'd always been great at mapping routes in his head and knowing where he was on those routes at any given time. The skill translated remarkably well to navigating the keep without being able to see where he was going. Vibius wondered if his wayfaring abilities had anything to do with that talent, or if it was some other natural gift.

"Sorry I'm late," Vibius said.

"Sit," Anson commanded. "It makes no difference. The morons in the kitchen mangled our meal anyway. I've sent it back to be remade."

Vibius felt his stomach pang in sorrow at that news. He'd been doing his best to ignore it but he was starving. His appetite had always been healthy, but it was even worse when he'd been using his gift to ply the ways. Or, as it turned out, to get into the mind of a behemoth.

He still hadn't managed to get one to do much more than shift its foot or sigh. But he could feel that his breakthrough was close. More than once he'd worried that Anson was going to find out somehow that he was using his gift to try to usurp his control over the behemoths, but nothing had come of it. Vibius knew if he kept at it, he would be able to command the beasts as well as any god.

It reminded him of his early training as a wayfarer. Vibius had known from a young age that he had a talent no one else could see. Utilizing that talent had been a little more difficult than identifying it.

But when it finally came to him, it had been in a flash. Sure, it had taken years and years of practice to master the craft. But actual proficiency happened all at once, as though a lever had been thrown in his mind. Vibius was confident that controlling a behemoth would be much the same.

One thing held Vibius back from pressing as hard as he could to make that connection. So far his focus had been on identifying the creatures around him rather than controlling them. If Vibius focused hard enough, he felt confident he could break through and control one. But he was unsure concerned that would be like lighting a flare and announcing to Anson exactly what he was doing.

That wasn't something that he was prepared to do yet. Vibius knew that if Anson thought that he was trying to usurp his control, he would kill him without a second thought, regardless of his usefulness. Men like Anson did not get to their positions without being cutthroat when it came to competition.

So Vibius would wait for a better opportunity. It wasn't as though he had anything better to do. Only a few more days were left until the end of Laran's deadline. Vibius doubted that anything of note would happen before then. Once they knew whether Laran was going to align himself with them or not, they would be able to move forward with more confidence. One way or another.

"My lord," one of the servants said from the doorway.

"I told you that if any of you came back before the meal is fully prepared," Anson said with barely restrained fury in his voice, "I would allow one of my pets to skin you alive and eat the hide in front of you."

Vibius heard an audible swallow from the doorway. The hairs on the back of his neck started to prick up. Something was wrong. There was no other reason the servant would be risking his life by standing in that doorway.

"I take it that since you are still here something is wrong?" Anson growled.

"My lord, someone is approaching the docks with a flag of truce flying."

A chair scraped the floor as Anson snapped to his feet. Vibius braced himself against the table as it shifted with the suddenness of his motion.

"You're certain?"

"Yes, my lord," the servant stammered. "A rider just came to the gate."

"This cannot be. I have not seen it."

"The ship bears the colors of Lord Laran."

The silence that followed stretched, but Vibius could practically hear Anson thinking. Laran was early, but that was not so out of the ordinary. Sea travel was not an exact science; any number of things could put a vessel well ahead of its schedule.

But Anson hadn't seen it. Vibius wasn't sure exactly what that meant, but he had an idea. Somehow, within hours of Vibius's own ship landing on Logathia, Anson had known they were there, in an uninhabited and unpatrolled part of the island. Whatever power had allowed him to do that should have allowed him to see someone sailing straight up to the de facto capital of his kingdom.

Vibius had long suspected that Anson was losing his grip on his sanity, but it seemed that he was losing command of his powers as well. Were the two connected? The idea left Vibius wondering whether his fear of being sniffed out was unfounded.

A shaky inhale and exhale broke his train of thought as Anson composed himself. The god was clearly trying to collect his thoughts. Vibius could imagine that it was difficult reacting to surprises when you were used to having information well in advance. Though he did have to hide a grin with a sip of wine. Just because he understood the feeling didn't mean he cared that Anson was uncomfortable.

"Prepare a carriage," Anson ordered. "We need to welcome our guest down at the docks."

***

Ferundun was as bustling a port town as Logathia possessed. Still, it had none of the soul of the larger towns Vibius had been in throughout his life. Rather than watch in awe as their deity passed through their streets as commoners in any of the other realms would have done, Vibius could hear parents as they pulled their children away from windows and hushed whispers as groups ducked into shaded alleyways. Fear, not adoration or worship, ruled here.

It amazed Vibius that Anson had managed to twist what he thought of as religion into such a perverse form. Vibius was agnostic at best, but if he could be convinced that the god he paid lip service to was walking down the street, he'd damn sure want to meet them. But the people of Ferundun knew that drawing their god's eye would bring no blessings or benedictions. Death or slavery awaited those who crossed path with this god.

The carriage rumbled along the deserted streets. The cool breeze that filtered through the windows brought the scent of lantern oil being burned, telling him dusk had fallen as they rode toward their destination. Vibius's growling stomach was informing him it was also well past dinnertime. He'd hoped the servants would at least bring out a little something for them to eat during the carriage ride, but no such luck. All thoughts of food had faded from Anson's mind.

Vibius found himself almost wishing Anson would say something as they bumped along in silence. Even thinking that threatened to make Vibius physically recoil, but anything would be better than the heavy silence that sat in the carriage with them. There was no telling what had Anson in such a foul mood. It could be the lack of forewarning, it could be the timing of Laran's arrival, or it could be any number of other things. Fortunately, Vibius didn't share a mind with him enough to know his thoughts.

Slowly, the scent of lantern oil was joined by another, much more familiar smell. The sea was nearby. From the research Calia had shared with him, the exact composition of the water that made up the oceans differed slightly from realm to realm, but for someone as travelled as he, there was no mistaking the scent. To Vibius it had always represented freedom. Once, freedom from his father's oppressive nature, and later, the freedom to make his own decisions as wayfarer of the *Mist Stalker*.

Now it taunted him, tantalizingly close but also impossibly unattainable. Vibius wondered if it would ever be a source of freedom again. Nostalgia, sadness, and anger mixed in his heart and he found that he was soon in as dark a mood as Anson.

Time dragged as the pair brooded, but soon enough they were at the docks. Only here did Vibius finally hear voices as men coordinated the landing of the galleys. It was easier to bring a galley under oar power in to dock than it was a sailing vessel, but it still took skill and direction. Anson had sent word to welcome their guests before they had embarked on their carriage ride. Vibius wondered what sounds they might have emerged to if he hadn't.

The carriage ground to a halt and footmen stepped up to help them out. Vibius took the help gladly. His mobility might be improving, but he still wasn't confident enough to leap down from a carriage. Though the thought of coming so far only to stumble out a carriage and snap his neck brought a wry smile to his lips.

"What are you smiling about?" Anson demanded.

"The smell of the ocean carries a lot of good memories."

"The ocean is a nightmare given form."

We'll just have to agree to disagree there, Vibius thought.

Aloud he said nothing, allowing the silence to stretch as the pair waited for Laran to disembark. Men shouted and replied, tying the ship to her moorings and lowering the gangplank. Eventually Vibius could hear the sound of boots making their way across the docks. It sounded like more than one pair, though he couldn't tell how many men were coming.

He could feel, more than hear, Anson stiffen next to him. Whatever was happening was still surprising to the god. Vibius couldn't decide whether that was a good or a bad thing for him. At one point, he would have thought that any inconvenience to Anson was a boon to him, but now he wasn't so sure. The unease that was radiating off of Anson was infectious, and Vibius was beginning to catch it.

"Lord Laran," Anson said. "We were not expecting you for a week still."

"I thought you might want to know as soon as I'd reached my decision," Laran replied. "If you'd like I can wait a week to deliver my answer."

"That's quite alright."

Vibius could almost hear the gears in Anson's mind turning. He was trying to put on the same show he had since Vibius arrived on Logathia—that of a god in complete control of everything around him. That façade was beginning to slip. Or more accurately, it was beginning to be stripped away.

Akos might have knocked on the gates with his betrayal and the wound he delivered to Anson, but Laran was widening the breach. Something about the way the man spoke made it clear that it was not mere friendly ribbing. And the way he had shown up, without Anson having any forewarning, might as well be a battering ram lined up right outside the gate of the keep.

"I considered your words carefully," Laran said. "And I think you are right. It is about time the gods set aside their petty squabbles and joined forces against the world. Now that they know we are here, it is only a matter of time before more come, and we need to present a united front to prevent them from picking us apart one at a time. If the use of force is necessary to get the others to put aside their grudges, then so be it. But first, I think an application of diplomacy is needed."

"I'm glad you agree," Anson said. "With you by my side I am sure that—"

"Vibius, a word if you please," Laran interjected.

"Ah, I'm sure that whatever you wish to ask me can wait until later," Vibius replied.

"No, I think this is the best time for it."

"Vibius is right. Perhaps we should continue this conversation back at the keep," Anson said, an edge of frustration creeping into his voice.

"Vibius, I want you to join me," Laran stated, ignoring Anson entirely. "After this is all over, I am going to need someone who knows the outside world, and who better than someone who has come from it?"

"Are you not joining us?" Vibius asked.

"What? Of course not."

"You little brat!" Anson roared, taking a step forward. "I should have crushed you when I first heard that you overthrew Cadrao."

"You should have," Laran agreed. "But you didn't. And now there is no point in pretending you even could anymore. Vibius, I will be frank with you. I know what you have been doing."

"Excuse me?"

"You've been training to take control of behemoths."

Silence hung in the air. Vibius's mind raced. He opened his mouth to deny it, but no words came out. It was as though his voice had been stolen. He could feel every eye turning toward him.

"Lies!" Anson spat. "I've felt no such thing."

"You've been blinded by your own arrogance and your madness," Laran stated. "If you'd been paying attention to anything other than your own schemes, you would have felt it too."

"I have no idea—" Vibius managed.

"At dinner, after Anson proposed his plan to me," Laran said. "I felt you command the behemoth in the corner to move. I thought Anson would have you killed on the spot, but he made no mention of it. I pondered that more than anything Anson had proposed. It was what led me to realize that Anson is too far gone to lead any kind of coalition. His madness has consumed him, blinded him to the world around him."

"I have more than enough control to crush you like the bug you are," Anson growled.

"Doubtful. If you could have done so, you would have the moment I began to speak out of turn. You're not sure that you could defeat me. Now, back to what I was saying. Vibius, I am willing to make this a worthwhile endeavor for you as well. I am sure Anson has promised you whatever you wish in exchange for your help, or at least guaranteed not to kill you. And I am sure you have promised to go along with his plan in exchange for your life, looking at every moment for a way to stymie his plans. That is why you have begun to explore your powers to control the behemoths, isn't it? As a way to gain some control back over a life that has come into the grasp of a madman?"

Vibius didn't answer. Some small part of him was sure this was all an elaborate setup for him to admit to his experimentation. The rest of him was interested in whatever it was Laran was offering.

"Obviously you haven't taken the plunge and tried to dominate a behemoth," Laran continued. "As mad as he is, even Anson wouldn't have been able to help but notice that. If you join me, I'll teach you to control that power."

"You'd put me on even footing with yourself?" Vibius asked.

Laran laughed. "Of course not. Being a god has nothing to do with controlling the behemoths; that just helps to hold onto it."

"And in exchange I help you conquer the realms?"

"No. That is Anson's dream, not mine. I just want information. The world is changing. Even if Anson cannot fathom it, the realms outside this one would overwhelm us eventually. If nothing else, they can strike at us and retreat, never having to fully commit, and we would have no way to retaliate beyond our own borders. Conquering the realms would be a fool's errand. What I want to do is unify this realm so that we can at least be seen as equals when the outside comes in. Enough of a threat that it is better to trade and barter with us than try to conquer us. Do you understand?"

"I do."

"What is your answer then?"

Vibius could hear Anson shouting at Laran, but he'd tuned him out. Laran was right; Anson was a madman. There would be no negotiating with him. And after this conversation, Vibius doubted that there would be any going back to the way things were.

A wry grin creased his face as Vibius realized how masterfully Laran had played this conversation. No matter what happened now, the idea that Vibius was working to undermine and usurp him would worm its way into Anson's mind. With him in the state that he was, there was only one outcome to that. Vibius could either agree to help Laran and hope for the best, or remain here and wait for the worst.

"You haven't left me much choice, have you?" Vibius asked.

"One thing I've learned in my many years is that there is no such thing as stacking the cards too much in your favor," Laran replied.

"Well then, I suppose I will help you."

"Traitors!" Anson shouted. Vibius took an involuntary step away, sure that the man would strike him. But no blow came. "I should have killed the lot of you the last time you were here."

"Once again, you should have," Laran said. "Vibius, would you like your first lesson?"

No time like the present, Vibius thought. "Why not?" he said aloud.

"There is a behemoth in the crow's nest of my galley," Laran informed him. "Do what you have been dancing around and take control of it."

"How?"

"Find it in your mind's eye, then push against it."

The words were cryptic, but Vibius felt that he knew what they meant anyway. It wasn't that different from when he'd been a young boy, learning to control his wayfaring powers. You took your mind's eye to the edge of the world, and then you pushed through the veil and you were into the ways. It seemed that the two powers were more interconnected than he could have possibly imagined.

He reached out with his senses. The practice Vibius had been getting had dulled the ache of looking into a realm to a bearable degree, and he hardly had to take a moment to get used to it this time. He searched the area near him and found the behemoth that Laran spoke of. He focused his gift on it the same way he would the edge of the world and pushed.

Chapter 23

The world swirled and shifted, jarring Vibius so hard that it drove him to his knees. Colors flashed and sparked through his mind, right behind where his eyes should be. It was like the worst case of proximity madness he'd ever experienced. For a brief moment, the part of his mind that could still think rationally wondered if he had made a mistake. Was this the process that drove the gods of this realm mad? Vibius tried to scream but could only manage a weak gasp.

Then it was over. Vibius caught himself with his hand right before his face hit the ground. Then he looked up. And he saw.

Vibius reached up to feel his eyes, but they were still nothing but empty sockets behind the fabric he'd tied over them. In the distance, he saw a figure moving, perhaps a hundred feet away. He focused in on it and realized that it was him. The shock of that jarred him. He could see himself, and Anson, and a man that he could only guess was Laran. He could see his own chest heaving as another part of his body panted for air.

"It can be jarring," Laran said.

Vibius heard the words as if Laran had a chorus softly repeating everything he said a moment after he heard it the first time. *I'm hearing from two different sets of ears*, Vibius realized. The words were reaching him and then reaching the behemoth he was dominating.

"You'll get better at managing it over time," Laran continued.

"As if I'd give either of you that time," Anson growled.

With his senses outstretched, Vibius could feel power flickering to life beside him. It was like a fire sputtering to life, though he could see through the behemoth's eyes that the man had simply raised one hand. Power flared from Laran as well. Neither man did more than stare at each other, Vibius lying a few paces away from Anson on the ground. He tried to push himself up but instead felt and saw the behemoth shift its weight instead.

Where Anson's power was flickering and ragged, Laran's felt like a bonfire. It rolled off him, threatening to force his inner eye closed. Vibius forced it open. There was no way he was going to miss what was about to happen.

"Kill them," Anson ordered.

His hand fell at the same time. Vibius refocused his attention on the now-moving figures. A behemoth was rushing straight toward him. He tried to reach out to dominate it, but his mind would not tear away from the one in the mast of the ship. Helpless, he watched as death sped toward him faster than a galloping horse. It reached out with clawed hands for what Vibius was sure would be a death stroke.

Vibius felt parts of his body tense for impact, and parts of the behemoth he was controlling tense as well. The sensation of being in two different bodies at once was making him nauseous. He tried once more to focus on himself, pushing to at least make an attempt to get away from the creature coming to kill him.

Elation ran through Vibius as he managed to push his arms and legs out under him and shove himself a half step back, away from the creature. It was too little to be of any use, but at least if he met any gods on the other side he could let them know he tried. He continued trying as he watched the creature prepare to disembowel him.

Instead, the behemoth scooped him up and turned. Rather than tearing his limbs off, it cradled him as one would a child. Vibius watched himself from a hundred feet away as he pushed weakly against the creature's chest and felt the steel cords of muscle against his palm a short distance from his mind. The sensation was too much. Vibius watched himself puke against the behemoth's chest.

The behemoth paid no attention to his feeble attempts at escape, and it didn't seem to notice the vomit. Instead, it turned its back to the city of Ferundun. Vibius watched as crossbow bolts buried themselves in its back, meant for him, and then it began to lope back to Laran.

Vibius let out a sigh of relief from both his own chest and the behemoth's as he realized this one was Laran's. The one chasing it down from behind was definitely not though, and neither were the dozens of soldiers charging toward the younger god's position. Just behind him, or maybe behind the behemoth he was controlling, Vibius could see more figures moving. His head swam as he tried to understand where everything was in relationship to him.

Perhaps he was coming at it the wrong way. Vibius focused on figuring out where things were in relation to his behemoth. Things focused in a little sharper and the world stopped spinning quite so fast. It wasn't perfect, but it helped him understand what was going on and calmed his stomach some.

There were a half dozen behemoths and five times as many men moving along the deck of Laran's ship. There was an equal force moving in from Anson's side. The behemoth carrying his body was trying to make its way back to the galley from the docks, but there was an enemy behemoth breathing down its back.

Just before Anson's creature could reach them, another behemoth flung itself from the deck of the galley. The behemoths met in a crash of muscle and fury as Laran's behemoth tackled its foe to the ground and started tearing at it with claws like razors. Vibius flinched. He'd seen what a behemoth could do to a man when unleashed, but this was something else. The two ripped and tore at each other with no regard for their own safety or health. The only thing that mattered was killing the other creature. Being able to walk away from the fight seemed to be the furthest concern from either of the creature's minds.

Laran's behemoth had the upper hand though. Anson's creature ripped and tore at anything it could reach, sinking its teeth deep into the shoulder of its foe. Blood sprayed from the wounds, but it wasn't enough. Like a boxer in the clinch, Laran's behemoth kept the other creature's claws from reaching anything vital while it had free rein to tear at its guts. Hide and muscle alike parted before its claws, spilling guts and organs out onto the stone of the dock. Anson's behemoth continued to struggle, but it was futile. Each motion became weaker until finally it was doing nothing more than scrabbling against its killer. Laran's beast wrenched to the side and tossed it to the cobblestone, looking about for its next foe.

The other behemoths had crashed together, jockeying for position in between Laran and Anson. These fights were a little more cautious, like wrestlers sizing each other up before moving in for a takedown. Soldiers from either side, too scared to get in the middle of the behemoth fight, were instead peppering their opponents with crossbows. Mostly they fired at each other, but from time to time one would take aim at the opposing god. There always seemed to be a behemoth in position to swat the bolt down or absorb it for their master though, and neither man broke eye contact as the battle raged around them.

Vibius felt the behemoth carrying him pull itself over the railing of the ship. It dumped him unceremoniously to the deck before turning and launching itself into back into the fray. Men moved to him, helping him to his feet and then dragging him away from the railing. They must have been ordered to keep him out of harm's way. Vibius realized there was no real point in him being in danger; he could still see the fight no matter where he was. So he allowed them to drag him away.

Once his body was safely stored in the oar deck of the galley, the soldiers returned to their battle. Vibius watched them emerge from the hold and resume their place at the railing. He turned his behemoth's attention back to the battle.

It seemed to be evenly matched for the moment. But Vibius could see more and more behemoths emerging from the streets of Ferundun by the moment. Before long, Laran would be overwhelmed by sheer numbers. Vibius wondered how he could stand there so nonchalantly while the battle lines were being pushed toward him.

Soldiers began to pour out as well, enough that they began to feel bravery in their numbers. Groups began to approach the behemoths, sliding in to strike when one was pinned by a friendly behemoth, or when its back was turned toward them. The minor wounds they were able to inflict with their swords were little compared to the massive injuries they were taking from the other behemoths, but over time they would add up. Vibius wondered when Laran would begin his retreat, or if this alliance was going to be a short-lived one.

Instead of backing off toward the boat, Laran strode forward into the fury of combat. His behemoths cleared the way, allowing him to walk unscathed through the maelstrom of clashing bodies. Anson's face twisted into one of pure hatred and rage, and Vibius could feel the energy pouring off him as he tried to match Laran. Vibius began to understand the plan as he watched Anson's behemoths freeze and begin to turn on their former allies.

Whatever this magic was that allowed men to control behemoths, it seemed to be tied to the willpower and the mental abilities of the user. Anson, in his maddened and weakened state, was faltering. That was allowing Laran to overwhelm his control and take his behemoths from him. With the amount of power Vibius could feel pouring from Laran, he was beginning to suspect the entire battle had been little more than bait. He was trying to draw as many of Anson's behemoths out into the open as he could so he could turn them into his own.

Now the battle was beginning to turn against Anson. Fear joined the other emotions on his face, and he began to back away. He was still powerful enough to retain control of the behemoths nearest to him, but the rest were beginning to turn. As Laran closed to within a few yards of Anson, the elder god broke and ran.

Laran stopped in his tracks as his foe turned and scrambled back toward the horses. Vibius watched as Anson dragged a man off his horse and swung up into the saddle in his place. Behemoths closed the street as he galloped away, preventing Laran's forces from following. It also had the effect of trapping many of Anson's human forces on the docks with Laran's behemoths.

The smart ones threw down their weapons and fled into the alleys and streets. Some tried to make a final stand, forming tight knots of men on the docks. Vibius could feel himself growing ill again as the behemoths rolled through these knots and left little more than gory chunks of flesh and armor behind them. Laran presided over the massacre, watching as his behemoths mopped up any resistance before turning back to the boats.

Vibius was somewhat surprised when none of the behemoths took off after the fleeing Anson. He'd half expected Laran to pursue him all the way to the keep if that's what it took. But it seemed the young god was content with allowing his foe to flee. The man took stock of his victory, and then motioned for his men to board the ship.

Now that the battle was over, Vibius closed his wayfarer's sight. Instantly the world went dark once more, and his consciousness flooded back. He no longer felt torn between two different bodies. Relief mingled with despair in his heart as he felt the world around him solely through his own senses once again. Relief because he once again had full control of his mind and faculties, and despair because his sight was once again gone.

Still, now that he knew how, Vibius could regain his sight any time he wished. The temptation to do so now was hard to resist. His roiling stomach and aching head made it a little easier. He didn't know if a god could sustain that kind of a consciousness split indefinitely, or if they dipped in and out as needed. Still, having experienced it for himself, Vibius was grudgingly impressed by some of Anson's and Laran's feats now. He couldn't even walk while controlling a behemoth; Anson had gone toe to toe with Akos in a sword fight while dominating one. It spoke of a level of control that Vibius hoped he would be able to match one day.

In that moment, Vibius realized he had never looked at the hold of the barge and as such, had no idea what was around him. He stumbled until his shins hit a bench, and then he turned to sit down on it. His stomach was still rolling. Controlling the behemoth had taken a lot out of him. Vibius hadn't realized he was exhausted. He put his head in his hands and let out a shaky breath.

"Tiring, isn't it?" Laran asked.

Vibius resisted the urge to snap his head around at the sudden sound. He wasn't sure if it was due to his fatigue or if Laran was just that quiet when he moved, but somehow he hadn't heard a single footfall. Instead, he straightened up, tilting one ear toward the god.

"It doesn't help to be on an empty stomach," Vibius said flatly.

"No, it certainly doesn't. I'll have one of the servants fetch you something to eat."

"First, I have some questions. If you don't mind."

"Of course not."

Vibius considered what to ask. What, exactly, was going to happen to him was the first thing that sprang to mind. Vibius dismissed it as fast as it came. Such a question wouldn't do any good and might make

Laran doubt his conviction. He would have to settle for something else that had been bothering him.

"Why didn't you pursue Anson?" Vibius asked.

"He was broken. There isn't any point in it anymore. He'll be able to command a few behemoths, those nearest to him, but it won't be long until his people realize that he is a god no more and turn on his rule."

"I thought you said that it took more than control of behemoths to be a god?"

"It does. But the most important thing is control. Did Anson seem like he had any control left to you?"

"No, I suppose he didn't. What will be my role here?"

"Straight to the point. I like that. You will be my advisor. I'll want to pick your mind for news of the outside world, and if you prove to be as intelligent as you seem, I might call on you for more than that."

"And how much freedom will I have?"

"Ah yes, Anson did mention that you'd had a stint in his dungeon, didn't he? I assume you would prefer more freedom than that?"

"That would be preferable."

"Well, I hope you will understand if I don't let you run back to your own realm yet. But at some point, I will have prepared as well as can be hoped for. At that point, I will need an ambassador to the other realms. I hope to impress you enough that you would like to take on that role."

"You'd give me that much freedom even though I now know how to control behemoths?"

Laran laughed.

"You know how to see through a behemoth's eyes. I wouldn't consider that control. But we can change that together."

"You'd train me? I have been operating with the understanding that gods do not take apprentices."

"There are many things that gods do not do. I believe that if we are to have any chance at changing this realm enough to survive the coming world, we must change ourselves. You provide a unique opportunity for this realm. For so long, we gods have 'operated with the understanding' that we would never leave this place. You are changing that by your mere presence. I may have been the only god to respond, but you can rest assured that I was not the only one that Anson invited into his scheme."

"What do you think will happen?"

"I'm not sure. I can see a few different outcomes from this. None of them are peaceful. Now is the time to make allies, not enemies."

Vibius couldn't help but feel like that last bit was pointed. A smile quirked the corners of his lips.

"If you don't mind," Vibius said with a sigh, "I'll take that meal now."

"Of course. Once we get underway I'll have the guards settle you in to your cabin, but for now I think it is safer for you here."

Vibius nodded. Laran turned and ascended back up to the deck. Vibius wasn't sure whether he could trust his new host yet. He promised virtually the same things that Anson had, but couched in a better light. Still, it wasn't as if he had a choice. Either way, Vibius would keep his cards close to his chest until Laran revealed exactly what kind of man he was.

The dark thoughts in Vibius's mind were driven away by the smell of roasted beef, and soon enough he was full and snoring on the bench without a care in the world.

CHAPTER 24

True to his word, Laran set sail almost immediately after their battle with Anson. Vibius could sense there was more that he wanted to do on Logathia, but he either didn't have the time or the resources to pursue it. Vibius didn't want to press the issue. Instead he sat at the railing of the galley, leaning on it for support as he reached out with his mind to the behemoth he knew was nearby.

Vibius found that the experience was less jarring the more often he practiced. It had only been a few days, and already he'd managed to advance to the point that he didn't vomit every time. It was something, a clear marker of progress that Vibius could latch onto. He still couldn't do anything so complex as dominate multiple behemoths or command them to fight, but it was still better than nothing.

Sight flooded back as he opened his mind's eye to see through the behemoth's eyes. The deck of the ship was a bustle of activity as men moved back and forth, performing the myriad of tasks that accompanied a ship under sail. Though, the beating of a drum below deck reminded him they were under oar rather than sail.

With that thought, the behemoth's gaze swiveled to Laran, standing at the helm of his galley. Or was it just Vibius's perception that changed focus? A behemoth had eyes all around its head. Vibius had managed to stave off the feeling of being overwhelmed by focusing in one direction at a time, but theoretically there was nothing to say he couldn't look in all directions at once.

Vibius shook his head, making sure it was his and not the behemoth's. He could think about and experiment with that later. For now, he wanted to focus his thoughts back on what was going on around him. Laran seemed to be unaware of his scrutiny, but Vibius had learned that the god had an uncanny knack for knowing when he was being observed. Still, Vibius took a moment to study his new companion. Or was it master? He still wasn't sure of the terminology of their relationship. Laran had made it clear that Vibius was not a servant or a slave, but Anson had started with that tack when they'd first met.

Laran was a few inches shorter than Vibius, which made him taller than most men. He looked to be much younger than Anson, though Vibius supposed that when it came to immortals, that metric was less relevant than others. His head and face were clean-shaven, his skin tone somewhere between Akos's deep tan and Leodysus's deep black.

But Vibius cared much more about his attitude than his looks. It was apparent that his men did not fear him in the same way that Anson's did. They didn't cast their gaze to their feet when he was near, and they didn't shrink under his gaze. Vibius also noted that the same men who had taken up arms and fought against Anson were the same rotating through shifts at the oars. That meant that either Laran employed slave soldiers or that the oarsmen were not slaves. After seeing the vast amount of slave labor that Anson employed, Vibius hoped that it was the latter.

Laran began to move about the deck, forcing Vibius out of his own mind and back to the present. He watched as the man moved about and greeted his men before realizing that Laran was moving toward him. Having an out-of-body perspective was going to take more getting used to than he'd imagined. Vibius couldn't help but grin as he thought about how absurd that thought was.

"I'm glad you are in such high spirits," Laran said.

"Something about being on a ship underway," Vibius responded, "has always soothed my soul."

"That is good to hear. I've felt you practicing quite a bit as well."

Vibius's heart skipped a beat. The words were not spoken with any audible malice, but he still didn't know enough about Laran to gauge whether he was angry or not. It wouldn't be good if he finally got away from Anson only to enrage his new host by doing something that could be construed as threatening or even uncourteous. Something of his concern must have shown, because Laran continued with a laugh.

"I thought I'd come over and encourage it. The more you can do the better. I'm afraid that the more I think about it, the more I am sure that I will need capable allies in the coming days."

"Why is that?" Vibius asked.

"Did you know that I am the youngest god in the realm?"

Vibius frowned. He wasn't sure if Laran was driving at something or if he had entirely ignored his question. He decided to give him the benefit of the doubt and see where this line of conversation went.

"I did not."

"It's all relative of course, but most of the present gods are well over a millennium old. I am a mere three hundred years."

"That's all?" Vibius asked dryly.

Laran laughed. "I understand how odd that must be to hear. But still, I am seen by the other gods as something of an upstart. A renegade of sorts."

"Why is that?"

"Because I am. I do not hold their values. I was not born into royalty. I am not so old as to forget the atrocities of my predecessor. I took power because the man who held it before me was a monster, and I was the only one who could stop him."

"An admirable cause. But I do not understand how that makes you any enemies."

"Since the first gods rose to immortality and the first of us learned how to dominate the behemoths, power in this realm has been determined by fear. The others wield fear as a weapon, enslaving those who would stand before them and making the others so scared of being subjected to the same fate that they will do anything to avoid it. I can only speculate, of course, but I do not imagine that the other realms have followed a similar development."

"There are still places where slavery is an institution." Vibius nodded. "But for the most part, it has died a well-deserved death."

"I'd like to ensure it meets the same fate in this realm as well. I've seen the horrors and cruelties it enforces firsthand, and I have no desire to rule over an empire of chains."

"But you do desire to rule?"

Laran grinned and tilted his head to acknowledge the point.

"A man is allowed some ambition."

Vibius wished he could look the man in the eyes, face to face, and judge his character that way. Laran was saying what Vibius wanted to hear, but what if he knew that? This could all be an act meant to put him off his guard to ensure that he did Laran's bidding when the time came. Vibius wanted to believe him, but it was for that very reason that he needed to keep a healthy level of skepticism.

"And when you've achieved that ambition and become the sole ruler of this realm? What then?"

"I supposed I will do what any other ruler does." Laran shrugged. "Attempt to grow the prosperity of my kingdom."

"Anson said much the same thing. His plan also required the complete subjugation of all other kingdoms and realms."

"I worried that Anson's influence might have poisoned your view of the rest of the realm. But I assure you that you will see my kingdom is not like Logathia."

"I hope that I do."

"Until then, feel free to continue practicing your new skills. I hope that you are as quick a study as you seem."

Laran nodded and moved away without another word. Vibius watched until he had resumed his place near the helm, and then let his control of the behemoth slip away. His sight blinked away and he was left with his own thoughts.

Vibius desperately wanted what Laran said to be true. He wanted Laran to be a good man, to have the well-being of his people at the top of his list of priorities. Nothing he had done to this point had indicated otherwise. Perhaps it was paranoia. Still, that paranoia had been hard earned.

Vibius sighed. There was nothing he could do to affect it at this point, one way or another. He would have to wait and see what Laran had in mind. With any luck, they would arrive in his kingdom to a cheering crowd that would parade him back to his keep, where there would be hundreds ready to testify to his goodwill. That might put Vibius's mind at ease.

Short of that, it would be difficult. If he'd abolished slavery in his own kingdom, as he claimed, Laran would have a much better leg to stand on than any of the other gods Vibius had heard of. There was more than one kind of slavery, though, and Vibius was all too aware that a man didn't need to wear chains to be controlled by another.

Instead of worrying about things he couldn't control, Vibius decided to enjoy the day. The spray of the sea on his face was a welcome distraction, and the heat of the sun beating down was like an old friend. It wasn't until now that he realized how much he loved being on the deck of a ship. Or perhaps it was the freedom he felt when he was at sea. Either way, he'd been deprived of it for far too long.

Chapter 25

The art of wayfaring was nowhere near a precise science. Entries and exits were always a little random, especially when the wayfarer performing them was high by necessity. Still, Vibia assured them she'd gotten as close to their original entry point as she could.

Calia stood by the bow railing, holding tight as the now-familiar waves of nausea rolled through her. It was mid-sunset when they transitioned into the void, or perhaps it was sunrise. There was no way to tell for sure until they'd had time to observe it, but if they'd come in anywhere near the point they'd aimed for, it would be sundown.

That would be good. The last time, they'd taken almost two full days to get to Ferundun, but they hadn't gone straight there either. Akos estimated they could make it in about a day and a half, which would put them there midmorning. They could always slow down if they needed to, but Calia got the sense that the captain was hesitant to do so. Akos stated that he believed they'd spent far too long in Tersun for his liking, and they needed to make up time any way they could.

Calia agreed with him. There was no way they could have foreseen anything that had happened from the moment her brother had Akos arrested. Still, they'd taken far more time than she would have liked. There was no telling what Anson had done to Vibius in that time.

So far, Calia had been able to push away the dark thoughts about what might have happened after they'd sailed away and left Vibius with an empty gun to face the wrath of a man who styled himself a god. But the closer they came to Logathia, the more worry began to creep into her heart. No matter what she occupied her mind with, the thoughts were always there. Dark visions sat on the periphery of her mind's eye, waiting for her concentration to lapse so that they could take center stage.

Hopefully she could keep her mind occupied long enough for them to get to Logathia and confront Anson. Then it wouldn't matter what she worried over; they would know one way or another. And they would be well within range to deliver swift justice should it be necessary.

Calia turned her eyes away from the horizon and back to the deck. Sailors went about their business after the successful shift, and Akos was lending an elbow to a visibly swaying Vibia as she made her way down from the helm. Calia was not surprised to see her so shaky. Vibia had been pushing them hard to get to their destination as fast as possible, and she'd barely had any time to rest or recuperate between the long days guiding their ship through the ways.

The wayfarer would get at least a little rest before they had to head back to the mist. Even after they rescued Vibius, they would need to find a place to stop and secure supplies. They were nearing the end of the supplies they'd been able to buy with Lord Galith's line of credit. There would be no way they'd be able to stretch what they had for the journey back to the realm of man. Calia and Akos had discussed making anchor near Sanctuary to hunt and forage for supplies. They agreed that would be their best bet. Calia doubted they would find a friendly port anywhere in the realm that would be generous enough to donate the supplies, or who would accept Macallian credit.

This all assumed, of course, that they defeated Lord Anson. Akos seemed to have no doubts about that, though how much of that was informed confidence and how much of it was his usual stoic outer mask she wasn't sure. They would have the edge in firepower. There was no doubt about that. Calia supposed that all the behemoths in the world wouldn't matter if they couldn't get within grapeshot range of the ship.

That thought reminded her of their short reprieve from Anson in the behemoth graveyard. The image of standing next to a tooth from a fallen behemoth, too wide to wrap her arms around and taller than Leodysus, was forefront among those memories. From the limited reading she'd managed to do, those gargantuan behemoths were a thing of the past, their use outlawed by the Accord of the Gods. Still, the thought nagged at the back of her mind.

There was nothing she could do for now though. A yawn crept past her lips as she straightened from the railing. Calia had been trying her best not to sleep. Her nights had not been restful since they'd entered the ways. But she wanted to be awake and aware when they entered Ferundun. Calia might not be able to help with the fighting, but she was sure she could find a way to be of use.

Calia turned away from the railing and spotted Valesa standing a respectful distance away. She walked back toward the stairs that led below deck and to the cabins, and Valesa fell into step at her elbow. They hadn't spoken much in the last few days. The stress of the journey had dampened Calia's talkative demeanor, and Valesa seemed to have a lot on her mind as well.

That struck Calia as unusual. Valesa was not the type to let much of anything bother her for more than a few moments. If it wasn't a threat or a possible threat, Valesa paid it no mind. To see her so clearly bothered by something was unnerving. Calia wondered if it was the same thing that was bothering her. Something told her it was not.

Something else told her that it was best not to ask right now. Valesa would open up when she was ready otherwise it was best not to push her. Calia had never been in this position with her maidservant before. Normally it was Calia trying to hide something that Valesa figured out on her own. Valesa had always told her everything, or at least Calia thought she had.

Calia was sure it had to do with her fight with Lusalin. She'd already confessed part of what had bothered her about the fight, but Calia was sure there was something more. More than simple confusion over why Akos would endanger himself to help her. It was possible Valesa wasn't even sure what it was yet. It didn't really matter. Calia couldn't force her to speak on it, and it would only lead to resentment if she tried. Valesa would open up to her when the time was right, if that time ever came. For now, the best thing either of them could do was rest.

***

The captain's cabin on the *Pride* was much larger than Akos was used to. Vanocian captains were all nobles, and if he remembered correctly, the minimum rank to be considered for admiral was duke.

Akos had never known a duke that would deny himself comfort. Even in a warship, where space was precious, they had to have more space than they needed.

Akos was thankful for their opulence. It had provided many rich hauls during his privateer career. And the dining table in this cabin was half the size of his entire cabin aboard the *Mist Stalker*. At the moment, Akos had it covered with weapons.

Down to the last dagger, they were borrowed or stolen. The last time that had been the case was right after he'd led a slave revolt aboard a pleasure galley with Vibius and Vibia's help. Since then, he'd always owned his fair share of trophies and captured weapons, but it had never been the entirety of his collection. Akos felt a smile tug at the corners of his mouth as he looked over the spread of weapons. When Vibius saw them coming to his rescue in a stolen ship, armed with stolen weapons, and with half a crew that wasn't theirs, would he laugh or would he wonder what happened?

The only weapons of his collection that Akos missed were the twinned dueling pistols that Vibius had gifted him. The rifling made it take an eternity to load them, but they were accurate and powerful. Akos wondered if he would ever see them again. One was in a lockbox in Geralis prison; the other was in the hands of Anson, and only the gods knew what he'd done with it.

The sword at the top of the table was a loan from Valesa—the blade they'd taken from Lusalin's corpse. Despite her insistence that she wanted nothing to do with the blade, Akos could see the glances she gave it when she was confident no one was watching. There was some connection there. It was something she was trying to deny, but there was no doubt in Akos's mind. Until she worked her way through whatever she needed to in order to come to terms with her duel with Lusalin, Akos could only consider it a loan.

The rest of the weapons were the pick of what they had taken from Garrot's skeleton crew and Felix's personal stash. Akos toyed with a dagger as he looked them over. This one was definitely Felix's. It was a glimmering silver blade with a gilded cross guard and pommel. Felix had always preferred the most dramatic weapon he could find.

It was hard to believe how much had changed since they'd been hired by Calia to take her into the void. The *Mist Stalker*, along with most of his personal possessions, was gone. Akos doubted he would ever see her again, much less be in a position to retake ownership of her. In fact, Akos doubted he would be welcome in Macallia for some time. No doubt Halis had already spun their escape as a kidnapping at the hands of the dread pirate Akos. Even if Calia could clear the water for him to return, what was there to go back to now?

Akos picked up one of the pistols, checking it over for signs of fouling or misuse. He needed to keep his mind here, focused on the present and the future rather than the past. If he allowed himself to begin to think of Anastasia, he would never stop, and his mind would be clouded when it came time for action. That could wait until Vibius was safely in their hands again and they were sailing away from this realm.

Despite himself, Akos found himself wishing he had more time, or more resources, for this rescue attempt. It was a useless thing to wish for. They were set on their course now, and there was nothing more they could count on than what they'd already gathered.

Still, they should be ready for Anson. They didn't have enough men to fight a ground battle against his forces. Even discounting his behemoths, he still had thousands of soldiers to Akos's two hundred some odd sailors. But they shouldn't even have to land to enforce their demands. Anson's keep was a massive target, close enough to the shore that Akos was certain they could pummel it down to the foundation without much difficulty.

There was a glaring gap in the plan that Calia had been quick to point out. If Anson packed up and went inland, where Akos's ship could not reach him, they would have no recourse. They would have to go and search for supplies before they could return and continue to make threats. Akos hoped the threat would be enough to make Anson capitulate, but he wasn't sure.

There were two ways that he could imagine it going. Men like Anson placed the utmost importance on appearances, with good reason. If the people started to believe that he wasn't a god, they would be more likely to rebel and fight back against his orders. Hopefully Anson would realize that Akos didn't need to physically endanger him to break the illusion that he was a god, and that would be enough to get him to hand over Vibius.

Of course, Anson could react the opposite way. In that scenario, Akos imagined that he would refuse, no matter the cost, out of pure spite. That would severely limit their options.

There was only one that he could think of. Just the thought of it was enough to make his skin crawl. But if Anson refused to hand over Vibius, Akos would have to make his underlings and followers fear him more than they did their god. He would raze every building on the coastline, tear apart any village, town, or ship that he came across. It didn't matter how long it took; given enough time, the populace would realize that it was either give Akos what he wanted or keep being shelled every time they approached the coast. Logathia was not a large enough island for a substantial population to live inland for very long, especially not when the majority of their infrastructure was on the coast.

Akos didn't want to do it. Hundreds, maybe thousands of people would die before they found the courage or desperation to turn on their lord. And who knew how many would die in the attempt. Any other man would wonder if one man was worth all that suffering and death.

But not Akos. Vibius had saved him from a life of servitude and slavery. There was no price Akos would be unwilling to pay to insure his freedom and safety. Even if that price included his conscience. Akos would steel his spine and do whatever it took.

Would Calia be able to handle that? Akos wasn't sure. She said she was willing to do whatever it took to free Vibius. It was clear that she loved him. But Akos had been dealing in death his entire life. He'd dispensed enough of it personally, and ordered far more. Akos never enjoyed it, but he'd become inured to it over the years. Calia didn't have the same decade of calluses to deaden the shock of seeing hundreds of dead the way he did.

Not that he would give her a choice. Akos wouldn't even consult her about it. Was that for her sake or for his? It had to be his. He could live with whatever he had to do to free his friend, but he didn't need to put that burden on anyone else. He was the captain, after all. Ultimately, anything that happened to any of his crew was his responsibility. Likewise for anything they did. That weight shouldn't have to rest on any shoulders but his.

Akos sighed, putting the pistol down and stepping away from the table. He'd allowed Remford to raid the cabin's liquor cabinet for his own stores. Akos was beginning to regret that decision. Perhaps it was better there was no alcohol readily available. He wasn't sure it would improve the black mood he found himself in. Instead, Akos decided it was time to try to get some rest. Though some small part of his mind told him he wouldn't be getting much sleep tonight.

CHAPTER 26

Something was wrong. Ferrundun was on fire.

Akos did his best to keep the surprise he felt off his face as the crew cut sails. They were drifting into the bay as the sun rose, their way lit by the blazing beacon that had been Anson's main port. Now that they were close enough for him to pick out the details, Akos could see that only portions of the city were on fire.

The fires were spread too far apart to be accidental. If there had been one fire, or if the different fires looked as though they had originated from the same place, Akos could understand. Cities were densely packed, and a dry season could turn them into a tinderbox. But these fires were in opposite parts of the city, with no connecting trail of destruction. That left only the idea that someone was deliberately setting fires throughout Ferrundun. And no matter how he tried to wrap his mind around it, Akos couldn't understand why.

That was a secondary concern at the moment. Dawn revealed half a dozen galleys anchored at their wharfs, helpfully silhouetted against the flames behind them. Crews were already pouring over them, trying to get them untied and out into the water where they would be safe from the encroaching fires. The glint of armor told him these were Anson's soldiers. If they managed to get out into the bay, they would have the advantage of maneuverability on him. Akos had to rely on the wind to take him where he needed to go; those galleys could row circles around him in the narrow confines of the bay.

It was time to see what the *Pride* had in her.

"Run out the guns," Akos ordered.

The call was taken up by Felix, who relayed it down to the gunnery deck. Akos directed the helmsman to bring their firepower to bear.

Soon enough they were aligned with their broadside to the port. Akos watched the men on the galley mill about, trying to get them untied and underway, with a trained eye. They must have noticed the *Pride* by now, but there was no indication they were letting it change their reaction. Not that their captains had much choice. They could either stay in port with the fires turning their way, or they could come out to face this strange new craft.

"The guns are ready, Captain," Felix said.

Akos hesitated for half a moment. Something had the hairs of his neck standing on end, but he couldn't decide what. It didn't matter. They needed to show their force. They needed to prove to Anson, and his followers, that the firepower they could bring to bear was overwhelming.

"Fire."

Within a moment, the thunderous roar of half a hundred guns ripped the air. Even Akos flinched from their report. The air between them and the dock was choked with billowing grey smoke, the familiar taste of spent powder hanging in the air for a moment before being whisked away on the morning breeze. Akos looked to see whether their volley had found home.

Within a moment he was rewarded. Wood splintered and exploded from the impact of steel shot. Men were tossed about, their faint screams carrying across the water. One of the galleys split in two, the ends flipping up into the air before beginning their slow descent into the bay. Another was blasted apart entirely, shots stitching down her side until there didn't seem to be two planks held together.

Two of the ships managed to run out their oars, but it was for naught. Akos could already see that they were dead. Anything they did now was a death throe, the sign of a beast that didn't know it was dead yet. *A mortally injured beast can be lethal to an unwary hunter*, Akos reminded himself.

"Give them another volley," Akos said.

The order was relayed. Within a minute the guns were firing again, though sporadically. Akos reminded himself that his men were privateers and pirates, not used to giving coordinated broadsides. To a privateer, a sunk vessel was wasted profit. Once they had more powder to spare and more time on their hands, Akos would have to drill his gunnery crews to correct that.

Still, the cannons did their deadly work. It only took a dozen more shots before the two remaining galleys were drifting wrecks. Akos could see men ditching their armor and diving into the bay, more willing to brave the deep water than the cannon fire. Now that they were taken care of, he turned his attention to the port itself.

"Make ready the longboats," Akos ordered.

The crew leapt into action once again, this time preparing the skiffs that would carry them to shore. The crews that would be going ashore with him were readying their weapons. Akos saw Leo counting the half dozen long knives he had along his belt, making sure they were all there. Unconsciously, his own hands went to his belt. He had a brace of pistols stuck through the back, as well as his borrowed sword riding his hip.

Akos resisted the urge to tap his foot or his fingers while he waited. The men needed to see an air of calm detachment. It wouldn't do for them to see that he was as nervous as the rest of them. Perhaps more so. The men were so assured of their superiority that Akos was sure they thought they could defeat an entire army alone. And they might have done a fair job of it if they had the proper positioning and the army was composed solely of human soldiers.

But that would not be the case. Akos knew there were behemoths in Ferrundun. Half of his crew had seen them before and would be as ready as any man could be to face them. The other half were fresh recruits from the ranks of Felix's men. Over the course of the trip, Akos found that Felix's men laughed off the descriptions of the behemoths as embellishments and tall tales. All Akos could do at this point was hope they did not break and run the moment one of the beasts descended on them. Coordination was the only hope they would have against the creatures.

The longboats were ready. The men lowered them into the water, then began clambering over the side and down onto them. Akos waited with as much patience as he could muster until they were all loaded before proceeding to the railing. Calia was waiting for him at the rails. For a moment, she looked as though she was going to demand to come along. Akos hoped she wouldn't. They'd already had that fight more than once. Akos would not rescue his best friend just to tell him that his love had been eaten by a behemoth halfway through.

Thankfully, she didn't try.

"Good luck, Captain," Calia said instead. "Do try to hurry."

"I'll do my best," Akos replied.

Then he was up and over the rails. He dropped down the rope ladder with the ease of long practice. When his feet hit the bottom of the longboat, he turned to the men waiting there. Their oars were poised and ready, waiting only for his order. Akos had boarded the lead skiff, so they would be the first to the docks. The men were silent, with none of the usual boisterousness that Akos always associated with the men who plied their trade.

"What are we waiting for, lads?" Akos asked. "An invitation?"

With that, the oars shoved hard against the side of the *Pride* and they were off. Akos settled into a seat, facing forward so he could see the city as they approached. Once they arrived, they would have to find someone who could summon Anson or at least deliver their demands to him. Akos wondered how long that would take in the chaos caused by the fires. Hopefully the word of what had happened to the galleys trying to escape the port had already spread and someone would be waiting for them.

To keep from fidgeting, Akos ran a final check over the bag he was carrying. It held a half dozen different colored signal flares that he could use to let the *Pride* know what was happening without having to send a boat back. White to wait, blue to dock, and red to fire. The gunners aboard the *Pride* knew their target, and Akos was confident that Felix would already be guiding her to a position where he could drop anchor and fire upon the keep if the order came.

Slowly but surely, the docks drew near. Rather than the ring of soldiers Akos was sure they would be met by, the only onlookers were loose knots of people. Few of them appeared to be soldiers. Most of them looked as though they were trying to get away from the fires. All of their eyes were fixed on the longboats as they approached.

As soon as he could, Akos rose and scrambled from the longboat and onto the docks. He was careful to keep his hands away from his weapons. This wasn't an assault, not yet at least, and he wanted to give the impression that they were there to talk. As he made his way down the long wharfs toward the shore, he looked for anyone with any kind of authority. None presented themselves. The hairs on his neck were still standing straight up. None of this felt right. Still, Akos kept his confident demeanor as his feet hit solid cobblestone.

"Who here can speak for Anson?" Akos shouted at the various crowds that had gathered.

At the mention of his name, the people quieted. No one stepped forward. Their eyes were wide, and Akos was beginning to wonder if he had taken the wrong tack. There was nothing for it now but to keep going, so he took another few steps and repeated his question. Still no one replied. Akos was getting angry now. He knew they understood him. Why were they holding their tongues?

"Who is the ranking officer here?" Akos asked instead.

Still no one spoke, backing away from Akos as his crew formed up behind him. Akos motioned for them to hold their place and stepped forward. The nearest knot of people shuffled away from him warily. Akos remembered that the people of Ferrundun were skittish, but he hadn't thought it was this bad. An alarm was ringing in the back of his mind, but he wasn't sure what it was trying to alert him to.

Then the screaming started.

A few dozen people burst from one of the side street leading down to the docks, scrambling as fast as they could. First among them were women and children, sprinting as fast as they could manage along the dock. After them came soldiers, equally distraught but still trying to keep themselves between the civilians and whatever was coming from behind them.

The screams were taken up by the people around them, and for the first time, Akos realized how much of the crowd was made up of women and children—well over half. They rushed past, trying to get as far away from the new arrivals as they could. *No*, Akos realized, *they are trying to get away from whatever is following them*. Akos could feel his men tensing up behind him, readying for anything. Akos's own hands went to the brace of pistols behind his back, not drawing yet, but ready all the same.

One of the guards turned to face the pursuer, only to be knocked from his feet and thrown several yards away. Akos watched him hit the cobblestone and rolll the front of his steel cuirass crumbled in. The alarm bells in his mind hit their crescendo and his pistols came out immediately. His gaze darted back and forth, scanning for the behemoth he knew had to be there.

Even when it finally bounded into view, its strange mottled-grey skin helped it blend in with the city behind it. Akos had a hard time tracking its movements as it loped out onto the docks. It had a strange gait, using its knuckles to propel itself along in bounds. It was on the soldier in a moment, punching its claws down through the steel that covered his back while its massive jaws silenced his weak screams forever.

"Muskets to the front!" Akos shouted.

Two more behemoths roared as they exited the side street. Akos saw his men hesitate at the sound of it. It shook the air around him, reverberating through his chest. Akos's legs threatened to turn to jelly beneath him, but he forced his stance and voice to stay steady.

"At the ready, lads," Akos ordered.

The creatures began to move down the docks. The first was distracted with its meal, but the other two were still on the hunt. One loped after the crowds trying their best to get away, but the other began to stalk toward them. Within a moment, it had covered half the distance between them, charging with another roar.

"Fire!" Akos shouted.

He took sight along the barrel of his own pistol, tracking the behemoth as quickly as he could. It moved far faster than any other target he'd ever taken aim at. Muskets cracked, their report pitiful compared to the savage roar the beast let loose when several of the balls found home in its flesh.

Miraculously, it staggered. Akos added his own shot to the bunch and was rewarded with a small plume of blood. For a brief moment, hope rushed through him. Perhaps the beasts were not so tough as they seemed. It only made sense. He'd been to their graveyard, after all, and seen firsthand that they were mortal beings. Flesh and blood, the same as any other opponent.

Then the creature leapt once more and it was among his men.

Men screamed as it milled about. Any sense of hope Akos had begun to foster was torn away in an instant. There was no form to its strikes, just a storm of claws and teeth that dashed through cloth and flesh alike. By the time he turned to bring his second pistol to bear, it had taken the leg clean off one man and thrown another one ten yards away, a bloody cavern where his chest had been.

Men slashed and hacked, but if the behemoth cared anything for the shallow cuts they left behind, it did not show. An axe buried itself up to the eye in the beast's triceps, and the axman was rewarded with a backhand blow that tore out his throat. While it was distracted, another man lunged forward and stuck his sword into its chest. Before he could withdraw, the creature had clamped a claw around his wrist and pulled him into those massive fangs.

Akos tried to line up his shot, but it was weaving a path of carnage through his men. He couldn't pull the trigger without fear of hitting one of his own men. Even if he hit his shot, he didn't know that it would stop the juggernaut plowing through their ranks. Akos cursed as he holstered his pistols and drew his blade, trying to maneuver close enough to strike without being swatted away.

Then a massive form met the creature, and for the first time, Akos saw it slow. Leodysus held a massive cutlass in one hand and a boarding axe in the other, using them to swat away the behemoth's claws whenever it tried to disembowel him. The fight was purely defensive, perfectly timed slashes and chops that deflected the behemoth's claws at the last moment. The behemoth roared again, shrinking back as its paws were turned into mangled masses of flesh and bone.

Still, it persisted. Leodysus advanced, meeting strength with strength. But it couldn't last. The orc blood that ran through Akos's first mate gave him superhuman strength, but the behemoth had decided it had enough. It rose up to its full height, a head and shoulders taller than Leo, and then dropped back down to charge.

Before his mind could stop him, Akos was charging after it. He didn't know what he expected to do once he got there, but he could try to get in a few lucky strikes while Leo distracted it.

The creature crashed into Leo like a cannon shot. Leo chopped at its head with his axe, keeping his cutlass free to fend off any last second blows from the claws. But it was no longer trying to use any sort of finesse. At the last moment, it dropped its head to tackle Leo, letting the axe sink harmlessly into the meat of its shoulder. Leo tried to catch the behemoth like a wrestler, but there was no matching it strength for strength. It bowled him over, pinning him beneath its massive weight.

The creature pinned Leodysus down with one mangled paw as the other raised to strike the killing blow. Akos arrived just before it could bring its paw down. He roared as he lunged, putting his entire weight behind the tip of his sword. The eyes on the back of its head must have seen him coming. It lashed backwards at him instead of down. But its balance was off from having to use the bulk of its weight to keep Leo down. Akos had just enough time to duck underneath the claw and ram his sword up to the hilt in its armpit.

He expected the creature to bring down its arm and tear his spine out through his back. When a second passed and his spine was still intact, Akos opened his eyes and glanced about. The rest of the crew had piled onto the creature behind him, and no less than three men were holding the beast's arm away from its body while another pair hacked at the shoulder joint with swords.

Akos wasn't sure whether he'd managed to pierce something vital or if the behemoth realized that it was overwhelmed. Its strength waned, and eventually it ceased fighting back as Akos's men swarmed over it like ants, tearing it limb from limb and hauling it off of Leodysus. Akos wrenched his blade free as his men let out a triumphant roar.

"Are you alright?" Akos asked.

Leodysus tried to prop himself up on his elbows, and then thought better of it and stayed on his back. Akos could see that his breathing was ragged, and there were three uneven holes in his chest. Despite Leo having hacked its claws to shreds, the behemoth had managed to sink them into Leo's chest like daggers. Part of Akos wondered if they had made it past the ribs while the rest of him began to panic.

"I think it broke some ribs," Leo wheezed. "But I think my innards are unpunctured.

"Well, that is the way we prefer them."

"I might not be good for the next fight though, Captain."

Akos shook his head, his panic draining away.

"I'd say you've earned a rest."

"What are the other two doing?"

Terror returned in an instant as Akos turned and cast about to see where the other two behemoths were. One had been enough to almost destroy his crew if it hadn't been for Leo's heroism. If the other two coordinated an attack on them, he didn't think they'd stand a chance.

The one that had bounded after the soldiers and their families had been cornered. Men with spears held it at bay while their families fled. Whenever it moved, a man jabbed it with a spear, keeping it pinned against the building it had its back to. Akos wondered how long it would be before it tried to bull its way through their spear wall the same way it had bulled through Leo's defenses.

The other one watched their group with dull black eyes, gore dripping down its chin. Akos supposed it could be watching both groups; it did have eyes all around the crown of its head.

Strangely enough, it didn't move to help its comrade, or attack them. Instead it picked up what remained of the man it had been feasting on, turned, and loped off further into the city. That shocked Akos. It was as if the behemoth was only worried about its meal, and not defeating the interlopers or what Akos was sure were rebels. That didn't make any sense. Anson controlled the behemoths, and he would have wanted one of the groups killed, or to at least help both creatures escape.

The behemoth had acted more like a predator, deciding that it had enough and unwilling to pick another fight with its stomach full.

"You four." Akos pointed to the nearest of his group. "Get Leo on a longboat and get him back to Krallek. The rest of you, form up. We're going to go help kill that other behemoth and find out what is going on."

Akos waited until the men had managed to drag Leodysus onto a longboat and get underway before he turned back to the dock. Once again he assumed his position at the front of the line and began to lead his crew toward the embattled soldiers. Along the way, Akos cast more than a few glances toward the street the behemoths had emerged from, wondering if more would spill out any moment. The thought crossed his mind that he should have returned to the *Pride* to wait this out, but he ignored it and pressed forward. If something strange was going on here, it was even more reason to push forward and find Vibius.

The women and children had disappeared, looking for a new safe haven amongst the burning rubble of Ferrundun, leaving only the soldiers behind. A few in the back started to talk amongst themselves as they approached, but none of them broke formation around the behemoth. To waver for even a second against such a beast could mean your life and the lives of all the men counting on you to keep your spear steady. Akos could see how a man could feel like he was caught between a hammer and an anvil in that situation. Instead of saying anything, Akos cocked his loaded pistol and walked to the back of the line.

"Hold steady!" Akos ordered.

He tried to put enough authority in his voice that the soldiers would instinctively follow his words without checking to see who they were coming from. Many of them did, though there were a few fearful glances toward him and his men. Akos raised the pistol and took careful aim. His eyes met one of the behemoth's down the barrel of his pistol, and he fired.

Many of the soldiers jumped when the weapon cracked. The one nearest Akos dropped his pike and reeled with his hands on his ears. Akos sometimes forgot that men who hadn't been around firearms their entire lives could have sensitive ears. *Ah well*, Akos thought, *I won't be asking him what's going on.* The rest of the men jumped back as well, taking Akos with them as they scrambled to get away from the dying behemoth.

It was good to know that *all* it took to down a behemoth was a point-blank shot to the eye.

Even with half of its brain splattered on the wall behind it, the behemoth tried to fight. It whirled, trying to swipe left and right at the same time. But its legs were no longer responding, and it flopped over onto the ground. It twitched and spasmed as more blood and grey matter leaked onto the cobblestones.

Akos looked up to see all eyes on him. *You did want to get their attention*, he reminded himself. Despite his confidence, Akos found himself making way to rejoin his own group before turning to speak to any of the soldiers.

"Who is in charge here?" Akos asked, desperately hoping it wasn't the man he'd deafened.

"I am." One of the soldier stepped forward.

He was old, his beard patched through with grey and his nose broken at least a dozen times. Most likely a sergeant, and a veteran one at that. There was no livery to indicate he was an officer, but Akos could see how the men were instinctively taking their cues from him.

"What is happening here?" Akos asked. "Is it a rebellion?"

The bearded man shook his head, and Akos could see weariness in the motion.

"No one knows," the sergeant said. "They say Lord Anson had a fight with another god here at the docks. After that, he locked himself inside his keep and set his behemoths on us."

"Why would he do that?" Akos asked.

"No one knows. We've been too busy fighting off behemoths and trying to keep the town from burning down to ask."

Akos could appreciate that. Still, that didn't bring him any closer to the answers he needed than before. It just confirmed his suspicion that something was going wrong here. Things must have been bad if Anson had set loose his behemoths on his own population. Who could divine the internal reasoning of a man who called himself a god though?

That thought caused Akos's mind to catch up to what the old sergeant had said.

"You said he fought another god?"

"Aye, right here on these docks. The boys who were there are all dead now, but word is that he didn't fare well."

"How many behemoths are there in the city?"

"Not really sure. They haven't been acting right. Only coming out to feed and then disappearing again."

So it wasn't just Akos who had noticed the strange behavior. Whatever was happening, he needed to make a decision fast. The safe play would be to return to the *Pride* and leave for Sanctuary. By the time they refitted and returned, this situation might have resolved itself, and they could make their demands of Anson then.

That would be the safest route. For everyone except Vibius, of course. He was stuck inside a fortress with a man who had turned his beasts on his own people. At least, Akos prayed that he was. The alternative wasn't something he could consider right now. Akos made his decision and turned back to his own men.

"Alright, lads," Akos said. "We're going to Anson's keep. It's several hours' march from here."

Akos looked from man to man, holding eye contact with each for a split second before moving on to the next.

"If any man wants to stay and guard the boats, I won't hold it against them. We all saw what those beasts did, and this town may be crawling with them."

To their credit, none of the men looked away when he met their eyes. Some of them looked as though they regretted ever signing on with him, but no one was examining his boots. Grips tightened on weapons and men swallowed hard, glancing amongst themselves. Akos felt a tap on his shoulder and turned.

"You're gonna take us with you," the sergeant said.

"To the keep?" Akos asked.

The grizzled man nodded. "Aye, and back onto that ship of yours and away from this hellhole."

"I only have room for a few hundred."

That wasn't strictly true. If they packed the ship to the gunwales they could cram over a thousand men on board, and he only had a complement of three hundred and some odd sailors. But to reach Sanctuary, they only had enough rations for about half of a full complement, and Akos wouldn't let his men starve to death on the way.

"That's fine," the sergeant said. "Doubt there's that many left."

Akos shuddered at the thought of a town like Ferrundun reduced to a few hundred breathing souls.

"Gather what you can then, and let's get going."

The man nodded and turned to talk to his men, Akos doing the same. To his surprise, none of the men had returned to the boats. He supposed that he shouldn't be surprised. They had followed him back into hell after all. What was a few miles more?

Akos turned his attention to Anson's keep in the distance. Its peak was visible over the tops of the buildings along the docks. It would be midday by the time they reached it, assuming they didn't have many more run-ins with behemoths. Hopefully, they would keep acting like predators and shy away from prey that looked like it could fight back, but they had already attacked them once. They needed to be prepared for it again.

It didn't matter though. If it were one behemoth or one hundred, Akos wouldn't let anything stop him from reaching his goal. Vibius would be free by the end of the day, no matter what.

CHAPTER 27

Akos wasn't sure whether if it was their numbers that kept the behemoths at bay, or if the creatures were all too full to try to make a meal of them. Whatever the case, they hadn't attacked them between the docks and the gates of Anson's fortress. Akos and his men had spotted a few lurking in the ruins of Ferrundun and watching them as they passed.

Their group was a ragged one. Logathian soldiers mixed with his own crew, all staring outward for threats. They'd even managed to scrounge together enough pikes to make assaulting them a challenging proposition for any behemoth. The soldiers had agreed to come with him in exchange for allowing their women and children to board the *Pride*, and a ticket off this island when their business here was done. It would stretch their supplies thin until they could forage at Sanctuary, but it was a small price to pay for reinforcements.

And now they were standing under the gate to Anson's keep. Their goal was so tantalizingly close that Akos swore he could hear Vibius laughing about his rescue already. Still, they needed to get inside, and there didn't seem to be anyone there willing to let them in.

In fact, there didn't seem to be anyone there at all. Akos and his men hailed up to the gates repeatedly, but no one responded. There was a chance that anyone inside had standing orders not to interact with anyone outside. With the way things were outside of the keep, though, Akos was willing to bet that something far stranger was going on.

"We've not enough gunpowder to blast her open," one of the men said.

"And not enough time to make a battering ram," Akos added. "We'll just have to get the *Pride* to do our heavy lifting."

Akos ordered his men back a safe distance and then readied his flare. He set the flare in the ground and then used one of the flints from his pistols to strike against his dagger and light the fuse. Soon after, a rocket shot into the sky, exploding in a bright red flash that would be visible out on the harbor. Then they waited.

Akos was beginning to wonder if they had seen his flare when they heard it—a faint scream, growing in volume until it was overhead. Cannonballs howled toward their target. Stone was no match for them, exploding away in showers of rock. The gate splintered and crumpled under the weight of fire. The top of the curtain wall began to fall away as the middle and bottom were demolished by cannon fire.

As quickly as it came, the bombardment ended. Akos held his men. They had agreed to three volleys unless the entire wall fell first. And while the first volley had done quite a number on it, the wall still stood. Akos passed the time by observing the gawking faces of the locals as they watched what they must have thought to be an impregnable fortress smashed from miles away.

The second volley came and went, followed by the third. By that point the wall was little more than rubble. Akos wondered if Anson was watching them from his window, staring in the same stark disbelief that covered the faces of his former soldiery. He certainly hoped so. This was the kind of display of power that a man like Anson could understand. Akos had a second red flare, just in case they needed to send another message like the first.

Now, though, it was time to go and see the man. Their group picked their way through the rubble. Akos didn't need any broken legs or twisted ankles slowing their escape down. Fortunately, there were several small paths blown clean through the rubble that they could use. Within moments, they were before the great door to the keep itself. Akos wasn't sure how he planned to get that door open. They hadn't brought much in the way of spare powder, and he wanted to have as much for his muskets as he could spare.

Akos strode up to the massive double doors, looking them up and down. They had brought plenty of boarding axes. If nothing else, he could have his men hack their way in, but that would take all afternoon and he still wanted some light to see by to get home to the *Pride*. In fact, he wouldn't go anywhere if it got too late. Placated or not, he wouldn't put his men in a position where they might have to fight a behemoth in the dark. Even the thought made him shudder.

Unsatisfied with all of the plans he was coming up with, Akos idly placed his hand against the wood of the door. With one part of his mind, he was trying to remember how thick it was, while the other part tried to think of how long it would take to chop through. Something felt off beneath his palm. Akos gave the door an experimental shove, and was surprised when it moved slightly. He snapped his mouth shut before turning to his men.

"Come help me push this open."

It took several men, but they managed to push the door wide open. Akos cautiously entered the dark grand entrance, scanning for any sign of a threat. Nothing leapt out at them immediately, and Akos wished they'd brought torches. There was enough light streaming into the hall to see the massive painting at the other end, but the side corridors and staircases were still shrouded in an impenetrable gloom. The torches and lanterns hanging on sconces on the wall were burned out.

"Go to the outbuildings," Akos ordered. "Groups of five. Do not engage anything, man or behemoth. If you run into something, fire off a shot and return here. Find us some torches or lanterns we can use."

The men ran off to do what they were told, and Akos stood vigil over the great hall while he waited. With every passing second, unease grew in his stomach. As the sun set behind him, more of the room was coming into view. The marble floor had been scratched, deeply, by what he could only assume was behemoth claws. Dark stains covered the walls and floors. Akos couldn't see it clearly from where he stood, but it didn't take a full analysis for him to know it was blood.

There were no bodies though. Sunlight glinted off discarded swords and spears laying scattered around the room. But not a single soul had come to see who was shoving open their doors. The lock beam sat in a rest next to the door, unused.

When the torches arrived, Akos proceeded into the keep with a pistol in front of him. Pikes would be useless inside, so the men armed with them stayed outside to guard the entrance. The men moved through the house, furtively glancing about with every few steps. Akos couldn't blame them. His own eyes darted back and forth, scanning for anything that could even be construed as a threat.

They made their way up the stairs cautiously. Akos hadn't spent as much time in the main keep as the others, but he still remembered his way to the dining room. That was where Anson held court; it was where they would begin their search for the god. If they didn't find him there, Akos wasn't sure where they would look. But they weren't leaving until he got some answers, even if it meant they had to cram their group into the main hall and sleep back-to-back to watch for any threats.

As they reached the higher levels, there were more windows set in the wall. High-set windows cast strange shadows in the midday sun. That combined with the dancing light of the torches cast the place in a hellish light. Akos thought he felt the very ground trembling in pace with his heart, but he dismissed it as his nerves. This place was unsettling him, and he wanted to be away from it as fast as possible. This was not how he had imagined the culmination of their rescue attempt.

After walking for what seemed miles, they finally stood outside of the massive double doors of the dining room. Akos took a deep breath to steel himself for whatever he might find on the other side, then raised a boot. A swift kick swung the doors open. Dust swirled as he rushed in with pistol raised, followed by a half dozen other men.

Nothing he could prepared him for what he saw. Anson sat alone at the head of the long table that dominated the center of the room. All around him were the husks of the strange golden fruit that he ate with every meal, in various states of decomposition. It looked as though they'd interrupted him midmeal; he still had a golden fruit in his mouth.

Akos's eyes were drawn to Anson's hand as it set the fruit down on the platter in front of Anson. Then his eyes traced back up to his face. That was the most shocking part of everything he'd seen so far.

Anson's face was blank. There was no surprise there, no fear, no hatred. The face that had stuck in Akos's mind, one of snarling fury and hatred, was nowhere to be seen. Stubble covered his chin, caked in what Akos could only assume was the juice of the fruit that was all around him. His normally smoothed hair was disheveled and wild.

But it was his eyes that were the most surprising. Despite Akos's disgust for Anson, he had always recognized his intelligence, but now, his eyes might as well have been a doll's eyes. No emotion, no thought, no spark of recognition showed in them.

Despite his growing unease, Akos kept his pistol trained on Anson as he scanned the room. Light flooded in from the massive window at the far end of the room, throwing long shadows toward them. As his men fanned out and lit the place, Akos could tell that they were alone. Not even a single servant to wait upon the god. Akos turned his attention back to Anson, who was watching the intruders with expressionless eyes.

Cold sweat beaded on Akos's neck. Nothing about this was right. Something jostled the table and a single fruit rolled off and fell to the floor with a wet slap that might as well have been a gunshot. Akos's pistol twitched toward the sound, and it took a moment to realize that he had been a twitch away from shooting the mushy core of some Logathian fruit.

"Where is Vibius?" Akos asked.

"Gone, gone, gone." Anson smiled. "Gone like the rest of them. Nothing left. Nothing but eternity."

Akos felt his heart sinking with every beat. He strode over to Anson's side, getting as close as he dared. The man had surprised him with his speed and strength in their swordfight. He could be trying to bait him to get a hold of a weapon, or just a hold of him.

"What are you going on about?" Akos asked.

"Nothing left. No control. I had everything under control, then you showed up."

Akos watched the god as he spoke, looking for any kind of tell that would indicate what was going on behind those blank eyes. There was nothing. None of the vitriol he'd expected behind the words. Just a calm acceptance, a statement of fact. Akos resisted the urge to shudder and continued to press him.

"Where is Vibius? If you give him to me, I'll leave you your life."

That was a lie, but if it led them to his friend he would tell Anson whatever he wanted to hear.

"Would that I could." Anson sighed. "But even I, a god, have no power to bring him back now."

Akos could feel his stomach roiling. His grip began to shake. Darkness was creeping into the edge of his vision, narrowing his world until only two things remained: Anson and his pistol.

"Taken from us, in my own seat of power. Given to a behemoth before my very eyes. By someone I'd trusted, tried to mentor no less."

The strength left Akos's legs, and he barely managed to stay upright. He jammed the barrel of his pistol into Anson's temple, almost knocking him out of his chair.

"Liar!" Akos shouted.

"Would you like to know who did it?" Anson whispered.

"Where is he?"

"In the gut of some behemoth. Actually, by now he's probably worked his way out."

Akos turned away from Anson and took several paces. His hands were shaking and his heart was hammering. Anson had to be lying. Vibius was here, somewhere. He had to be.

But the vision of bloody hallways and scratches in the marble filled Akos's mind. What if one of those smears had been Vibius? Akos had seen what a feeding behemoth could do to a horse, much less a man, and it wouldn't have left much. Suddenly, Akos felt very tired.

"Will you avenge him?" Anson asked.

"Who killed him?" Akos asked.

"Lord Laran. God of Craislund."

"How long ago?"

"A month? Maybe more. Time has ceased to hold any meaning for me."

"Is that why you set your behemoths on your own people?"

"In the attack that took your friend's life, Laran broke my control over the behemoths. I am no longer setting them on anything. They won't attack me, but anyone else is prey. I'll ask you once more. Are you going to avenge him?"

"Aye."

"Good, I—"

Akos didn't let him finish. He dropped his pistol and turned back to Anson. He wrapped his hands around his neck and squeezed. He drove him from his chair and to the floor, straddling his chest and putting all his weight behind it. Anson flopped beneath him, unable or unwilling to find the strength to attempt to fight back. His face slowly turned blue, but the expression in his eyes never changed.

As the life left Anson's eyes, Akos had hoped to find some sort of understanding or remorse there. Something to show that Anson knew he deserved it. Instead, he saw only blank acceptance. As though Anson couldn't care less that his life was being choked from him. Rage built in Akos's chest as the light left Anson's eyes. Soon enough, the life was gone from them entirely.

Akos slowly loosened his grip and stumbled to his feet. His legs were weak, and his vision was swimming. He found where he'd dropped his pistol and picked it back up. For a moment he examined it, considering holstering it. Instead he took a moment's aim and fired. Every man in the room jumped as Anson's skull was splattered across the floor. Akos dropped the pistol into its holster. Even that hadn't made him feel better.

In fact, he didn't feel anything right now other than pure, hot rage. Akos roared and slapped the plate full of fruit off the table. Men scrambled back as Akos picked up the chair he'd dragged Anson out of and threw it at the window behind the table. It shattered, and the chair tumbled along with shards of glass down the tower to the outside. Only after he'd thrown it did he realize that some of his men might still be down there.

Akos didn't have to fight back tears. None were coming. He was numb. He sank down to his haunches, staring at nothing in particular, and then down to his seat. Everything they'd done had been for nothing. They'd come all this way, and Vibius had been killed in the crossfire of two feuding gods. If there were any real gods out there, they hated him. Akos wasn't sure how long he sat there before one of his men snapped him out of his daze.

"Sir!" Gasci shouted in his face.

"What in the hells do you want?" Akos roared back.

Gasci answered by pointing. Akos followed his finger to the window he had knocked out. Akos clenched his fists as the cold numbness was replaced once again with hot rage.

"What does it matter? You think I care about some window?"

"Look out the window, Captain."

Akos glared at the young man as he dragged himself to his feet. He strode over to the glass and looked out. For a moment he wasn't sure what he was supposed to be looking for. To the right was the town of Ferrundun; to the left was the beginning of the mountain range that the keep was backed against. Akos could feel an angry retort forming in his chest, but it died before it ever reached his throat.

Something moved. The ground shook. And then one of the mountains turned its head toward the keep.

It took his mind some time to process what he was looking at. It wasn't a mountain, it was a behemoth. Easily the same height as the curtain wall they'd knocked down, if not taller. Akos recalled the painting in the entrance hall depicting Anson dueling some other god with massive behemoths fighting in the background. Then he remembered the massive skulls, each the size of a longboat, that Calia had found in the behemoth graveyard.

It took another step toward them and the ground trembled. It was some miles away, maybe, and heading toward them at a leisurely pace. Akos heard his men around him whispering and gasping in shock. He wasn't sure how Anson had managed to hide something like this the first time they were here. Considering he thought it was a small mountain the first time he saw it, Akos imagined they probably hid in the mountain range that dominated the center of Logathia when Anson didn't need them.

Akos's idle thoughts were interrupted when the creature's mouth lolled open, letting a tongue the size of a mainsail slip out. The numbness was back, which Akos supposed was a good thing. Otherwise he might be too terrified to act. Instead he turned to his men.

"Get downstairs. We need to get to the *Pride* before that thing does."

CHAPTER 28

Calia drummed her fingers against the railing of the *Pride*. The ground crew was taking too long. Everything had gone wrong from the moment they'd arrived. They hadn't planned for Ferrundun to be on fire. They hadn't planned on being attacked by behemoths on the docks before they could even speak to anyone. They hadn't planned to take on refugees. Calia supposed this was what people meant when they said that no plan ever survived contact with the enemy.

Akos had been gone for far too long. Calia had just finished helping all the refugees settle into the hold when they'd seen the red flare. Felix had gladly ordered the bombardment of the keep. Calia couldn't see from the deck, even with the spyglass that Vibia had lent her, but the man in the crow's nest told them they'd demolished the wall. Then he'd reported as the crew entered the courtyard and then the keep itself.

Now they were waiting for any other news. There had been no flares to let them know it was all clear. Once they'd entered the keep, Calia had expected a short wait before they'd seen the signal to dock. But it had been at least twenty minutes and no signal. The sun crept across the sky. Calia felt her patience wearing thin with each passing minute, and the urge to convince someone to take her ashore to find out what was going on was almost too much to bear.

Whenever Calia felt she might find the courage to do it, the memory of four men hauling Leodysus aboard, bloody and unable to move under his own power, crossed her mind and kept her in place. Valesa would have her restrained before she allowed it anyway. All Calia could do was sit on the deck, drumming her fingers and thinking of dozens of different scenarios in which things could be going wrong.

It was only when she was nearing the edge of her imagination that the man in the crow's nest shouted down to the deck.

"Blue flare!" he called.

Calia sighed with relief. That meant that they would be returning soon. Akos wouldn't risk the *Pride* if he weren't sure things were safe enough for them to dock. Either that or something had gone horribly wrong and they needed a quick exit. Calia was still debating which it might be when the crewman settled her mind for her.

"They're running out of the keep!"

Calia and Valesa exchanged glances. Successful negotiations, at least in Calia's experience, did not end with hasty retreats. Had they walked into an ambush? The people belowdecks had all told her the same thing—that Anson had locked out the world and unleashed his wrath on them following an altercation at the docks. It would stand to reason that even the sight of Akos might be enough to set Anson off considering their past, but Calia didn't know why he'd allow them all the way into his inner sanctuary before he tried to attack them.

There were too many things it could be, and the topman had stopped relaying information as the ship swung around. Calia's fingers drummed against the wood until she was sure she would bore right through, but the railing held up against her assault.

A man caught her eye as he descended the rigging to take care of some duty on deck. Calia stared at the rigging for a moment before glancing down at her own legs. She'd worn trousers today in case she needed to go ashore for any reason. The rigging was knotted and strung up like a ladder, and Calia had climbed ladders before. She'd seen Akos and dozens of men clamber up them as naturally as walking. How hard could it possibly be?

Before the rational part of her mind could provide her with an actual answer, Calia shoved the spyglass in a pocket and started toward the rigging. Valesa was either too confused or too preoccupied with what was going on around them to stop her. Calia made it all the way to the rigging before she heard her maidservant call her name.

Calia was on a timer now. She had to get up the rigging before Valesa tackled her. If she could at least get a few rungs up, it would slow her bodyguard down, maybe long enough for Calia to get a good view of what was going on. She tried to recall what she'd seen the men do when they started up the rigging before.

First, plant a boot on the railing. Calia swung her foot up and planted it right in the middle. Grab the rope and swing out around the edge so that you weren't climbing upside down. Simple.

Calia pushed off and around the rope, and for a moment her opposite leg and half her body were above nothing but open water. She looked down. It was a mistake. Blue so deep it might as well be black frothed against the side of the boat, churning into white wake before being swept along the bow. For the briefest moment, Calia thought she could see eternity in that water. By the time her foot and her other hand were firmly on the rope, her heart was hammering along. Apparently it was trying to make up for the beats it had skipped while she was over the water by thumping triple time.

"What in the hells do you think you're doing?" Valesa shouted at her.

No time for panic now. She needed to get up several feet to see what was going on. Calia pried her white-knuckled fingers away from the rope and grabbed a little further up, lifting an unsteady leg to haul herself upward. Fear of Valesa's chiding warred with fear of falling, and eventually won out. Calia pushed herself to put rung after rung beneath her.

She kept her eyes fixed on the rope in front of her, refusing to look down or out. If she did that, she might not be able to go any further. She was already unsure how she was going to get down, but that was a problem for the future. For now she needed to get to where she could see over the skyline of the city.

"Get down!" Valesa shouted up at her.

"I need to see what's going on," Calia shouted back.

"You'll break your neck!"

"Only if I fall."

Calia glanced down at her maidservant and saw that she had somehow made it twenty feet up into the air. That would be far enough. At least, Calia hoped it would be. She didn't think she could go much further without freezing in place. She hooked one arm through the rope, the way she'd seen many of the topmen do, and turned toward Ferrundun.

As she looked down on the city, all of her fear disappeared. The town sprawled out before her, rising and falling with every swell as the *Pride* barreled forward. A triumphant giggle escaped her throat as Calia realized where she was. She'd scaled the rigging of a warship to get a view of the rescue party that had gone to save her love from the clutches of an evil lord. It could have been the script of one of the romances she'd read. A year ago, she wouldn't have even dreamed of doing something like this.

Once the moment passed, Calia carefully used her free hand to pull the spyglass to her eye. Vibia had told her it was worth a small fortune, and Calia doubted it would still be as valuable if she dropped it three stories onto the deck. Or even worse, straight into the ocean. And it wasn't as if she still had a fortune to replace it with.

It didn't take long for Calia's gaze to sweep over to the keep. It was a great spike in the earth, taller even than the small mountains around it. The bobbing of the ship made her feel a little ill, but she swallowed it down and forced her gaze to remain steady as she followed the spike down to its base. There she could see the rubble of the wall and men clambering over it.

It was too far for Calia to make out any detail, but she could see that they were hurrying. She panned back over the courtyard and saw nothing. Calia frowned. Why were they in such a hurry? There didn't seem to be anything chasing them. She turned her sight back to the men and saw that one of them had stopped on top of the rubble, and was bent over and fiddling with something. Perhaps his foot had gotten stuck and he was trying to get it loose? Calia couldn't tell.

Then there was a bright spark and red trailed off out of her sight-line. Calia blinked. She lowered the glass and saw that a second red flare had been shot. She followed it until it impacted a nearby mountainside. Then the mountain moved, and Calia almost dropped the spyglass along with her jaw. She snapped the glass back up, cursing as she tried to get her bearings again. Then she finally spotted the remnants of the flare sputtering against what she'd thought was a mountain.

It was a behemoth. It had to be. And of all the ones Calia had seen so far, it exemplified the name. It was the largest creature she had ever seen. Certainly large enough to leave behind skeletons of the size that they'd seen in the behemoth graveyard further inland.

And it was walking their way.

Calia panicked as the beast trudged along. Each step was covering massive ground, and it wouldn't be long before it reached the docks. Would the shore crew reach the ship before it did? Would it matter if they did? There was nothing to say that the monster couldn't swim. And they were sailing directly toward it.

The spyglass in Calia's hand swung back toward the group of men running down the road to Ferrundun. Many of them had dropped their weapons, and the Logathians among them were ditching their armor as they ran. One figure trailed behind them, setting flares in the road and lighting them before turning to catch up with the group. Calia wasn't sure, but she thought that it must be Akos, trying to buy them time by distracting the creature.

Before they could get close enough to confirm her suspicions, Ferrundun rose up and cut off her view. They were close to the docks, and Calia could no longer see over the roofs between them. She considered trying to get further up the rigging, but there was a spar not far above her and she didn't want to try to navigate her way around it.

Slowly, Calia made her way down the rigging. Once she had swung back onto the railing, Valesa grabbed her and brought her the rest of the way down to the deck. The maidservant looked as though she was about to scold her charge when she looked her in the eye. Calia didn't know what exactly she saw there, but it was enough to stay whatever she was about to say.

"You're white as a sheet," Valesa said. "What did you see?"

"A behemoth," Calia said. "The size of a mountain. We need to warn the others. Go tell Felix and I'll let the gun crews know to be ready."

Valesa looked hesitant to leave Calia on her own. There was no time for hesitation. They needed to be ready for anything at a moment's notice. Without waiting for Valesa to finish her internal debate, Calia took off to descend to the gun deck. A glance over her shoulder told her that Valesa had obeyed her and had left to find Felix.

Once she was below deck and out of sight, Calia took a moment to compose herself. There would be time to panic once they'd escaped that creature. For now they needed to be able to act, all of them. Calia grabbed the first sailor she could find and began to relay instructions to be ready. Hopefully it would make a difference.

***

Akos cursed the flint, steel, and the fuse of the flare, in that order, as he tried to get the damned thing to light. It took a half dozen strikes before the sparks found home and the fuse sputtered to life. There was no time to wait and see if his aim was true. The behemoth was gaining on them far too quickly for Akos's liking.

The half empty bag of flares smacked against his back as he sprinted to catch up to his crew. His sword threatened to trip him with every step, so he yanked loose the scabbard and carried it instead. The city of Ferrundun was only a few hundred yards away. If they could get there, they had a chance to at least lose the beast in the ruins if they had to. *The ruins that are infested with hungry behemoths beholden to no master*, Akos thought, unbidden.

Akos pushed away that thought as something to worry about *if* they weren't trampled and consumed in the next few minutes. That unbidden thought was followed by another—wondering whether the beast would chew or if it would pop them into its mouth whole and swallow them that way. Akos wasn't sure which option sounded worse, and he didn't intend to find out the hard way.

It wouldn't be difficult to push a little harder, but then he would start to leave behind members of the crew who weren't as physically able. Akos wouldn't leave any more of his men to die on Logathia. A man in front of him stumbled. Akos ran up behind him and hauled him to his feet, setting him back on the path and risking a glance back at their pursuer.

The behemoth was still gaining on them, slowly but surely. Each of its steps seemed to cover a mile. It towered over them, glaring down at them with a half dozen glazed-over eyes. Akos turned back and continued to run, shouting at his men to keep going whenever his breath allowed.

At any moment he expected to see behemoths launching themselves from windows and alleyways as they passed, taking advantage of their now disorganized and unarmed prey. But nothing barred their path as they barreled through the streets toward the docks. Akos thought he saw a behemoth grinning at them out of the window, but it recoiled back inside when the massive behemoth's footstep shook the ground.

Akos ran until the air was fire in his lungs and his feet felt like lead weights. He ran until the ship was in sight, docked at the end of one of the wharfs with as many ladders dropped as would fit in the space. He could see the crewmen of his ship gawking at the beast behind them and encouraging their fellows to run faster.

Cobblestone turned to wood beneath their feet as the shore team sprinted toward the *Pride*. Akos's heart sank as he watched the men stack up at the ladders. A glance back confirmed his suspicions. There were too many of them on the docks. Even if they scaled the ladders faster than they ever had in their lives, there were still too many of them to get up the ladders before the creature caught up to them. Akos hesitated at the entrance to the wharf, alternating between watching his crew clamber up the side of the *Pride* and the behemoth knock down small buildings as it pursued them through the city.

Akos would not leave any more of his men to die on Logathia.

Before he had time to think, Akos was running back to the center of the docks. He could hear men behind him shouting questions and curses at him, but he ignored them. He cast about, looking for anything that could be used to anchor one more flare. Every second he slowed the behemoth down was another second his crew could use to escape. Unfortunately, it looked as though the docks had been stripped of anything useable.

Except for bodies. Several of the Logathians had been killed by the assaulting behemoths earlier, and unlike the crew of the *Pride*, no one had bothered to recover their bodies. Akos ran over to them and found two that looked as though they were intact enough to hold up a flare.

"Sorry about this," Akos muttered as he hauled on the smaller corpse.

Within moments, he'd stacked them well enough to wedge the flare in at the angle he wanted. Now all there was to do was wait for the creature to show its head over the rooftops to strike the fuse. Despite his heart hammering in his chest from all the running, Akos felt surprisingly calm.

Footsteps shook the ground like a slow drumbeat, marking the behemoth's approach as he waited. Akos scanned the roofline, hands ready to make a quick adjustment if it came in at a different angle. Stinging sweat dripped into his eyes, and he scrubbed at them with his sleeve.

The beast appeared.

Akos jerked the flare to face the direction it was coming from, making sure the corpses wouldn't suddenly shift and throw off his aim. Then he took up the flint and steel.

Sparks showered the fuse. A booming footstep brought the creature out onto the docks. A second strike, a second shower of sparks. Akos refused to look up. If he looked at that massive creature, he would freeze, and he would fail. A third strike. The end of the fuse lit for a brief moment, but the wind snuffed the flame before it could take.

Akos struck once more. This time the fuse took, burning toward the distraction that he would need to get to the *Pride*. Instead of taking off immediately, Akos finally looked up to make sure he had his aim right.

The creature was directly in front of him, the distance between them the same as its massive arm span. It either hadn't noticed him yet, or it had deemed him unworthy of its attention. Akos adjusted the flare, aware that as soon as it went off, there would be no more ignoring him. There was still time; he could cut the fuse and let it sputter out.

Akos glanced at the *Pride*. The last of his men were clambering over the railing. The creature would be able to grab them before they had the chance to cast off. Akos stepped away from the flare, readying himself to run as soon as it went off.

The flare roared as it launched, almost straight up, into the underside of the behemoth's chin. The creature jerked backward, stumbling. The ground shook so hard that Akos was almost jarred from his feet.

His sprint was turned into a barely controlled sprawl. Akos somehow managed to keep his feet. He aimed himself toward the wharf holding the *Pride*.

"Cast off!" Akos shouted.

The men leapt to obey his orders, cutting away the ropes mooring them to the dock. They began to unfurl sails, preparing to leave as wood thumped beneath his feet. Men were shouting encouragements, waving him along as he moved toward them.

Their encouragement turned to warning, and Akos glanced behind him. The behemoth was swiping its massive paw, and it was aiming right for him. Its arm was more than long enough to sweep the wharf, and Akos wouldn't be able to outrun it. It swept toward him like a wall of death. With no other options, Akos dove into the black water of the bay.

The cool water enveloped him. Akos watched the shadow pass overhead as he dove deep. The creature's arm tried to dip into the water with him, but he'd timed it well enough to avoid it. Still, the wake of its massive arm plunging into the water swept him aside. He hit something, hard, and he realized it was the wreckage of one of the ships they'd sunk earlier. The blow drove the air from his lungs and put stars behind his eyes.

Only years of swimming experience kept him from sucking in water. Instead, Akos turned toward the surface and kicked hard. He was sure his lungs would burst before he reached it, the light dancing just out of reach. Akos managed to break the surface and suck down another lungful of fire. Despite the burn, Akos thought that air was the sweetest thing he'd ever tasted. He cast about to get his bearings and then began to kick toward the *Pride*.

The sun disappeared around him, and Akos turned on his back to see the behemoth taking another swing at him. This time it was straight down. In the water he was an easy target. Akos couldn't move fast enough to get out of the way, and he couldn't dive deeper than the behemoth's arm could reach. Akos stopped kicking and waited for death to take him. At least the rest of his crew would get away. Hopefully he would get to see Vibius on the other side so that he could apologize.

Before he could start composing his apology, Akos heard the crack of a cannon. And then another. Akos watched as cannonballs crashed into the chest of the behemoth. The blows staggered it, tearing massive chunks of flesh out of it. The behemoth's arm retracted, covering its face as if to stop the balls from taking its eyes. It covered its chest with its other arm. The *Pride* continued to pour fire into the beast as fast as it could.

Akos watched as dozens of cannonballs blasted into the monster. It staggered, taking several involuntary steps away from the water. The force of the shot was enough to drive it backward, but the wounds didn't appear deep enough to cause mortal damage. Akos felt his heart sink as it dawned on him how tough these massive behemoths were. Valesa's voice broke him from his reverie.

"Swim, jackass!"

Akos turned around and started to kick toward the *Pride*. He wasn't that far away. But the men had finished tying down the sails, and the *Pride* was beginning to pull away from the dock. Akos didn't think he could outswim a ship under sail.

A rope sailed toward him, landing a few yards away. Akos struggled toward it as the ship began to pick up speed. The slack was quickly being taken out of the rope. Akos reached out a hand, watching as it started to whip past.

Akos managed to get a hold of the rope right before the slack snapped out of it and it began to move away from him. There was a weight on the end that allowed them to throw it far enough to reach him, and he used it as a stop to hold on to. Even with that, the rope almost jerked out of his hand. The evening wind was pushing away from Logathia and propelling the *Pride* out into the bay.

Akos managed to drag himself a little further up the rope and wrap the length of it around his forearm. Then it was all he could do to keep on his back and his face away from the frothing water. It would be a shame if they'd tried so hard to rescue him only for him to drown from being <u>hauled</u> behind the ship.

Fortunately, it seemed everyone but the helmsman was working to pull him aboard. Akos was reeled in, bumping his way up the side of the *Pride* as it turned out to open water. A dozen pairs of hands grabbed him as soon as they could and hauled him up over the railing, dumping him unceremoniously on the deck.

White-knuckled hands peeled themselves away from their grip on the rope. All the exertion of the past few hours caught up to him at once. Akos closed his eyes and took a minute to breathe. At least, he tried. Someone grabbed him by the front of his shirt and pulled him up to his seat.

Akos opened his eyes as Vibia crushed him in a hug. She was saying something about being glad that he was alive. Akos barely had time to register what was happening before Vibia alternated to slapping his arm for being so reckless. She switched between the two for some time.

Then Akos saw Calia over Vibia's shoulder. She was pushing between the men who were gathered around Akos, looking from face to face. Looking for someone. Akos felt all the strength leave his limbs again.

"Help me up please," Akos said.

Vibia gave him an elbow and Akos managed to make it to his feet. He was dripping from head to toe, saltwater stinging his eyes as it poured from his hair. Akos waved to Calia, making sure he caught her eye.

"I'm glad you made it alr—" Calia started.

Akos cut her off. "I . . ." I don't know how to say this."

Akos kept his composure as long as he could. But as he stumbled over his explanation, he saw Calia's eyes begin to fill with tears; he looked over to Vibia and saw the same. Then he couldn't meet their eyes anymore.

"Vibius is dead," Akos managed.

Calia turned and wrapped her arms around Valesa, weeping on her shoulder. Akos did his best to keep up his captain's mask. Then he decided it didn't matter anymore. He turned and hugged Vibia, and they cried on each other's shoulders.

Even though they'd escaped Logathia, the *Pride* was in mourning.

CHAPTER 29

Valesa had never seen Calia like this. To make matters worse, she wasn't sure how to help her. She'd never been one for romance and couldn't really sympathize with what it was like to lose a lover.

Not that she wasn't hurting. Valesa had grown to like Vibius over the course of their interment on Logathia. He had been polite, witty, and intelligent. He clearly cared about Calia, and he was one of the few men that Valesa felt would be able to keep up with her on an intellectual level. He was the first man to show interest in Calia that hadn't been more interested in her title or wealth.

Still, Valesa knew that he meant far more than that to Calia. She hadn't said a word since she'd gotten the news. Every now and then, she would stop crying, and Valesa thought it might be over. But then the tears would start right back up. Even after Akos had dried his tears and told them what happened at the keep, and what Anson told him, she hadn't changed.

It didn't help that they were under sail. There was nothing they could do to keep their minds busy to distract them from their feelings. Though Valesa wasn't sure that there would be any distracting from this, at least not for some time.

Just as Valesa was about to leave the cabin to get them something to eat from the galley, Calia rose from her bed. Valesa watched as she began to rummage through the small desk that was bolted to the floor of the room, and then through the dresser. After a few moments, curiosity outweighed her fear of upsetting Calia and Valesa made her way over to see what was going on.

After rummaging through much of their stuff, Calia took out a rolled-up piece of parchment. She smoothed it out on the desk, weighting the corners with anything that was close at hand. Valesa peered over her shoulder as she leaned over to study the parchment.

It was a map. Valesa had never been a cartographer, but she realized that it was a map of the realm of behemoths. Her curiosity deepened as Calia traced across the map with a finger. Finally, Calia found what she was looking for and tapped it with a triumphant finger.

"Craislund," Calia whispered.

The name tickled at her mind, until the realization dawned that Craislund was the name of the island where the god that killed Vibius was from. Valesa began to realize what was going through Calia's mind, and she didn't like it at all. Valesa hadn't wanted to allow Calia to return to the realm of behemoths in the first place, and she definitely didn't want her to be here now that they'd seen what the realm was capable of.

"Calia I don't think—" Valesa began.

"Don't," Calia said.

Her voice was hoarse from crying. Valesa met her eyes. They were puffy and bloodshot, but there was something else there. A determination that Valesa had rarely seen.

"If not us, then who?" Calia asked.

"Soon enough the entire realm of man will know of the existence of this place," Valesa said. "And they'll know the secret of how to get in and out. Once they begin to move in, the gods will all get their comeuppance."

Calia shook her head and turned away from the map. She returned to the edge of her bed and sat down. Valesa joined her.

"Galith wants to colonize," Calia said. "To make money. They'll look for diplomatic solutions first. They'll bargain with the gods and work with them, so long as they get their piece."

Calia was right. There would be a rush to colonize the new realm, but it would be easier to work with the already established kingdoms rather than to try to bull over them. There was no way to know for sure, but a smart man would try to put off conflict until he was sure he could win. Still, if Anson provided any indication of the temperament and attitude of the rest of the gods, conflict would eventually arise.

"Still, they'll fight eventually," Valesa said. "And we've seen that the gods are killable, just like any other men. The realm of man will be triumphant and wipe out the gods, Laran among them."

"Not soon enough," Calia replied. "I'll have justice for Vibius before we leave."

"And if I put my foot down?"

"It won't matter. Akos is of the same mind."

"You can't know that. You haven't spoken with him."

Even as she said the words, Valesa knew she was wrong. Akos had sailed back into the void without a moment's hesitation to save his friend. She could only imagine the lengths he would go to avenge him. That didn't need to include them, though, and Valesa wouldn't let him put Calia in harm's way on a vengeance quest.

"We'll have him take us back to the realm of man before he returns to dispense justice to Laran," Valesa said. "You'll still have your justice, sooner rather than later."

"I won't go," Calia said. "I've made up my mind. I'm going to see this through."

Valesa considered how she could respond to that and decided that she couldn't. Instead she rose, crossing over to the door. Calia watched her go without comment. Valesa wondered if they would think a little clearer on a full stomach, but something told her that it wouldn't change anything.

She might not be able to change Calia's mind, but Valesa wouldn't allow her to die in the void. Valesa swore a silent oath, not for the first time, that she would keep Calia safe no matter what it took.

Even if that meant taking vengeance on a god.

ABOUT THE AUTHOR

Taylor Gregory is a lifetime reader who has been writing stories of some form since a young age. He obtained a Bachelor's Degree from Texas Tech University in History, which he uses to infuse his fantasy worlds with an air of realism. He currently resides in West Texas. For news on upcoming works and random musings, head to taylorgregorywriting.com to keep up with him.